Praise for *FreeK Camp*

Steve hit it out of the park with *FreeK Camp*. It's a terrific mystery with elements of sci-fi that made me happy. And while it's really aimed at teens, it kept me engaged all the way through (like the Harry Potter stories are fun for adults as well as the kids they are intended for). At the end I was literally holding my breath, waiting to see what would happen next!

— LAREN BRIGHT, AWARD WINNING ANIMATION WRITER

FreeK Camp reminds us about the importance of unique gifts in our society—an important message for all adolescents struggling to fit in. Teachers will discover in Burt's artistry a "mentor text" for use in character analysis for young readers and character development for young writers.

—JOYCE HITT GORDON, NATIONALLY KNOWN LITERACY SPECIALIST, LONG BEACH, CA

Steve Burt takes us beyond the "normal" to the paranormal, pitting his FreeKs—psychic teens—and their powers against a deadly psychopath. An incredible page-turner with an ending that will leave you breathless.

— CINDY CORRIVEAU, PARANORMAL INVESTIGATOR AND
CO-HOST OF TV'S GHOST CHAT NEW ENGLAND

Your best book yet. Other kids my age will really enjoy this one. It's scary and suspenseful, but it still has some funny parts. I didn't want to put it down.

— STEVEN SAWAN, AGE 12, DOVER-SHERBORN MIDDLE SCHOOL (IN MA),
WHO READ THE MANUSCRIPT BEFORE PUBLICATION

It must be magic. Somehow Steve Burt manages to hook both teen readers and adult readers with the same story—and he delivers for both.

— JIM DONGWECK, AUTHOR, MOONBEAM CHILDREN'S BOOK AWARD-WINNER

FreeK Camp takes readers on a wonderfully scary trip into the wilds and wonder of a Maine summer camp—but not a typical one. Captivating, fascinating, heroic and weird characters weave their way through this tale to the delight of readers. Another great read by a terrific storyteller.

— RICHARD WAINWRIGHT, CHILDREN'S BOOK AUTHOR AND WINNER OF THE
BENJAMIN FRANKLIN AWARD

Praise for *Stories to Chill the Heart* Series

Steve Burt's stories are set in a recognizable world, but they never go in the obvious direction, preferring instead to take off down dark alleys and twisting roads which leave the reader shivering and looking nervously into dark corners when the book is closed.

— BARBARA RODEN, EDITOR, *ALL HALLOWS: THE MAGAZINE OF THE GHOST STORY SOCIETY*

These are stories kids want to read and talk about! They're asking for his books and want to know when we can have him back. The most successful author visit we've ever had.

— FRAN JOHNSON, MEDIA SPECIALIST, NEWFOUND MEMORIAL MIDDLE SCHOOL, BRISTOL, NH

When I teach high school seniors story-writing, I always include Steve Burt's books. Teens know the real thing when they read it. The next best thing to camping in the woods.

— MARYLIN WARNER, PIKE'S PEAK BRANCH, NATIONAL LEAGUE OF AMERICAN PEN WOMEN, COLORADO SPRINGS, CO

Just when you think you have the story cornered, you'll find it's sneaked up and gripped you by the back of the neck instead.

— BILL HUGHES, EDITOR, *DREAD MAGAZINE*

Burt relies more on atmosphere and skillful plotting than blood and gore, making his stories old-fashioned in the best sense of the term. If you think, "they just don't write them like that anymore," you'll be pleased to discover that Burt does.

— GARRETT PECK, THE HELLNOTES BOOK REVIEW

Your kids will love these stories and so will you! Spooktacularly entertaining summertime reading! Highly recommended.

— J.L. COMEAU, EDITOR, THE CREATURE FEATURE REVIEW PAGE, WWW.COUNTGORE.COM

If ever there was an author to rival the storytelling genius of M.R. James and E.F. Benson, Steve Burt is it.

— DON H. LAIRD, PUBLISHER, *CROSSOVER PRESS, THRESHOLD MAGAZINE*

Bram Stoker winner Steve Burt's stories have entertained—and frightened—my children for years, not to mention me. My son is in college now and still talks about stories from the *Stories to Chill the Heart* series' four collections. In fact, his scariest nightmare came about after reading one of them. You can't give a better compliment than that to a horror writer!

— DAN KEOHANE, AUTHOR, *SOLOMON'S GRAVE*

Awards for Steve Burt

Winner, **Bram Stoker Award** (young readers dark fiction)

Winner, **Paris Book Festival Award** (young adult fiction)

Winner, **San Francisco Book Festival Award** (teen fiction)

Winner, **New York Book Festival Award** (teen fiction)

Winner, **Mom's Choice Award** (teen fiction)

Winner, **Mom's Choice Award** (young adult fiction)

Winner, **Beach Book Festival Award** (2010 teen fiction)

Winner, 2011 **Beach Book Festival Award** (2011 teen fiction)

Runner-up, **Hollywood Book Festival Award** (teen fiction)

Runner-up, **Benjamin Franklin Award** (adult mystery/suspense)

3 **Ray Bradbury** Creative Writing prizes

Runner-up, **Moonbeam Children's Book Award** (young adult mystery/horror)

Runner-up, **Next Generation Indie Award** (young adult fiction)

Honorable mention, **London Book Festival Award** (teen fiction)

Runner-up, **New England Book Festival** (young adult/teen fiction)

Sole Honorable Mention, **ForeWord Award** (adult suspense/horror)

Honorable Mention, **Independent Publisher Award** (young adult fiction)

Honorable Mention, **New England Book Festival** (anthologies)

Honorable Mention, **New England Book Festival** (spiritual)

Runner-Up, **Writer's Digest Self-Published Books Award** (genre fiction)

Finalist, **ForeWord Award** (young adult fiction)

Nominee/Finalist, **Bram Stoker Award** (young readers dark fiction)

Runner-Up, **Writer's Digest Self-Published Books Award** (inspirational fiction)

Finalist, **ForeWord Award** (adult audio fiction)

Storyteller Magazine **Short Fiction Award**

Poetic Eloquence **Readers' Choice Award**

8 Honorable Mentions, **Year's Best Fantasy & Horror**

Recent Fiction by Steve Burt

The FreeKs series

FreeK Camp: Psychic Teens in a Paranormal Thriller (2010), winner
of 12 major awards including the Paris, San Francisco, New York,
London, New England, and Hollywood Book Festival Awards; 2
Mom's Choice Awards; a Moonbeam Children's Book Award; a Next
Generation Indie Award; and Beach Book of the Year for 2010 and
2011

The Stories to Chill the Heart series

Odd Lot: Stories to Chill the Heart (2001), winner of the Benjamin
Franklin Award (silver) for Best Mystery/Suspense Book

Even Odder: More Stories to Chill the Heart (2003), Bram Stoker
Award Nominee (runner-up to J.K. Rowling, *Harry Potter and the
Order of the Phoenix*)

Oddest Yet: Even More Stories to Chill the Heart (2004), winner of
the Bram Stoker Award (tie with Clive Barker)

Wicked Odd: Still More Stories to Chill the Heart (2005), Honorable
Mention for Independent Publisher Award

Inspirational books

A Christmas Dozen: Christmas Stories to Warm the Heart (2000),
runner-up for Writer's Digest 10th International Self-Published
Book Awards for Best Inspirational Book; finalist for ForeWord
Audio Book of the Year; New England Book Festival Best Spiritual
Honorable Mention

Unk's Fiddle: Stories to Touch the Heart (2001)

FREEK SHOW

Where Nothing Is As It Appears

Steve Burt

*To Derek
Enjoy the solving!
Steve Burt*

Burt
Creations

NORWICH, CT

FreeK Show
Where Nothing Is as It Appears

FIRST EDITION
Copyright © 2012 by Steven E. Burt

First Trade Paperback Edition
13 digit ISBN 978-0-9741407-3-5
10 digit ISBN 0-9741407-3-2

Printed in USA

Inquiries should be addressed to:

Burt
Creations

Burt Creations
Steve Burt
29 Arnold Place
Norwich, CT 06360

Tel: 860-405-5183
www.burtcreations.com

TEXT DESIGN BY DOTTI ALBERTINE, WWW.ALBERTINEBOOKDESIGN.COM

ACKNOWLEDGMENTS

MY THANKS to the following people who read through the draft copy of FreeK Show and offered corrections and suggestions: Connie Hurtt, Mobby Larson, Lorraine and Bruce Grey, Bob Rochford, and my daughter and editor extraordinaire Wendy Burt-Thomas. And I cannot say thank you enough to my wife Jolyn for her support, editing, major suggestions, and conscientious 15 readings.

I am also grateful to my "California team" (all award-winners in their fields) for their hard work and patience with me as we took the manuscript and turned it into a real book: copywriter Laren Bright (www.larenbright.com) and book/cover designer Dotti Albertine (www. dotdesign.net). I highly recommend them.

Haven't we always had a fascination with the psychic and paranormal? I mean, really, come on. And it's not just when we were little. We still find it intriguing. When I do a school author visit, it's always an energized discussion that everyone contributes to.

On the TV show "Crossing Over," medium John Edward "reads" the spirits of the dead who have connections to audience members. In 2012 a new phenom, "The Long Island Medium," has appeared, "reading" the departed spirits around people in a way similar to John Edward. Still other psychics help police on missing persons cases. This locating of people, pets, or objects is called dowsing, as in dowsing for water with a split branch, also known as divination or water-witching. (I once had a friend who was a cat dowser.) Can people really find things this way, and if so, how do they do it?

In 2012 I saw The Amazing Kreskin perform in New London, CT. He's the mentalist made famous by Johnny Carson on The Tonight Show. In his late seventies now, Kreskin has entertained audiences with his mental feats for 60+ years—guessing cards, telling you what number you wrote on a slip of paper, calling out the obscure name of someone's dog and then saying, "That was when you lived in Wisconsin, right?" His signature closer is locating the night's paycheck that audience members have hidden somewhere in the theater. No one's ever been able to expose him. Is he for real? Can a person actually develop such psychic powers?

Other people have been reputed to have "the sight," an Appalachian term for one's ability to sense something about to happen (forebodings and premonitions). General Ulysses Grant's wife Julia had such a foreboding and insisted she and he not accept the Lincolns' invitation to join them at the Ford Theater the night Lincoln was assassinated by John Wilkes Booth. Years later she had a similar sense of doom and pressed Ulysses to get them out of Chicago; they barely missed the Great Chicago Fire. Is there anything to it? Maybe you've had a similar experience yourself?

How about out-of-body experiences? Thousands of people insist their astral bodies have left their physical bodies during an operation or at an accident scene, and they've looked down on the scene from above, maybe approached a bright light before being drawn back. Similarly, some Eastern mystics swear they've entered deep states of meditation and intentionally traveled out-of-body in the astral plane. What's up with that? Can we separate the astral body from the physical body, and if we can, is it possible to see without an optic nerve or hear without eardrums?

We now know that someone who has an artificial limb can be "wired" (electronically) so his or her brain waves operate the new battery-operated limb. If science can help us do that now, isn't it possible that certain individuals have been able to move things by telekinesis and psycho-kinesis (brain power) all along?

How many of us knew the phone was going to ring, knew who was calling, and knew what the call was about? How many have seen the ghost of a loved one shortly after the death or funeral?

Science has a lot of answers, of course. But there's still a lot left unknown. Who knows what's possible in the world of the psychic and paranormal? Another interesting question: if we can develop some of these "gifts," how can they help us?

For the Freeks, these teens who possess a variety of these "gifts," using them wisely and together may mean the difference between life and death. It may mean stopping a murderer.

FRIDAY

CHAPTER 1

THE BATTERED BLUE van marked *FreeK Camp, Bridgton, Maine* crunched up the long driveway and parked by the dining hall. The blood-red K wasn't just graffiti; it hinted at the camp's true populace—"different" teens with psychic or paranormal gifts.

A woman over six feet tall came to the screen door, looked out at the van, and yelled back inside, "Caroline, Dad's back from the Post Office. Tell Bando, please." She descended the steps and walked to the driver's door as it opened.

A tiny man atop a booster seat unhooked leg extenders from his calves then swung his stubby legs out to the side and clambered down to the ground.

"Anything good, Twait?" she asked, towering two feet over the little man.

He slammed the driver's door with a little too much force.

"Whoops," she said. "I guess that means no."

"Sorry, Rose. I didn't mean to take it out on you. But no, there's no good mail, only junk mail. No new applications. Any last-minute phone-ins while I was gone?"

"Nope."

He cursed softly. "It's because of last year and Bronson, isn't it? Their parents won't let them come back. Or maybe it's the kids themselves who are afraid."

"Maybe both, or something else. Sweetie, you've got to remember they're teenagers, a year older than last year. And it's summertime. They're 15 and 16 now."

"What are you saying—that sports and hormones are more of a draw than a week working on psychic development?"

"For some, yes." She let him stew a minute. "We'll adjust. Last year 10 signed up and only half of them made it here. This year we've got five—four back plus a newcomer. And Caroline makes six. We can work with that. It is what it is." She reached out a hand. "Come on, let's go break the news to Bando and Caroline."

Bando was on the phone when they walked into the office. He hung up and began massaging the bridge of his nose with thumb and forefinger.

"Trouble in Paradise?" Twait asked. He climbed up onto his usual stool while Rose took a chair.

Bando nodded. "That was Juan and Juanita's mother. Last month she thought the twins might make it if they finished up the case they were helping the cops on. No such luck. It was a long shot. And all the others have commitments."

"I thought Mo was a possible, too," Rose said.

"I spoke with his mother awhile ago. Mo had to choose between Free Camp and that new place in North Carolina. He thought they'd be stronger in his area, telekinesis."

"They may be," Rose said. "That's good for him, bad for us."

"Do you think there's a fear factor with the others?" Twait asked.

"Could be," Bando answered. "Would that be so surprising after Bronson?"

"But the man had a brain tumor twisting his thinking. We had nothing to do with placing them in harm's way. Bronson grabbed them before they even got here. It doesn't make sense."

"Oh, come on, Twait. You and Rose are parents. You know parents sometimes make decisions based on emotion and not just reason. The bottom line is, tomorrow we get four of ten back—Charlie and Maggie from the safe group, Atlanta and Mouse from the abducted group—plus a new kid on the block."

"So we have a dreamer, a spoon bender, a levitator, and a question mark. What do we know about this new one?"

Bando picked up a sheet of paper. "His name is Damon. He's almost seventeen, so he's older than the others. He lives here in Bridgton with his uncle. No sports, no hobbies, no interests listed. I have no idea how he got our application."

"Psychic experiences or gifts?" Rose asked.

Bando scanned the page. "He didn't check a single box on your psychic-and- paranormal experiences questionnaire, Rose. And he didn't answer any of the three narrative questions."

"Then why are you accepting him?" Twait asked.

"Two reasons. In the margin here he sketched a vortex, a funnel cloud almost identical to one that several of last year's teens sketched when we were dealing with Bronson. He'd have no reason to add it to his application, so why'd he do it? My guess is he doesn't know why. The other reason: at the end of the questionnaire he added a new category: *hunches.*"

CHAPTER 2

THAT NIGHT IN Burlington, Vermont, after she had packed her bag for Free Camp, Atlanta and her cousin Wendy drew the bedroom shades and lit a candle on the night table between the twin beds. They turned off the lights and lay on the beds, staring up at the flickering shadows on the ceiling.

"You're changing, Atlanta. You know that, don't you? I can see it in your looks, in your attitude, at school, even when we're just talking like this. What's going on?"

Atlanta rolled onto her side and stared across the gulf between them.

"It's Mom. She just royally pisses me off. Since she and Dad divorced she wants to keep me like I was when he left, and that's just not going to happen. When I went to Free Camp last year I was younger and I felt younger. I was almost fifteen and I was still the model of sweet and innocent. But Donnie Bronson changed that. I had to adjust, make choices for myself just so I could survive and help my friends. Now I'm almost sixteen. Last summer taught me that I *can* make decisions on my own, but Mom has never accepted that. She insists on treating me like the little girl I was before I went to camp."

"She just cares. You know that."

"Easy for you to say. Your Mom and Dad aren't like that. You're a year younger than me and already your curfew is later, you've got two nose rings, a tattoo—and your clothes are way cooler than what Mom lets me wear. I'm different this year and I'm going to let the camp know it."

Wendy let the topic drop then after a few minutes said, "Is that why you're going back to camp—to prove to them you're changed? Or is there another reason? You already know how to levitate."

"Actually, I've been reading up on psychic development and paranormal powers, and this stuff is really neat. I want to see if I can do anything besides levitate. Last week I bought a pendulum so I can ask it questions. There's supposed to be a teaching session on it that I can't wait to go to. There's other neat stuff, too."

"A pendulum? I don't know what that is. What kind of questions can you ask it? Have you got it here?"

Atlanta pulled something out of her backpack—a quartz crystal on a chain.

"Can I try it?" Wendy asked.

"Won't work. I programmed this one for my energy force." Atlanta held the top of the chain between her thumb and forefinger so the crystal hung motionless. She closed her eyes. "Is Wendy my cousin?" she asked, and after a moment the crystal started swaying away from her and back. She opened her eyes. "That's a yes."

"How do I know you're not making it do that, forcing it?"

"You don't. And I am making it happen, just not consciously. I'll close my eyes and do it again."

"Ask it if your parents are getting back together."

Atlanta said nothing out loud and kept her eyes shut. "What's it doing?"

"It's circling."

Atlanta cursed under her breath. "That's a maybe or a don't-know-yet. Let's try a different one. Is camp going to be safer this year?"

A moment later Atlanta heard Wendy suck in her breath. She opened her eyes. They widened in surprise. The pendulum swung side-to-side. She dropped the chain into her palm with the crystal and closed her hand over it then returned it to the backpack.

"You don't really believe it works, do you?" Wendy asked. "Isn't it like one of those Magic Eight Balls you shake up—made for party entertainment? You don't trust it, do you?"

"I don't know. I'll tell you next week. For now, though, we don't tell Mom."

"Agreed. Let's change the subject. Tell me about levitating. Do you think it runs in families? Like ours? Your Mom can't do it, can she, or your little sister Gia?"

"Mom would have told me if she or Gia could do it. They don't know about me. Only my camp friends know, and even they haven't seen me do it."

"I have."

"You're the only one in the world. And your first time was this week and you swore you wouldn't tell."

"All week I've been dreaming about it, wondering if maybe it's in my blood, too. Can you teach me?"

Atlanta locked the door. "We don't want Mom walking in on us."

Wendy lay back on the bed.

"Not there," Atlanta said, stretching out on the rug. "Get down here beside me on your stomach. It helps if you can feel the hard surface under you for contrast."

Wendy joined her on the floor. "When did you first do it?"

"I was four."

"What did it feel like?"

"Weird at first, like mild seasickness, but that was just the first time."

"Did you chant a spell in your dream? I mean does it take magic words?"

"It's not about magic. It's about emptying yourself. Just lie flat on your stomach with your hands at your sides. Take a deep breath in through your nose and hold it a few seconds, then exhale it. Do that about ten times so you've got a slow rhythm. As you do it, tell your muscles to totally relax. Start with your head, neck, and shoulders and work your way down to your toes. Let go of all your tension. Clear your mind. It's like meditation."

Two minutes later, "Now what?"

"Pretend you're on an air mattress with no air in it. Feel the floor through it?"

"I feel like I'm in a cheap sleeping bag on frozen ground."

"Okay, then imagine a hair dryer is inflating the air mattress under you, little by little expanding and supporting you. Your ankles and knees and pelvic bones and ribs and shoulders and cheekbone are still touching the floor, but the spaces between are filling up and lifting you. Feel the difference?"

"I think so. Can I look?"

"No, don't open your eyes. It takes imagination at first. Later you'll gain better control. The hair dryer is still pumping air into the mattress and it's inflating. Your bony parts are being lifted off the floor now. Feel it?"

Wendy didn't answer.

"Wendy, can you feel yourself rising off the floor?"

No answer.

Atlanta opened her own eyes and realized she herself was gazing downward from the ceiling. Below her—six inches above the rug—hovered her cousin. "Wendy," she whispered, don't open your eyes yet. "Maybe it does run in families. You're doing it."

"Am I high up?" She didn't open her eyes.

"Less than a foot. Keep your concentration while you slowly open your eyes."

Wendy opened her eyes fast. "I did it!" She crashed to the floor with a thud and groaned, "That hurt. I think I broke something."

"I told you to open them slowly," Atlanta said, halfway down. "Lost your concentration. And don't be such a drama queen. You're fine. It wasn't like a skydiving accident."

"I really was up, wasn't I?"

"You really were. Maybe it's a family thing after all."

A small dog yapped at the door, followed by a woman's voice and a rattling of the doorknob. "Girls! Atlanta. Wendy. I heard a crash. Are you okay in there?"

"We're fine, Mom." The girls looked at each other and rolled their eyes in unison. "Girl talk. Just go away."

"Well, don't be too late. You and I are off to Maine at 5 a.m. Wendy needs to get her sleep so she can take care of your sister and the dog while I'm gone."

"My alarm is set, Mom. Good night."

"Good night. I love you, girls."

"Back at you, Mom," Atlanta said sarcastically, and the girls rolled their eyes.

"Are we really going to sleep this early?" Wendy asked.

"Soon. I do have to wake up early enough to get myself ready for camp. I plan to make an impression."

"Okay, but before we go to sleep, tell me again how you escaped Donnie Bronson's blockhouse and that buried school bus. Then I want to levitate again once more tonight. That was amazing. I'll practice until you get back next Saturday. Maybe next year I can go to camp, too."

SATURDAY

CHAPTER 3

Next morning Twait and Caroline drove to Portland to pick up Maggie and Charlie. The two of them were waiting on a motel bench with Maggie's parents when the van pulled in.

"Ah, the infamous *FreeK Camp #2*," said Maggie's father, a fortyish man in khaki shorts. "It's good to see it again." He patted the van then shook hands with Twait. "Love that bright red *K* and the third eye. Did the police ever locate *FreeK Camp #1*?"

Twait shook his head. "It's probably at the bottom of some swamp. Bando didn't even bother trying to replace it. This year it's this van and Rose's new car."

"Oh, that's right. Her old one took a dunking in that lake. Well, Maggie has pointed out numerous times—and I agree—that none of last year's mess was your fault. Her mother here was a little nervous about filling out the application this time, but Maggie can be very persuasive. I'm not worried. Besides, how could anything top last year for drama? With any luck this year summer camp will seem pretty dull."

Twait smiled. "We hope so. Maybe we'll get through a whole week this time."

"And the kids will get their money's worth," Maggie's father added. When Twait didn't laugh, he added, "*Free* Camp?"

"Good one," Twait said.

Caroline helped load the backpacks and bags.

Maggie's brown hair was still frizzy and she wore the same peace-symbol necklace and earrings as the year before. "Where is everybody? Are we stopping at another motel?"

Caroline slammed the tailgate door. "Tell you later."

Maggie gave her parents a quick hug and said, "Okay, got to go. Long ride back to the camp. Places to go, people to see, adventures to have."

"Easy on the adventures," her father joked sardonically.

"Right, Dad. Low stress week. That's what Caroline, Charlie, and I live for—a week of boring old summer camp."

Charlie shifted the conversation. "Thanks for letting me hitch a ride."

Caroline and her father climbed in front while Maggie and Charlie took the captain's chairs. Twait was still strapping on his leg extenders when Maggie's mother rested a hand on his arm. Her eyes were moist.

"Don't worry," he whispered. "We'll take good care of them. I promise." He squeezed her hand.

A minute later, as FreeK Camp #2 left the parents in the rearview mirror, Maggie asked, "Who's coming besides us?"

"Atlanta and Mouse," Twait said. "Their parents are driving them straight to the camp."

"And?" Maggie pressed. "Who else?"

Twait hemmed then said, "The twins didn't finish up a police case in time. But how cool is that? Crime busting."

"Yeah, cool," Maggie said sourly, "for them. What about team loyalty—at least to our five? Charlie and I are here. I thought we had a bond. Mohawk Mo is coming, right?"

"Mo had to make a choice—Free Camp or a camp in the Carolinas with a really strong telekinesis emphasis."

"Well, isn't this just freaking great?" Maggie spat, unable to contain her disappointment. "Me, Charlie, Atlanta, and Mouse. What about Tim, Celine, and BJ? They have excuses, too?"

"Not excuses. *Plans*," Caroline said. "They have other plans."

"So it's just the four of us?" Maggie kept on.

"I think you forgot someone," Twait said, and nodded at Caroline.

"Oh, right. Sorry, Caroline. I wasn't thinking of staff family members. Okay, five of us."

"Six," Caroline corrected. "A new boy signed up. Damon."

"Oh great. So we've got somebody who wasn't with us for Bronson last year? How's that going to work? I thought we already had a great team. Does this Damon even have a gift?"

"What we know," Twait said, "is that he's almost seventeen and comes from town."

"But no gift?"

"Not on his application," Twait answered. "Didn't attach a picture either, so don't bother asking me if he's cute."

*   *   *

Around the time Twait and Caroline were leaving Portland, Rose was finishing up in the kitchen. She came out onto the dining hall porch.

"Bando? You out here?" She looked around the driveway area and scanned the ball field and cabins. She turned to the screened window and called into the camp office, "Bando? That you?" No reply. "Someone out here? I can feel you. Come out, come out, wherever you are."

A tall boy who looked like a muscular Johnny Depp stepped from behind the corner of the building. He wore a backpack, hiking boots, tattered jeans, and a black tee shirt silk-screened with a classic dragon. Showing from under the right arm of his tee shirt was a tattooed skull, under it an inscription: *2008 Veni, Vidi, Vici.*

"You must be Damon."

"Yes, ma'am."

"You're early."

"That's why I was waiting out here. The letter said between 10:00 and 11:00. I didn't know somebody would stop and offer me a ride."

"You walked from town?"

"Part of it. Somebody gave me a ride here from the five corners."

"So you walked about six miles?"

"Five and a half maybe."

"Well, you may as well come in and sit down. I'm Rose. I'm the camp cook and one of your instructors. Bando is the director and is wandering around here someplace. My husband Twait—he's a little person, a midget, you'll notice—is off with our daughter Caroline in the camp van picking up two campers. Come in. Let me get you something to eat and drink. You must have worked up an appetite on a walk like that. After you have some food you can take your gear over to the boys' cabin and pick yourself a bunk. First come, first served. This is the dining hall."

"I know. I've walked around the camp many times."

"You have?"

"Well, when nobody was here, of course."

"Of course."

CHAPTER 4

WHEN THE VAN reached camp around 10:00 Rose and Bando met it. They hugged Maggie and Charlie and oohed and aahed over them while Twait and Caroline unloaded the bags.

Before everyone could go inside a Volvo station wagon rolled up the driveway with Mouse and his mother inside, so the process started over.

"See you've still got the hat, Mouse," Rose said, pointing to the *Call Me Mouse* cap from Disney World.

"You still da Mouse man," Twait said.

"Actually, I'm not," the boy said, his voice cracking and deepening. "I hit six feet this spring and have outgrown my nickname." He removed the cap and handed it to his mother. From his bag he pulled a new one that he set on his head: *Harley Davidson*.

"Motorcycle Boy?" Maggie asked. "You got a motorcycle?" Then she turned to his mother. "You got him a motorcycle? Talk about a cool mother!"

Mouse's mother smiled, embarrassed, and shook her head.

"Not Motorcycle Boy," Mouse said. "Harley. It's my name."

"Harley Davidson?" Caroline asked, puzzled. "You're from the motorcycle family?"

He grinned. "No, Caroline. Harley and Davidson were two different men. I'm not from the motorcycle family. But my first name—which was also my grandfather's--is Harley."

"But your last name is Davidson?" Maggie asked.

"No, it's Abernathy," his mother said. "My husband is David." She blushed, couldn't say the punch line.

Mouse could. "My Dad is David. So I'm Harley, David's son! Get it? It's the perfect hat. Harley David's son."

Everyone groaned. Mouse's mother—now Harley's mother—shrugged. "For years it was Mouse and now he wants back to Harley. What can I say?"

Another car crunched up the gravel and dirt, a Subaru wagon.

"Atlanta and her mother," Rose announced.

It came to a stop and the driver got out, slammed the door, and stood shaking her head. She muttered aloud, "We made it. At times I wasn't sure we would, but we made it."

The passenger door opened and the drama queen emerged, a curvy blonde with pink and purple streaked hair. She put a hand on her hip and with one hand pulled her sunglasses down an inch to peer over the top of them coquettishly. She wore an eyebrow ring, a lip ring, and a tank top that ended two inches above her hip-hugger jeans. When she had everyone's attention she removed the sunglasses the rest of the way, revealing dazzling blue eyes accented by neon-blue eyeliner. She extended a leg, drawing everyone's vision downward, where pink sandals and sparkling blue toenails completed the effect.

"Holy crap," Caroline muttered. "What happened to Atlanta?"

Mouse-turned-Harley gasped, "I don't know, but wow!"

Charlie seconded that. "Wow is right!"

For a few seconds nobody spoke or moved. It was as if they had looked Medusa in the eye.

Atlanta's mother shook her head.

Then in the blink of an eye, as if she had made her point and was ready for camp, Atlanta changed back. She said with true enthusiasm, "Hi, everybody. My God, it feels great to be back. Are the others inside?"

Before anyone could answer, the screen door swung open and an unfamiliar male voice asked, "Rose, you want me to put those cinnamon buns out now?"

Every head turned and saw the young man on the porch in his jeans and black tee shirt.

"Woof!" Caroline grunted.

"Everybody, meet Damon," Rose announced. "He's our newest camper."

The greetings began, but Damon heard the voices as if he were underwater as his eyes and Atlanta's locked onto each other like heat-seeking missiles.

Rose saw it and acted. "Everybody inside," she announced. "Hot cinnamon buns fresh from the oven."

But before anyone could move, a State Police cruiser drove in and parked. A patrolman got out and as he did Damon slipped back inside.

"Bando, Twait, Rose, folks," the Trooper nodded. "Don't worry, it's not a speeding stop. No tickets today." He smiled, hoping his humor had broken the ice. "We're just passing out a poster in case this man wanders in. He's got Alzheimer's and walked away from his home in Sebago." He handed around several photocopies. "He once owned a camp up this way and may have headed this direction on automatic pilot. We trust he'll turn up soon, but until he does, please keep an eye out. If you see him, stay with him and have someone call us." A minute later the cop and cruiser were gone.

Bando held the door and everyone streamed inside. Atlanta's mother passed him and paused, touching his arm and looking him in the eye. He saw her exhaustion and exasperation when she asked, "Before I leave, can we talk about Atlanta?"

CHAPTER 5

THE TWO MOTHERS and all the cinnamon buns were gone by 11:00, giving the campers an hour before lunch to settle into their cabins.

"So, Atlanta, what got into you over the winter?" Maggie asked. "Too much *Jersey Shore?*"

"Funny," Atlanta replied and primped her hair.

"Maggie's serious," Caroline said from a bottom bunk. "The look is interesting, but don't you think it's a bit over the top? Why no tattoos and a tongue stud?"

"Because Mom's being a bitch, that's why. My cousin Wendy has way more pierced jewelry than I do. She's got three eyebrow rings on one side and five studs in one ear. And several tattoos, which I may do, too, after this week—with or without Mom's permission."

"Why?" Maggie asked.

"Because I can. Because I want to."

Caroline sat up. "But why would you want to?"

"Because people notice. Did you see how Damon noticed me today?"

"Atlanta, wake up," Maggie advised. "He'd have noticed you without the colored hair and cosmic eye makeup. Caroline with her red hair and me with my frizz, we're the ones who need the extra help."

"Exactly my point. Did he notice you?"

"Hey, wait a minute!" Caroline warned. "You might want to lighten up on those insensitivity pills you're popping. Cut down from six a day to one."

"Sorry. That was cruel. I apologize."

"What we're trying to say as your friends," Maggie explained, "is some girls are naturally gorgeous and already have so many things going for them—like you. What the heck is going on here? And what is it with your clothes and hardware? You may be trying a little too hard. What are you trying for here, the Marilyn Monroe look or the slut look?"

Atlanta turned from the mirror and in her stage persona shot Maggie an eye dagger. "The slut look, obviously." And she walked out.

"What's up with her?" Caroline asked.

"Teenage rebellion combined with hormones," Maggie said, shrugging. "Not that I'm familiar with either firsthand."

"Me either. So let's get off Atlanta. What's new in your life? Boyfriend?"

"No. A lot of the tenth-graders have paired off, but most of my friends—boys and girls—travel in groups, not couples. You?"

"Trying to figure things out. I may be lesbian or bisexual—or maybe asexual. I don't seem to have much interest." Then she imitated Atlanta and over-dramatically throwing her hand across her forehead said, "I'm so confused."

They both laughed at her acting ability compared to Atlanta's.

Then Caroline said, "Really?"

"Yes, seriously. Today when I saw Damon, I thought he was really hot. And I also thought Atlanta looked hot. But I wasn't really attracted to them. I just thought, *damn, they're gorgeous specimens.*"

"No sexual desire?"

"Not yet. I wonder if I'm just a few quarts low on hormones. Which doesn't bother me. I like to think I'll find some nice relationship someday, but it's not high on my list right now. Neither is sex. How about you?"

"I've got four months until I'm sixteen. Right now nothing's pressing. Maybe the red hair is working against me."

"You think Atlanta's on the pill?" Maggie wondered.

"Not if her mother had to approve it. Seeing her with Damon this morning, though, I hope one of them has protection. The way they looked at each other had mud-wrestling match written all over it."

"What about Charlie?"

"What about him?" Caroline asked.

"He's shy but he's liked you since last year."

"He has? I thought we clashed on everything."

"He clashes with me, too. But your problem, Caroline, is that you and he are both head people, know-it-alls. I think he really likes you."

"You really think he likes me?"

"Definitely. He's just awkward, unsure of himself. He's more comfortable with books and information, which is your common ground. Why do you think he reads all that paranormal and psychic stuff? It's so he can one-up us, so he can feel secure with knowledge when he feels insecure with relationships. But don't shortchange him. He's a stand-up guy. He'd jump in front of a speeding bus to save you."

"Thanks for the heads-up. By the way, how's the spoon bending? Getting better?"

"A little stronger. How about you? Any more close encounters with ghosts?"

"Too busy with high school. I don't look for them and they haven't looked for me, not since Addie and Karen last summer."

Maggie got up. "Guess that catches us up for now. My watch says lunch in five. Ready?"

Caroline threw a dramatic hand across her forehead and drew out her answer, "Oh, dahling, is the limo here already?"

CHAPTER 6

AFTER LUNCH ROSE handed out the schedule for the week.

"First of all, let me say that we're very happy to see all of you. It's been a while since we were last together. And we're glad Damon could come and join us. I've passed out a timeline for the week. Everybody got one?"

Twait raised a hand and joked, "I didn't get one, teacher," and everybody laughed. Someone passed him a page and Rose continued.

"Today is arrival day. Unpack, explore, and get acquainted. Please note that we purposely did not schedule anything for you until 7:30 p.m. See where it says Fireplace Chat? That's when we'll say why each of us is here and get a chance to share our psychic experiences."

Caroline raised her hand. "My mother and father made me come." The others laughed.

"The other lightly programmed day is next Friday, when your families arrive before noon to get you. The five days in between you'll be very busy learning and trying new things having to do with the psychic and paranormal. That doesn't mean it's all work and no play, because if you look at the schedule you'll see we've also worked in the usual summer camp activities like swimming, canoeing and kayaking, hiking, games, and campfires."

Twait said, "Realizing you are teenagers, we took pity on you this year and scheduled no programs before breakfast at 8 a.m. Your morning class or activity will generally be 10:00, the afternoon class or activity at 1:30 or 2:00 depending on the day."

"Looks like a busy week," Harley commented.

Charlie whispered to Caroline, "Has your Mom ever taught 8th grade? She's a natural."

"No. Just college. Why?"

"Just thinking that kids wouldn't give her any lip."

"The three field trips look interesting," Damon commented. "The first one, Horton Farm and Cemetery in North Bridgton was on that TV show, American Ghost Story, last year."

"Horton Farm is set for tomorrow. Monday is the scavenger hunt in Bridgton. It's a chance to see if you can work together in teams. Tuesday is a whole day away. We'll take box lunches and learn grave rubbing in Durham, the small town where Stephen King the horror author grew up, and when we finish we'll go on to Freeport and check out the original L.L. Bean store."

Maggie raised a hand. "Is the word Meditation a misprint? Every morning it says 9 a.m. Meditation with Bando. I thought Meditation was just tomorrow's class."

"Bando?" Rose said.

"That's not a misprint. Tomorrow's is indeed a class-length session with instruction and practice. Starting Monday we'll sit in meditation for about a half hour each day. That's why you see it listed at 9 a.m. It'll still mean you have a half hour afterward to get ready for the morning class or activity. Let me stress that the half hour of daily meditation is not optional; it's mandatory. Meditation is a major element in many things psychic."

Charlie's hand went up. "My grandmother meditates to manage her arthritis pain." The others looked at him in surprise. "It's been proven that some people can mentally lower their blood pressure and heart rate. It's called biofeedback."

Before Bando could regain the floor Harley said, "A lot of stuff is psychic. In sixth grade my friend Paul was digging a tunnel and it collapsed on him. The night of his funeral I saw him at the end of my bed. I wasn't meditating, though."

Nobody questioned or challenged Harley.

"I wasn't dreaming," he continued. "Really, I was awake. He stayed by my bed close to a minute. He didn't disappear until I sat up and reached for him."

"Did he come back?" Caroline asked.

"No. Why?"

"Karen and Addie did last summer. They kept coming to me until Bronson died."

Charlie asked, "But now they're all crossed over, right, and haven't been back?"

Bando turned the conversation. "Let's continue this tonight."

Rose briefly discussed some of the class topics: Pendulums and Dowsing, Automatic Writing, and Psychic Awareness. Then she asked, "Have we missed anything?"

"Ghosts?" Harley asked.

"We'll see," Rose said.

"Yeah, you and Caroline," Harley joked. "How about the rest of us?"

"Anything else?" Bando asked.

Charlie said, "Out-of-body experiences."

"Understanding that will be an outgrowth of meditation."

"Will it be discussion or practice?" Maggie kidded.

Bando shrugged. "With this group, who knows? Any other questions?"

When no one spoke up, Atlanta asked, "Who wants to go to the waterfall? Mouse and I—I mean Harley and I--never got to see it last year. And Damon hasn't seen it."

"Actually, I have," Damon said.

Atlanta's disappointment showed.

"Last summer after the Bronson story came out, a lot of townies went up there. So I've seen it." Then seeing her pout he smiled and said, "But I've never seen it with you."

Caroline and Maggie exchanged eye rolls and finger gags.

"Before you go," Twait said. "Remember that we've let you bring cell phones this year, but you need to leave them with us now. Put them here on the table. You can get them out of the office and use them each night in the half hour after supper. That's the only time."

"And for emergencies," Maggie amended.

"Real emergencies," Twait clarified. "Not to phone or text a boyfriend or girlfriend. *Emergencies as in life or death.*"

As the words left Twait's mouth, Rose and Bando found themselves wincing.

The herd got to its feet and began to migrate.

CHAPTER 7

THE SIX TEENS headed up the waterfall trail, Caroline leading the way, Atlanta and Damon lagging at the rear out of earshot of the group.

"So you're from Bridgton?" she asked.

"Last couple of years."

"Where before that?"

"Portland."

"I hear it's a neat city. Why'd they move to the sticks?"

"They didn't. I did."

"Alone?"

"My uncle took me in after my parents died."

"Oh, God, I'm sorry. That's terrible. What happened?"

"A house fire."

Atlanta stopped and turned to face him. "Were you there?"

His voice hardened. "I was downtown. We'd had an argument and I walked out. Later when I started for home I heard the fire engines. Something in my gut told me it had to be our house, so I ran the rest of the way back. By the time I got there the whole place was in flames. The firemen held me back."

"Did they find out what happened?"

Damon clenched his teeth. "The fire was set."

"Oh, my God."

"They found my parents upstairs."

"But who would do that? Who would set a fire? They don't think your parents did it, do they? Did they have enemies? Who would do such a sick thing?"

Damon looked up, his own eyes full of pain. "They tried to pin it on me."

Atlanta sucked in a breath.

"It wasn't me. I swear."

"I believe you. Are there suspects? Leads?"

"No. Nobody. Nothing. That's why I signed up for this."

"Signed up for what?"

"This camp. Jerry, the guy driving your van last year—when Bronson carjacked you—he's from Bridgton. He gave my uncle a Free Camp brochure and my uncle gave it to me. I thought I could develop some psychic powers and maybe see who murdered my parents."

"But at this point you don't know what your gift is?"

"No idea. You know yours?"

"I do."

"Can you see ghosts? Sounds like Caroline and Rose can."

"No. I levitate."

Damon's jaw dropped. "Seriously?"

"Seriously. But I don't do it in front of people."

He looked skeptical.

"Don't you believe me? I believed you when you said you didn't set the fire."

"Yeah, I guess. I suppose I believe you. But it'd be easier if I could see you do it."

"We'd have to know each other a lot better."

"I'm up for that."

Charlie's voice called back from the group, "Hey, you two. You're falling behind."

"Right there," Damon shouted. "Tying a shoe."

Ten minutes later Caroline stopped them all before the last bend in the trail so they could hear the water's roar before they saw it.

"Ready?" she asked.

They nodded and she led them around the bend quietly as if approaching a shrine. They silently fanned out beside the pool like mourners by a grave. Harley unconsciously took off his hat and they gazed in awe at the falls cascading down into the whirlpool basin.

Harley cleared his throat. "So that's where Bronson—"

"Shut it, Harley," Maggie rasped out the side of her mouth.

"No, I think it's okay," Charlie said. "Harley and Atlanta weren't in our group that made it here to camp. Neither was Damon. And Maggie, you and I weren't here when it happened. We were up at the lake for the rescue. Only Rose, Juanita, and Caroline were here when Twait and Bronson fell off. And Caroline's the only one here now. Let her tell the story and we can talk about it."

Caroline led them to two granite memorial benches.

"Karen and Addie's benches," she said. "Bronson's wife and daughter who had drowned here five years earlier."

"Bronson had the benches made?" Harley asked. "Like the stone he shackled us to in the sinking boat?"

"Not Bronson. Karen's parents donated these."

"Harley, let Caroline tell her story," Maggie said.

Caroline told how Bronson and her father had fought at the top of the waterfall after the cloudburst and how they had tumbled together into the whirlpool. She finished in tears.

The others sat spellbound. Hearing unfamiliar parts of the terrible story was different from trying to picture it alone in isolation as they'd been trying to do since the event. Both groups of five—the ten teens plus Caroline—had been forced to say goodbye the day after the ordeal ended. Their final meal together at the motel had been the only time they'd all been able to tell and piece together some of their stories, and that evening was a blur.

They talked quietly for over an hour—with no claims of heroics, no victory gloating—until Maggie finally said, "It's time to head back."

"I'm really glad we did this," Charlie said.

"Me, too," Caroline agreed. "Together."

The others nodded. After an unplanned moment of silence that was like a prayer, they started down the trail.

Caroline and Atlanta stayed on the bench.

"You coming?" Damon asked.

"We'll catch up in a minute," Caroline said.

Maggie started down the trail, passing Harley as he shaded his eyes with his hand, staring once more at the top of the falls, his eyes following an imaginary freefall line from promontory to pool. Then he shook his head in disbelief and fell in line behind Maggie, Charlie, and Damon. "Hell of a dive," he muttered.

Back on the bench Atlanta asked, "So you and your Mom haven't seen them since?"

Silence. Caroline stared into the pool.

"Caroline?"

"Shh." Caroline's eyes were glued to the curtain of water splashing into the pool.

"Caroline, don't screw around. You're scaring me."

"Shh!"

"What is it?"

"Addie. With somebody behind her."

"Her mother?"

"Don't think so."

"Bronson?"

"No."

"Male or female?"

"Male. Head tilted to one side. Mouth is moving."

"What's he saying?"

Caroline held up a hand saying wait. She stood slowly. So did Atlanta.

"Where are you going?" Atlanta whispered loudly.

Caroline edged toward the pool.

"Caroline, don't!"

Caroline stopped near the edge. Atlanta gripped her arm.

"He's fuzzy, but I think he's the man who wandered away. He's trying to mouth something but there's no sound."

"You're sure it's him?"

Caroline didn't answer, but instead called out to the water curtain, "Addie. Addie Beals. Why are you back?"

"Did she answer?"

"Addie Beals, what's your friend saying?"

They waited, and Atlanta asked, "Is she answering?"

Caroline said nothing then "Addie says, 'Help him. He's dead.'"

"Help him, he's dead? Kind of late, isn't it? Come on, Caroline, let's get out of here."

Caroline called to the curtain, "Addie, how can we help?"

A voice from behind broke the spell—Harley's. "Who you talking to? Are you two coming?"

CHAPTER 8

By 2:30 THE temperature had risen to 85 degrees, hot for Maine, so everyone showed up at the waterfront. Charlie was taking a swimming lesson with Twait near the far rope.

"Dad, where's Mom?" Caroline called as she and Maggie walked onto the beach.

"Town. Back any time. You need her for something?"

"It'll wait."

Twenty yards offshore Atlanta lay on the diving float like a supermodel at a photo shoot. Damon hung from the edge of the platform, chin on muscled forearms, body tapering into the depths as if his legs might end in a merman's tail. Both the goddess and the god wore sunglasses, allowing them to safely check each other out.

"What's the tattoo mean?" she asked.

"Skull. Death."

"I know that. I meant the wording."

"*Veni, vidi, vici*. It's a famous Latin message sent home by Julius Caesar after his legions kicked Gaul's butt. Gaul back then was what's now France. *I came, I saw, I conquered*."

"You got a tattoo for Julius Caesar?"

"Funny girl. No, it's not for Caesar, and it's not gang-related. I got it six months after the fire. When the tat-man did the skull, I had him add the words. I was in a really dark place. It hit me that no matter what the priest said about heaven at the funeral, in the end Death conquers all. *Veni, vidi, vici.*"

Atlanta said, "Hmm," then she came back with, "France isn't still under Caesar, is it? So *Veni, vidi, vici* isn't forever."

Damon looked puzzled.

"Life goes on. Things change. Not everybody's dead. You and I aren't."

Fifteen feet from the float and neck-deep in water stood Harley in his sunglasses and Harley Davidson cap, trying occasionally to insinuate himself into some of the conversations. But Atlanta and Damon weren't speaking his language—Disney, old pop songs, movies, nothing remotely in his range of subjects. He didn't know Latin, didn't care about tattoos, and hadn't yet learned the art of adolescent small talk. The onslaught of testosterone and puberty were only now paying their first belated visit, leaving their parting gift—a cracking voice. He was out of his league with the merman, the god, but he had enough hormones to recognize that this summer Atlanta had become a super hot goddess.

Caroline and Maggie opted for towels and sun on the beach, slathering themselves with sunscreen on those body parts not covered by their one-piece bathing suits. But after 20 minutes of baking they picked up their towels and water bottles and moved uphill from the beach to the shade of a towering oak, where they lay down and gazed up into the overhanging branches.

"Caroline?"

"What?"

"I've been thinking."

"About what?"

"Last year."

"What about it?"

"Well, Harley told me that last year when his group was in Bronson's bomb shelter, they had two jackknives. They talked about what they might do if Bronson came down the ladder and they could overpower him. Could they—would they—slit his throat?"

"And?"

"I guess Celine answered for all of them saying she couldn't do it."

The topic hung over them like a sword.

"I could do it," Maggie said finally. "Maybe it's because we're all a year older, but I really think if I were in that situation I could do it. I know Bronson was a sad man and lost his family and had a brain tumor and all, but—."

"No need to explain. If it came down to him or us, if he or somebody else threatened any of the FreeKs, or my parents, or Bando, Rose, or Twait, I could do it, too. You're right, we're all a year older, and last summer changed us. We're not as naïve. We're not kids anymore. We're less innocent, more practical. I hate to say this, but I may be—colder."

"So we're not just desensitized, callous? We're just growing up?"

"I don't know. Maybe we're more realistic about life. I just know that if I had to now, I could do it."

"Still, I hope we never have to make that choice."

Rose walked down the path in her swimsuit, announcing, "I'm back." She walked to the boathouse, rolled down the awning over the garage doors, and unfolded a chaise lounge in its shade. "Lifeguard number two on duty," she called to Twait, who waved.

Caroline and Maggie got up and walked over to her.

"Hi, Mom. Mind if we sit?" Caroline fished two lawn chairs out of the boathouse.

"Not swimming today?"

"I saw Addie."

Rose pulled the sunglasses down on her nose and looked over them.

"At the waterfall. Not her mother. Just Addie."

"She's back? I thought she and her family had crossed over when Bronson died."

"Me, too."

Rose made a megaphone of her hands. "Atlanta! Hey, out there! Atlanta, if you don't get in the water once in awhile, you're going to burn."

Atlanta glanced toward the boathouse and offered the Queen's wave.

Damon turned his head shoreward then looked back at the goddess as she held up a water bottle for Rose to see. With Damon and the floating head in the motorcycle cap watching, she tilted her chin up exposing her neck in a classic Marilyn Monroe pose and slowly drank some water.

Rose yelled, "Atlanta, I said get *into* the water. I didn't say drink it." She knew that behind her sunglasses Atlanta was rolling her eyes.

Finally the goddess eased toward the edge of the float and slid into the water. She propped her forearms on the platform by Damon's, their backs to Harley and Rose.

"That idea backfired," Maggie said.

"I can only control so much from here. At least their arms and hands are on the float."

"Addie brought a man with her," Caroline said. "I'm positive it was Mr. Alley, the one everybody's looking for."

"Did you see or hear anything, Maggie?"

"I'm the spoon bender, not the ghost whisperer, remember? Besides, I wasn't there. It was Caroline and Atlanta. Atlanta says she didn't see anybody."

"Remember how clear Addie and her mother were last year, Mom? Today Mr. Alley's spirit was fuzzy, like he was struggling to make himself visible. His head was cocked to the side and he was trying to move his mouth. When I asked Addie what he wanted, she said, 'Help him. He's dead.'"

"You're sure it's Alley?"

"Yes."

"Maybe he walked into a pond or fell and hit his head?" Maggie suggested. "And nobody knows he's dead yet."

"They'll have something on the news at 5 o'clock," Rose said. "At this point we can't call and report him dead. They'll ask how we know."

"So what are we supposed to do?" Maggie asked.

Rose massaged the center of her forehead, her mind's eye. "If this is Alley and he's dead, he's earthbound for a reason and has latched onto Addie, probably because she has a connection to a living person that might be able to help free him—you, Caroline. Any other voices, visions, or feelings from you two or the others?"

"Let's ask those questions tonight after supper," Bando said, seeming to materialize from behind the canoe racks. He stepped toward them. "Remember the tea leaves this morning, Rose—those patterns? We didn't take them seriously. And the vortex Damon drew in the margin of his application—he didn't explain it, but he said he was prone to hunches? I don't know if our gathering all these psychic energies together—these gifted teens plus ourselves—attracts extreme negative energies or what, but I'm afraid something's coming our way again just like Bronson did last summer—and may already be here. Whatever that negative energy is, Free Camp appears to be right in its path."

Rose got to her feet and blew her lifeguard whistle. "Atlanta, Damon, let a little bit of light shine between you, please!"

CHAPTER 9

AT 7:30 THEY arranged the furniture in a rough circle by the hall's stone fireplace. Everyone settled in and Rose started the discussion.

"We're here tonight to tell our stories."

"What about the ghosts at the waterfall?" Harley wanted to know. "Was the man Mr. Alley or not?"

"We don't know for sure," Rose answered. "Probably. There was nothing on the evening news. And when Bando called the State Police to ask if Alley was found safe, they said it was still a Missing Person case. We'll check TV late tonight and if there's still nothing, in the morning."

After the grumbling subsided, Twait said, "We want to remind you that what we divulge here is in confidence. Meaning you don't go and blab to your friends or family back home what anybody's gift is or confidential details about their stories."

"Because government scientists would run tests on us and want to dissect our brains, right?" Harley joked.

"More truth to that than you know, Harley," Twait replied sternly. "But yes, there is the potential for exploitation."

"Exploitation like having to leave the country?" Harley asked in a serious voice.

"That's deportation, Dweeb," Maggie said. "Exploitation is using somebody."

"Like King Kong when they put him on stage," Harley grinned. "Before he broke the chains."

"Let's get back on track," Rose said. "We want to talk about our psychic experiences and what brought us here. We'll use the Native American talking-stick approach." She set a stick out on the coffee table. "The one who's holding the stick is the main storyteller. Pick it up when you're ready."

They waited.

Finally Charlie cleared his throat and put a gnarled hand around the stick.

"I dream things then forget them, same as you. But sometimes, just before something is about to happen, it comes back to me, the details, like the lake rescue last summer. I knew we couldn't waste time getting Bando out from under those collapsed shelves even though he was seriously injured. I knew I had to drive Rose's old car into the lake."

"When did it first happen?" Rose asked.

"When I was seven. That was the year my parents died."

"We have something in common then," Damon pointed out. "Deceased parents. Mine burned in a house fire. What happened to yours?"

"They left me with my grandmother that summer to go camping with five other couples in Rocky Mountain National Park. A cloudburst set off a flash flood that swept down the canyon through their campground while they were sleeping. Only one couple survived." Charlie's voice was flat, as if he'd told the story many times and had little emotion left. "That's why my grandmother raised me."

"That's horrible," Caroline said. "So your precognitive dreaming started after that?"

"No, *before*." Charlie's face clouded over. "That night it happened I dreamed it—before it happened—but I thought it was just a nightmare. When I woke my grandmother up and told her, she thought that, too. But it was so real I couldn't get back to sleep. The next day the news on TV reported the story. Nineteen people died. The news announcer told it word-for-word the way I knew he would, and a couple hours later the phone call came. I knew it two minutes before it rang. I even knew that

Gram would say goodbye to the person on the other end and drop the phone and knock the candy dish over and break it. And I knew she'd break into tears and sit on the couch and pull me close without telling me what was wrong even though I knew what was wrong. I heard my own voice before I spoke, when I asked her, 'Mom and Dad died in the water, didn't they?'"

Charlie took a deep breath. "Nobody believed my dream story. The therapist insists my psyche created it after the flood as a way of coping. He said I felt guilty about not being able to warn them, save them. But I didn't feel guilty; I still don't. I truly believe I dreamed it, forgot it, and then saw it as it became true. My problem with that dream was that I wasn't part of the solution. In the lake rescue last summer, I was. I knew the solution and just had to choose to take part."

"Your grandmother must have told the shrink about your nightmare," Atlanta said. "That would back up your story."

"The therapist believes Gram's mind played the same tricks mine did. He says her mind made up the supporting story—also after the tragedy—as a coping device."

"Well, I hope you both got a second opinion," Damon said.

"I was seven. Gram and I were devastated. We let it drop. It didn't matter. We couldn't get my parents back. And we weren't invested in arguing that I had precognitive dreams. We were in therapy to work on our grief."

"But you do believe you dreamed it first, don't you?" Damon asked. "You have faith in your gift, I hope."

"I do. But it doesn't stop me from wishing I'd had enough time to warn my parents." Charlie locked eyes with Damon. "Know what I mean?"

Damon nodded, affected by his own sadness.

"Charlie," Rose said. "Even if you *know* what's about to happen, you can't *control* everything. Your parents' deaths were an accident. Bad things happen to good people. Their deaths weren't your fault."

Charlie dropped his gaze to the floor. "I was mad at them for not taking me along."

Damon finished the thought. "And so for awhile you imagined that you made it happen, by secretly wishing them bad luck—because you were angry at them. Charlie, you didn't. That's called magical thinking. It's bogus. We can't make things happen by wishing them. I thought that, too, for a year or more after my parents were murdered. But believe me, you weren't responsible for your parents' death any more than I was responsible for mine."

"I know what magical thinking is. I've read up on it. In my head I know I didn't wish that rain or that flood. But every so often when I'm missing them that idea creeps back in. I'll bet it does with you, too."

Damon nodded.

"Let me tell you a little more and then I'll pass the stick. As I said, I live with my Gram. I read a lot and I don't have a lot of friends."

"You seem to read and remember everything, Charlie," Maggie said. "With me, I read and it goes in one side and out the other. I can't believe you remember the stuff you do. That's a gift, too."

Charlie continued as if he hadn't heard her. "I have these claws for hands, which people are always asking me about, so I tend to keep them hidden in my pockets most of the time. I've got a whole collection of sweatshirts with a monk's pocket in the front. I've had these hands all my life, so I'm used to them; they're my hands. It's other people who are uncomfortable seeing them and want me to get them fixed so they look and work like theirs."

The silence deepened until finally Bando asked, "You haven't given up the talking-stick, Charlie. Is there more?"

Charlie looked thoughtful. "Yes. Last summer Twait taught me to swim. I trusted him. Maybe my parents' drowning was why I chose not to learn when I was younger. Whenever I was invited to learn, I used my hands as an excuse. But I knew the day Twait offered to teach me that I had to learn right then. It must have been an early fragment of the larger Bronson dream. I knew I had to say yes. I learned to swim just in time to get out of Rose's car at the bottom of that lake. Then you, Bando, helped me trust my dreaming again, helped me see it could be a good thing, not always a nightmare. And it showed me the rescue plan in the nick of time. Last summer Free Camp changed my life, and that's why I'm back."

There was no applause, but heads nodded.

After a lull Maggie took the stick. "As you've seen, I bend spoons with my mind. At least that's how I think I do it. I'm not really sure. My parents tell me I've always been able to. I can also move small metal objects—only metal—without touching them. So it's not telekinesis like Mo did last year; it's specific to metal. He could move things through the air. It never seemed like a big deal to me, because my parents told me lots of people do it. They said spoon bending became a worldwide phenomenon in the 1970s after a mentalist named Uri Geller did it a few times on the Johnny Carson show. So, even though my older brother and sister and parents can't do it, I've never felt special. I mean, what can you do with it? If anything, it was like a magic trick I could do to amuse a couple of my friends. They still can't figure it out. They think I'm just refusing to give away the secret of the trick. In all these years no newspapers or TV shows have knocked on my parents' door to interview me or ask for a demonstration. Spoon bending just isn't all that big a deal. It wasn't until last summer here when I lined up the pins in those padlocks at the bottom of the lake that I understood I have a gift that can make a difference. So I'm back to develop it further or to learn something new."

"Maybe one day you'll lift a car off somebody," Caroline said.

"I don't know about a car, but I have been practicing. Last month in a supermarket parking lot I had a man chasing a shopping cart. It was like teasing a cat with a laser beam. Every time he'd get close, I'd move it, which wasn't too hard since it was on wheels."

"Kind of sick," Harley kidded with approval.

"I know, I know. I finally let the poor guy catch it, and when he pushed it past me he asked, 'Did you feel any wind?'"

Everyone laughed. Then Harley said, "I want to say seriously, spoon bender, that you saved my butt and three others. You can't imagine what it's like being chained to a granite headstone on the lake bottom with no breath left in your lungs. Not only for myself but also for Tim, Celine, and BJ." He swallowed hard. "Thank you."

Maggie's face reddened. She passed Harley the stick.

"Youngest of five boys. All grown or in college except me, so I'm sort of an only child. Dad's a scientist at M.I.T. He works on space-age radar systems. Mom's an elementary school principal. I'm in the top ten percent in school without much studying and average in tennis and cross-country. And I don't remember things the way Charlie does, that's for sure."

"But you're the class clown, right?" Maggie asked.

"I try. But even there I'm barely in the 50th percentile."

"As class clown?"

"Yeah. I think I'm funny, but only half the teachers and half the other kids do. Which means half don't—50th percentile. Stupid and sometimes funny things just pop out of my mouth. I can't help it. My uncle is a guidance counselor and says I'm just trying to find myself and my place in society."

The group waited, eyes on Harley.

"What?" he asked.

"Gift?" Atlanta pressed. "We're talking about psychic gifts, remember?"

"No idea," he answered, and began to babble. "No freaking idea. That's why I'm here again—to find it. Hey, I'd be happy to learn knife throwing. Oh, wait. Knife throwing is a skill, not a psychic gift. Spoon bending, knife throwing, whatever—I'm not choosy. Like my uncle said, I'm trying to find myself. If it's not my athletic prowess or my good looks or my sense of humor, then what is it? I don't see dead people. I don't dream stuff. I can't get off the ground by jumping, much less levitating. I don't know what I do, but it's certainly nothing special like you guys do."

"At least it doesn't seem to bother you," Damon said sarcastically.

"Of course it bothers me! I'm jealous and frustrated. I admit it."

"Then join the club," Damon replied. "I don't have a gift either. I'm here to see if I can learn or acquire one—something, anything—the way Charlie learned to swim. Swimming may not be a psychic gift, but it sounds like it was a useful one that paid off at the right time. I need to see if some of these psychic things can be taught or uncovered."

"Which we'll work on this week," Rose said. She took the stick out of Harley's hand and held it out toward Atlanta. "Ready?"

Atlanta accepted it. "What do you want to know? I levitate."

Rose said, "Does all that extra hardware weigh you down? It's hard not to notice the nose and eyebrow rings. They're new this year."

"Don't start sounding like my mother, Rose. She's a pain lately. Just to get her to let me come here this week I had to promise not to get the hip tattoo I was planning."

"Guess you wanted to come here pretty badly," Caroline said, "to pass up a hip tattoo."

"Or you're not so sure about the tattoo after all," Maggie suggested.

Atlanta didn't answer.

"Do you have to take the rings out at night?" Harley asked, slipping back into clown mode. "Maggie can do it for you, no hands." Nobody laughed.

"Fiftieth percentile and slipping," Maggie said, drawing snickers.

"Good one," he replied. "Maybe we're a comedy team."

Maggie gave an eye roll and a headshake.

"All right, my *so-called* friends," Atlanta said, dragging the words out. "Is it my turn to talk or not? I appear to have the stick." She held it up.

"What I want to know," Harley asked, "is do your parents know you can levitate? Does anybody?"

"I'm pretty sure my mother and sister don't know. And I'm so mad at my mother now that I'm not going to talk to her about it. My Dad lives in Florida. I'd ask him if I got the chance. I doubt he knows, though. I don't know where I got the genes, but now I'm thinking it may actually run in families. Last night I started teaching my cousin Wendy. She got a few inches off the floor. She's also the only one who's seen me do it."

"When did it start?" Charlie asked. "Last year Mo was talking about his telekinesis and said his parents said they watched him spin the mobile over his crib."

"The first time I was four. I was in the back yard on our swing. The neighbors' pit bull came into our yard, snarling. I knew he saw me, so I parachuted off the swing, planning to run for the back door. But I hit the ground and fell on my face. I could see he was about to charge. I remembered a movie on TV about people in a hot air balloon throwing baggage off so they could stay above the waves. So I imagined myself getting rid of excess weight. I started to rise. The dog was startled, and by the time he did charge and reached me, I was out of reach. He jumped and nipped, but he couldn't get me."

"What happened?" Charlie asked.

"I was tiring and I couldn't go anywhere but up or down, so I was stuck. The neighbor whistled and the dog went home. I floated down onto my hands and knees and went inside."

"Did you tell your parents?" Damon asked.

"Nope. They were caught up in their own drama and were about to divorce. I levitated for fun when I was alone."

"It wasn't for fun last year," Harley said. "You did it in Bronson's cement blockhouse and again at the buried school bus, both times so you could go find help. Thank you."

"You're welcome."

Damon asked the obvious. "If you're teaching your cousin to levitate, can you teach us?" The idea drew excited chatter.

"I don't know. I can try."

"Individual instruction?" Damon asked, grinning.

"Group might be better," Rose said. "We'll see if we can work time into the schedule."

Damon leaned close to Atlanta and whispered, "I'd prefer individual."

SUNDAY

CHAPTER 10

THEY WERE TEN minutes into Sunday breakfast when Caroline walked in and sat down. "Nothing," she said, and reached for the scrambled eggs.

"Nothing what?" Maggie asked.

"On the missing man. The morning news. Hundreds of volunteers and the National Guard searching, thousands of posters handed out, and they haven't a clue."

"No news is good news," Harley said. "He could still be alive."

"He's not," Caroline said.

"He could be," Harley countered.

"I saw him, Harley. With Addie."

"But—."

She froze him with her eyes. "Harley and the rest of you, Ted Alley is dead. They just haven't found his body yet. There's nothing we can do to get him back alive."

"Maybe not alive," Atlanta said. "But we could volunteer to help search, couldn't we? There are nine of us. Addie said, 'Help him, he's dead.'"

"Bando? What do you think?" Twait asked. "Rose? It's eighteen more boots on the ground, nine more pairs of eyes and ears."

"I can call and check with the police," Bando said.

"Sir?" Damon raised a hand and looked to Bando. "I don't think you need to. I'm pretty sure they're going to find his body today."

"Why would you say something like that?" Charlie asked. "Did you dream it?"

Damon shrugged. "I didn't dream anything. But something tells me he'll be found. I don't know where. They're searching the wrong area. Somebody will find him—not the searchers, though, somebody by accident. It's just a strong hunch."

* * *

By the time the teens gathered in the hall again for 9 a.m. meditation, Bando had already done a half hour of yoga stretches and Tai Chi. Now he sat cross-legged on a floor mat. The five campers and Caroline took their places on a semi-circle of rubber mats facing him.

"Everyone is on time. Good." He instructed them how to sit. "Wear loose clothing if you can. Harley, you might want to remove your hat so your scalp can expand on the outside and your brain can expand on the inside."

"Seriously?"

"No. Just the part about the removing the hat."

Bando had them close their eyes so his voice could guide them. He helped them learn breathing technique, muscle relaxation, and how to empty their minds. After awhile they heard him saying, "You may open your eyes when you're ready."

"Holy cow," Charlie said. "It's 9:30. I swear I just closed my eyes. Did I fall asleep?"

"How do you all feel?" Bando asked.

"Relaxed."

"Rested."

"Refreshed."

"Great."

"Like when I came out of anesthesia."

Bando nodded. "That's typical. So far we've used it for relaxation."

"And a way of connecting with the universe," Caroline added.

"That, too, yes," he agreed. "This isn't Caroline's first time meditating. But it appears that it is for some of you. Since most of what we'll do this week has a connection to meditation, let's talk about it, about what we're doing and how it might apply. Anybody want to jump in first?"

Charlie raised a hand. "Sleeping, dreaming, daydreaming, being hypnotized—those are all altered states of consciousness that are different from our everyday states."

"Thank you, Mr. Encyclopedia," Maggie said.

"Charlie's correct," Bando said. "It has to do with our brain wave frequencies. When we're awake and walking around, walking, playing, working, eating—when we're normally *conscious*—our brain activity is heavy with *beta* waves. When we're knocked out—literally *unconscious*—our brains are emitting more *delta* waves, a very slow, low frequency wave. So conscious is more *beta* and unconscious is more *delta*. In between are two other brain waves: *theta* and *alpha*."

"Is there a quiz on these later?" Harley asked.

"No. Don't memorize the words, just get the concepts. *Theta* waves increase during emotional experiences. There's the fourth, and I've saved the best for last: *alpha* waves. Sleep scientists measure higher *alpha* wave production in the brain during four states—what Charlie referred to as altered states. The first is dreaming, the second is daydreaming, and the third is hypnosis. Know when the fourth is?"

"Meditation?" Harley guessed.

"Excellent guess," Bando said. "But put it on hold for a second and I'll come back to it. The answer is: during times of psychic activity and awareness."

"I see where you're going with this," Charlie said. "Meditation will help us work the process in reverse. We use meditation to intentionally raise our *alpha* levels, putting us in a more receptive state, a more psychically aware state."

"Exactly. Waiting for a dream or a daydream to give us psychic awareness is too haphazard. With hypnosis it's somebody else controlling the situation."

"But," Maggie interrupted, "by using meditation rather than

hypnosis, we're maintaining more self-control while increasing our *alpha* and our psychic awareness."

"We slow down our brains," Bando said, "and lower the frequency. More alpha but plenty of beta in the mix."

A couple of them looked bewildered.

"Okay," he said. "Try this. Make the sound of rumbling thunder for me." They did.

"Now imagine your toast is stuck in the toaster and burning. It sets off the smoke detector. Know that high-pitched alarm sound? Let me hear you recreate that."

They all made some variation of the sound.

"That was an act of will, wasn't it? For the thunder you told your vocal cords to produce low frequency sounds and to suppress middle and high frequencies. Then for the smoke detector you told your vocal cords to suppress the low and middle but allow the highs. You manipulated the situation, didn't you?"

Maggie grinned. "Meditation can be a mild self-hypnosis. We slow our minds down, produce more *alpha* waves, and increase our psychic awareness."

"Nicely put, Maggie," Bando said.

"So we can know what we don't know we know," Harley said. "I know it sounds like a riddle, but it makes sense to me."

The others agreed it that it made perfect sense.

Bando said, "I like the way you're all thinking. Now here's another question. There are two violins in a room, but only one violinist. The violinist picks up the first violin and starts to play. What does the other violin do?"

Charlie said, "The second violin mimics the first. It's a sympathetic response."

The others stared at him as if he'd spoken Russian.

"The first violin plays. The strings of the second vibrate at the same frequency," he explained.

Bando replied, "Yes. They communicate, *connect*, because they share a certain range of frequencies."

Caroline said, "Last summer Mom and I connected with the spirits of Karen and Addie, who were no longer living. Ghosts must vibrate at a different frequency than when they were living. Mom and I must overlap with them at some common frequency." Charlie said, "I read a book by this psychic named John Edward. He had a TV show called *Crossing Over*. The reruns are great. He connects with dead spirits who want to communicate with some of the audience members."

"Some people say he's a fake," Atlanta commented.

"Same people who don't believe a girl can levitate," Maggie muttered.

"I didn't say he was a fake," Atlanta responded defensively. "I said other people say it. Like, does he actually see them? Do they look like they did when they were alive?"

"He says they're not really visible to him," Charlie answered. "He gets impressions of them. You have to train yourself to do it. But listen to this. He says he gets ready for psychic readings by *meditating*. He slows his mind down like we're talking about doing. It's the frequencies. He has to slow his down and the dead have to speed theirs up so they can overlap—which is where they meet. He can't stay in that state for long because real life sets back in—beta waves, I guess—and the dead have a hard time maintaining it for long as well."

"Sounds like a relay team in track at the handoff," Harley said. "Runner with the baton slows down as the next runner speeds up so they can make the transfer. In that split second when they're both touching the baton—speed, frequency, kind of the same thing—they're connected."

The others nodded.

"So," Maggie said. "This John guy meditates to increase his alpha waves and goes ghost hunting. But he doesn't actually see them. How come Caroline and Rose see and hear them?"

"He's not ghost *hunting*," Charlie said. "He's making himself *receptive* to spirits who want to speed up and approach him. I don't know why Caroline and Rose are so receptive without even meditating, but they are."

"If they start meditating, they'll have ghosts lined up at the door," Harley half joked.

Bando cleared his throat. "Rose and I know of John Edward and his use of meditation. Other psychics have claimed they can meditate to a lower frequency and then engage in astral travel—what some call the out-of-body experience—which we'll save for a different discussion."

Suddenly Rose was there towering over the group. "I overheard the last minute. I want to go back to John Edward and the idea of living people communicating with the dead. Using meditation to prepare is a centuries-old practice. However, very few have legitimately used it to that end. Most mediums who offer séances or meetings with the dead are charlatans, hucksters, and con artists. They prey on the grieving and the gullible so they can separate them from their money. Their time is spent less in meditation and more on perfecting the con. So be skeptical and beware. Bando, back to you for the last word."

"Rose, Caroline, and this John Edward may have similar gifts, but they are also different persons. John Edward seems to see it as a calling— his mission in life—to bring messages of comfort to the living day after day. He may be legitimate. Caroline is still developing her gifts and will have to decide for herself how and when to use them. I have known Rose for a long time and I'm certain she doesn't feel called to do what John Edward does. Otherwise, thousands and thousands of people would line up and demand readings, treating her like a candy machine they could pay into, expecting to get what they want in return."

Harley raised an index finger. "Rose and Caroline are also different from John what's-his-name in other ways. They get clearer images than he does. And it's the ghosts who come looking for them, not them sitting and waiting for the ghosts in a TV studio. My question about Caroline and Rose isn't whether it's true, but *why?* These ghosts must have to work pretty hard to get to you. Why come here?"

"They need our help," Caroline said.

"They sense we're the ones they can ask," Rose added.

Damon spoke up. "Here's the way I imagine it. A group of dead people has been riding the train that goes from this side to the other side, life to death. They've stopped at a station for a rest stop. This Addie and her mother and Donnie Bronson all have their tickets punched. But they get talking to this poor Alley guy who's wandering around the station without a ticket, or maybe he's lost it. Either way he can't get back on the train. You see? Something's blocking him from crossing over, some unfinished business. Addie feels sorry for him, because she and her Mom had the same holdup last year—unfinished business while they waited for Bronson. So she tells this man she knows somebody among the living who might be able to help—maybe two people—a girl named Caroline and her mother Rose who have learned to set aside their fear of ghosts and help. Addie knows a good place for this Alley ghost to appear—at the waterfall, which has worked for her before. Problem is, Alley can't go alone because he's a newbie; he isn't good at changing his frequency yet. He'll come across fuzzy and won't be able to speak very well. So Addie agrees to be his guide and mouthpiece."

"Makes sense," Atlanta said, playing with her nose ring. "So what we need is to find out what's keeping him from crossing over."

CHAPTER 11

ATLANTA SAT ON the log bench overlooking the swimming area watching Damon skip rocks on the water.

"Damon?"

"The answer is yes."

"You don't even know what I was going to say."

"You were wondering if I think you're hot. The answer is yes. We have chemistry."

She smiled. "That's not what I was going to ask."

"Oops. There goes my gift for reading minds."

"Actually, I think you did know, but you didn't want to hear it and gave me an answer you thought might block it."

"So now you're psychic, flying girl?"

"Not psychic. Intuitive. It's women's intuition. And I don't fly, I levitate."

"Same difference."

"No, it's not. It's like a plane and a blimp. They both get up in the air, but the plane flies and the balloon floats. I'm a blimp."

"No, you're not. You look great."

She forced a smile. "You're avoiding the subject."

"What subject?"

"Why did you make yourself scarce when that policeman showed up yesterday? Are you afraid they're checking up on you?"

Damon sat down beside her and stared out over the lake. "I have bad dreams about cops. A couple of them tried to sweat a confession out of me the night my parents died. They came at me all night."

"So your mind tells you to keep looking over your shoulder?"

"Always." He stared down at the sand. "And it won't stop until they—or I—"

"Or we—find out who set the fire."

She reached an arm around his shoulder and they sat quietly for several minutes.

"I like the piercings," he said finally.

"My Mom didn't want me to get them. I can't remember the last time we agreed on something. She doesn't want me to grow up. Last week I wanted a tattoo. She said if I got it, I couldn't come to camp."

"Get it after you get home."

"I may. Most likely I will. Oh, I don't know. I'm not so sure now. The piercing and the hair I'd have probably done anyway, but even then I'm not a hundred percent certain. It's all mixed up with me being pissed at her for everything lately and I want her to know it."

"Like what else are you pissed at?"

"The divorce. I blame her for it, and for driving Dad away and for forcing us to move to Vermont."

"Sounds confusing. Do you get to see him?"

"Twice a year."

"Why only twice a year?"

"He moved to Florida, near Orlando. We lived in Georgia before the divorce. Now we're in Vermont, which seems like the boonies. But Mom insisted she had to be near her parents."

"But you do get to see your Dad." It was a statement, not a question. "And you talk to him on the phone."

"Yes."

"Consider yourself lucky. They're both still alive—separate but alive. And their marriage wasn't all about you."

She didn't answer but she got his message and looked like she was thinking.

CHAPTER 12

MAGGIE AND CHARLIE kicked a hacky sack in front of the dining hall while Harley sat admiring their footwork.

"My feet work better than my hands," Charlie said, and flipped the little beanbag from his toes up to the opposite kneecap and then across to the other foot.

"Unless you're eating," Harley said, tearing a blueberry muffin in half.

A pickup crunched up the driveway, parked, and a man got out. He walked toward them, a thick rolled newspaper under his arm.

"Morning," he said with a broad smile. "Great day for hacky sack. Sun's nice and warm." He motioned toward the screen door. "Bando and Twait in?"

"Both inside. Rose, too," Harley answered. "You're Jerry, right, last year's driver?"

The man's smile vanished and he lowered his eyes as if he'd been caught stealing. He nodded and started for the steps.

"Wait," Harley said, standing and blocking the man's way. He extended his right hand. "I'm Harley, formerly known as Mouse. I'm sorry for what happened to you. We're all sorry."

Jerry looked puzzled.

"I was in your van, the one Bronson carjacked. He had already tied you up by the time we got in." He shook Jerry's hand. "We know Bronson had a gun. You must have been terrified."

Jerry's eyes met the boy's. He swallowed hard and said hoarsely, "I'm so thankful you all made it out alive."

"Us, too."

The man seemed to relax a little. "How many of your five came back to camp?"

"Me and Atlanta."

"She's the one who walked for help?"

Harley nodded.

Jerry broke off the handshake and stepped past Harley. He paused with his hand on the screen door, looked back, said thanks and went inside.

Twait saw him coming. "Hey, stranger, long time no see."

Bando and Rose looked up from the table.

"Still some muffins and coffee," Rose said, pointing. "You know the drill. Grab something and come sit down."

Jerry fixed two muffins, sweetened a cup of coffee, and came to the table.

"You're a better man than I am," Twait said. "I can't finish two muffins nowadays."

"Metabolism," the slim man said. "Turned fifty-five, but I've still got this nervous energy. Food runs through me like seed through a goose."

"So how have you been?" Bando asked.

"Getting better. It's been slow. Got the therapist visits down to one a month. Fewer nightmares."

The other three nodded.

"No Caroline this summer? What'd you do—farm her out to relatives?"

"She's here," Rose said. "We have computer and TV in the cabin this year."

"Ah," he said. "Alternating babysitters."

"So, what brings you out on a Sunday morning?" Twait asked. "All the churches closed?"

Jerry almost choked on a piece of muffin. "Hah. Good one." He unrolled the *Maine Sunday Telegram* and smoothed it on the table. "This is why I'm out. Obviously you haven't seen the paper."

"Sundays I pick it up in town at noon," Twait said.

Jerry separated the sections. "You know about the missing man, right?"

"Yeah. Ted Alley," Rose answered. "Caroline caught the morning news, which said he's still missing. Any change?"

"No. I just came from the diner. Searchers stayed out all night. They're still at it."

"You think he's okay?" Rose asked.

"I hope so. With luck he'll walk out of the woods soon and try thumbing a ride home. He was a fisherman before the Alzheimer's, so maybe his automatic pilot will kick in and he'll follow a stream downhill until it crosses a road. It's not cold at night, so exposure won't be the problem. Bugs maybe. Or a fall."

"I worry the longer this goes on," Rose said, "the poorer his chances."

"True. But Alley's not why I stopped by. I wanted to show you the stupid spread the *Telegram* did. Look at this. It's a rehash of camp-related accidents and disasters over the years. What are they trying to do, drive away all the tourists and summer visitors? I'll bet the Governor's hot over this."

He pushed a section of the paper across the table.

Twait scanned it and cursed softly. "Look at all this. Sensationalism. Here's the Bronson story—so much for not calling attention to us this year. Why'd they have to dredge that up again? The *Telegram's* turning into a damn supermarket tabloid."

"Can we see, too?" Charlie asked as he, Maggie, and Harley appeared behind Twait.

The section included a roundup article listing accidents, tragedies, and disasters at different Sebago and Bridgton area summer camps. It mentioned fires, a child paralyzed after being thrown from a horse, a bee-sting death, two suicides, and an electrocution.

A gray-shaded sidebar gave the names and death dates for drowning victims at the Free Camp waterfall, including Karen and Addie Beals in the Mixmaster and Donnie Bronson in the plunge from the top that

Twait survived. The Bronson paragraph referred readers to another story—with photos—recapping his commandeering of Jerry's van and his abduction of five campers.

"We do everything we can to not draw attention to ourselves," Twait moaned.

"Look at this, Twait," Rose said. She pointed to some photos on the back page. "They found one of your old publicity shots, probably on the Internet."

Embedded in the Bronson story was a pair of photos. One was of the waterfall. The other was very old and showed a little person with long, thick, curly red hair. It was either a publicity photo or a promotional postcard. The fine print read *Tiny Twait the High Diving Midget*. He stood on a stool next to *Atlas the World's Strongest Man*, who looked like a seven-footer. Both men had the sculpted bodies of competitive bodybuilders. The caption noted that Theodosius Wilfred Waight, Twait, had survived the fall from the waterfall that killed Bronson. He was listed as the assistant director at Free Camp, serving the needs of gifted children.

"I know you don't want the spotlight on the camp," Harley said. "But you've got to love that old photograph."

***

Not far away in Raymond on the east side of Sebago Lake a man sat in a diner drinking coffee and reading the same articles. He skimmed the missing-man story, already knowing everything he needed to know. His eyes focused on the 8C photo of the High Diving Midget. Like Harley, he also loved the old photograph—but for a different reason. Here was another suitable subject being revealed to him. Thanks to Lady Luck, he'd been discovering them one by one. The Crazy Switch snapped on in his head once again.

CHAPTER 13

THAT AFTERNOON THEY drove to the Horton Farm and Cemetery in North Bridgton. The family's matriarch, Carmen, gave them the history and showed them the segment that had been taped for *American Ghost Story*. A tour of the house and grounds followed, ending at the family cemetery. Needing to get off to town for a school meeting, she invited them to stay as long as they liked then bade everyone farewell and left.

"Did any of you sense a ghost or spirit in the house?" Twait asked. "Like maybe in that room with the rocking chair?"

Nobody had.

"Rose? Caroline? You're the ghost-busters," he pressed. "Anything?"

They shook their heads.

"Maybe Horton ghosts are shy around visitors," Maggie suggested.

"It was kind of a dud," Harley lamented. "I expected more."

"Let's give it awhile," Bando suggested. "Remember what we said about *alpha* waves? Why don't we try sitting and meditating?"

"Right here in the graveyard?" Atlanta asked.

They chose their spots, most of them near the little perimeter fence. Damon moved to a gravestone in a corner and sat with his back against it. Bando took them through a brief meditation session.

"Anything?" Atlanta asked when they finished. "Anybody?"

They all shook their heads except Harley, who sat with his legs still crossed and his back against the fence. His head lolled forward on his chest.

"Harley fell asleep!" Charlie said, and the others laughed. But the laughter didn't awaken him. "Harley!" Charlie said loudly in his ear. "Wake up!" He prodded his friend's shoulder. Harley slumped sideways onto the grass. "Bando!" he said with alarm. "What' wrong with Harley?"

Before Bando could answer, Harley opened his eyes, sat up slowly, and stretched himself awake.

"Wow, that was weird. I dreamed I was standing right there next to the fence, looking at you and at myself until Charlie pushed me over."

"Yeah, right," Charlie said. "Maybe you were having an out-of-body experience—you know, like floating over an operating table while they're working on you."

"It's a side-effect of the anesthesia," Maggie said.

"Actually, you've got two different things," Damon said. "The operating table is a near-death experience. It could happen at a car wreck, too. Something pulls you back. The anesthesia is closer to what they call *astral projection*. Seems to me the difference might be that you *choose* to leave your body for a while and check things out."

"Did you see anything more specific?" Rose asked. "Like somebody pulling out a wallet or writing down a message, something you couldn't have known otherwise? I don't mean to be skeptical, but when you started meditating you knew Charlie was next to you. You could have woken up lying on your side and assumed he pushed you over."

"No, I literally saw him push me over. Other than that I didn't see anything special. You were all just sitting and meditating until the session was over. Then you all got up and I didn't. Charlie pushed my shoulder and I fell over. I wish I could verify more, but nobody was doing anything. It's not like a fox ran by. And even if it had, none of you would have seen it with your eyes closed. But I get your point. It's questionable. Even now it's starting to feel like I dreamed it. Maybe it was that, a dream."

Bando said, "Let's assume it happened as you said. It's not going to hurt anything. Don't talk yourself out of it. Let it ride."

They all dusted the dry grass from their seats and walked out the little gate single file. Caroline and Rose were the last out, and as they cleared the gate, it slammed on its own. They spun, but no one was there. So they went back, opened the gate, and stepped back inside the graveyard. The gate slammed again.

"Caroline, don't move," Rose said. "Bando, Twait, keep everyone out. Somebody wants us to visit." The two of them stood perfectly still. "See anyone?"

"Something like a dust cloud coming together in that corner by the rose bushes. Right in front of that grave marker Damon was leaning against. Getting thicker, like a swarm of bees. You see it, too?"

"Yes. Someone's working hard to come through."

A gauzy form slowly took shape.

"It's a man," Caroline said.

"Ted Alley?"

"Don't think so. Younger. And look at him—he's burned."

"Burned?" Damon called from outside the fence. "Is it my father? I was sitting right on that spot where you say he is."

"I don't think so, Damon," Rose answered. "This man isn't very tall, and I'm guessing he was in his twenties when he died. His mouth is moving, but there's no sound. Can you hear anything, Caroline?"

"No."

"Let's take a couple of deep breaths, relax, and slow our brains down."

Rose and Caroline stood quietly, their shoulders slumping as they relaxed.

"He's fading, Mom. He's tiring."

"Young man, focus! We're losing you. One word is all we need. One word!"

"He's gone, Mom. I got a word, though. Did you get it, too?"

"I did. *Scarecrow?* That the word?"

"Sounded like it to me."

Behind them the gate eased open of its own accord.

CHAPTER 14

IT WAS LATE afternoon when they got back to Free Camp. The teens headed to their cabins while Caroline made a beeline for the computer. Bando, Twait, and Rose went into the kitchen.

"Answering machine's blinking," Rose said as she passed the office, and the three of them stepped in. Bando pressed the Play button.

"Bando, Rose, Twait? This is Jerry calling around 4:15. I know you were going out to the Horton Farm, so you probably haven't heard. They found Ted Alley's body. Sounds like he may have hanged himself in the highlands above Sandy Point. Two mountain bikers from Camp Sojourner—counselors, I heard—found him in a clearing. The 5 o'clock news should have something on it."

* * *

Caroline ran a Google search using the key words *charred body, burn victim,* and *scarecrow.* Google returned more than 45,000 possibilities. So she dropped out the words *burn victim* and ran it again—still a phenomenal number of links to consider. A quick check of the first three pages repeatedly referenced the TV show, *Bones,* Season 2 Episode 11, "Judas on a Pole," in which the show's star investigators are called to the roof of the Federal Building and find the burned remains of a street snitch hung on a cross like a scarecrow. Other links led to arts and crafts sites or gardening sites: How to Make a Scarecrow for Halloween and How to Make a Scarecrow for Your Garden. Of the three-dozen web addresses Caroline skimmed, none looked promising.

The door opened and her father walked in and clicked on the TV. Bando was only a step behind.

"They found Ted Alley's body," Twait said. "Need to catch the news."

The story was already in progress, the police photo of Alley on the screen behind a woman newscaster.

"The body was discovered this afternoon by two camp counselors out mountain biking near Sandy Creek, south of Bridgton. That part of Cumberland County, from Sebago Lake north, is known for its many church summer camps."

The sportscaster beside her looked like he might be a young father himself. He commented, "Imagine if a group of kids from one those camps found him."

"Absolutely," the newswoman responded, "That would have been traumatic." She finished the report with, "How the man got there and the cause of his death are under investigation."

"Jerry's message said the rumors have him hanging himself," Twait said. "She didn't mention that."

"Isn't Sandy Creek close?" Caroline asked. "What is it, maybe ten miles?"

"Fifteen, give or take a mile," Twait answered.

"Maybe we can find out more. I knew he was dead yesterday when Addie brought him through at the waterfall. You think it's true that he hanged himself? If he did, why would Addie say he needed our help?"

"Maybe he was hanged," Twait said. Maybe it's not a suicide. If it's not that, and if it's not an accident, what's left?"

"Murder," Rose said through the screen door. "Bando? Twait? Smitty's waiting in the kitchen."

CHAPTER 15

T HE TROOPER'S NAMETAG read *Smith*, but Bando, Twait, and Rose knew her as Smitty. She worked the afternoon/evening shift. Sometimes when they went to Slices and Ices for pizza or ice cream they'd see her cruise the parking lot noting license plates. On several occasions she had come inside and stopped at their table to chat. Once a week she managed to stop by Free Camp on a courtesy call.

Twait climbed up onto the serving counter and dangled his stubby legs over the edge. Rose leaned against the counter next to him. Together they looked like a ventriloquist act.

Bando sat on a wooden stool at the end of the center worktable.

"What Smitty has come here to say *officially*," Rose started off, "is that Ted Alley's body has been found and the public needn't worry."

"So say Top Cop and the Governor," Smitty added, emphasizing "*officially*."

"They don't want to spook the tourists whose wallets we depend on," Twait commented.

Smitty shrugged. "They don't just bring money. They also bring their children, and if they're scared they can pull them out anytime. I heard your numbers are down this year, maybe for that reason."

"Point taken," he said. "But back to the Alley death. Speak *unofficially*."

"Well," she said, looking across at the odd couple.

"Okay, not unofficially," Rose said. "But how about *personally?*" At the drop of the word she saw Smitty's gaze flicker to Bando and back to her. "You might advise us to be careful and on the lookout for suspicious characters and unusual activity. You might suggest we keep our campers close to home and have them travel in pairs or more. You might say there's no need to panic, but why throw caution to the wind. And you might say that even we adults need to be on our guard until this is resolved, right?"

"Right. Everybody."

Bando jumped in. "Everything's not fine. We can feel it, these campers sense it, and your stopping by tells us something's fishy. You wouldn't drive in here if Alley's death had been an accident or a suicide. Rumors abound he was found hanging in a clearing."

"You're welcome," was all she said, and turned for the door.

"Wait."

She turned back. An eyebrow went up.

"I'm sorry. I—," fumbled the man who was seldom at a loss for words. "I-I appreciate your coming out, Smitty, to check on us, warn us—even if you have to do it between the lines. Thank you."

Rose and Twait exchanged a sideways glance, tickled to see Bando flustered.

He finally said, "Did you see the scene?"

"I did. Trooper Ward and I were first on the scene before the Crime Scene guys took it over. This was my first stop after they let me go."

"First?"

She nodded and gave him a what's-so-odd-about-that look.

"Well. I, uh, I'm sorry you had to see him like that. Even with experience, it's got to be hard."

"As I said, I didn't see it alone. Ward was with me. Pity the poor couple that found the body. Recently married, just a couple of twenty-something church camp counselors out for a bike ride."

"Are they okay?" Rose asked.

"They're pretty shaken up."

There was an awkward lull in the conversation so Bando said, "Well, we won't keep you from your appointed rounds." When he finished the sentence, Smitty stared at him, shook her head slightly, and started for the door again.

"Oh, one last thing, Smitty," Rose said. "We've known you for a couple of years, but we don't know your real name--Smith, obviously. But what's your first name?"

"Alicia. Why?"

"Alicia," Rose repeated, avoiding the why. "That's lovely."

Twait agreed.

Bando said, "I wish we'd asked before."

She smiled and some color came into her cheeks. "Well, this isn't my only stop. I've got a few other camps to see, too. I'd better hit the road."

"Thank you, Alicia," Rose said.

Bando stood and walked toward her, extending his right hand so they could shake. "Yes, thank you, Alicia. It's too bad the State Police got you before we could. Something tells me you'd be great."

"Great?" Rose asked.

"With the teens," he amended. His eyes locked on Alicia Smith's for a moment.

"She's got to go back to work, Bando," Rose reminded. "You need to let go of her hand."

The three of them walked Smitty to the porch and watched her drive off.

"She saw the scene," Bando said. "She knows something's wrong with it. Either she hasn't put her finger on it or the Crime Team won't let her say anything yet."

"When you shook her hand," Twait asked, "did you get a mental picture of it?"

"No. It's like she knew I was fishing."

"A picture isn't what I saw developing in that handshake," Rose ribbed.

Bando blushed. "Get off it, Rose. I know the line is trite, but I'm old enough to be her father."

"The only time I've heard you use a trite line," she parried, "is when you're at a loss for words."

"No, that's not true. Trite it may be, but that phrase describes perfectly the ridiculousness of your implication. She's attractive, yes, and interesting, yes. But I've got thirty years on her."

"Twenty-five," Twait said. "Don't exaggerate the age difference. And Rose didn't ask you if the woman was attractive and interesting. You volunteered that observation."

"All right, enough, you two. She's attractive and interesting, period. Back to Ted Alley's body hanging in the clearing."

"Okay," Rose said. "It's clear we may have a killer wandering around our back yard. We'll talk to the campers over supper."

"Rose?" Bando asked in a beggy voice. "A favor?"

"Yes, you can borrow my brand new car in the morning."

"You must be a mind reader."

"I am. Retired. When do you want to borrow it—right after meditation? And why? So you can pay a visit to Camp Sojourner. How am I doing so far?"

"You're just as good as you ever were, Madame Rosario."

CHAPTER 16

Once everyone sat down for supper the questions started.

"Why was the cop here?"

"It was about the dead guy, Ted Alley, right?"

"It was murder, wasn't it?"

"Yes, it was about Ted Alley," Rose answered. "They haven't declared foul play yet. But they want us to be on the safe side just in case there's a bad guy running around. Stay on the camp property and travel in groups, pairs at a minimum. Nobody alone."

That started a round of chatter that ended with Caroline saying, "Oh, come on. The man was murdered. We know it. The cops know it. It's just not public yet."

All eyes fell on her.

"If it was an accident or a suicide, the news would have had that right away. And Smitty wouldn't come out here if there were no danger. Alley was dead yesterday when he showed up at the waterfall with Addie. Now we've got a second victim who was burned—the guy we saw at the cemetery. My guess is he came through on that spot because Damon was sitting there—and Damon's Dad was also burned. That makes sense to me. Whether Alley and the burned man are connected I don't know."

"Any luck with Internet searches?" Charlie asked her.

"From Alley's home to Sandy Point is over 20 miles. So he didn't walk it all. At least one driver gave him a ride. It's probably the person who killed him."

Bando let the gasps and whispers subside and said, "This is a good teaching moment. While we're eating let's talk about how we receive data."

"Fax, email, and cell phone," Harley blurted out.

"You'll have to excuse Harley," Maggie said. "He can't help it— fiftieth percentile class clown. Fifty out of a hundred—do the math— half wit." A couple of the others snickered but Maggie's support quickly died.

"Okay," Bando said. "Hard data and soft data. What's hard data?"

"Facts and figures," Charlie said. "Or evidence—a letter, phone record, fingerprint, DNA. Mainly it's stuff that's admissible in court."

"Good examples," Twait noted. "What about a ghost sighting or a hunch or a feeling?"

"Soft data," Harley said. "May be helpful but not admissible."

"Very good," Bando said. "Now, in addition to hard and soft data, we have a third area—interpreting those data. I'm referring to theories, deductions, and conclusions."

"Here's a good example of putting hard and soft data together," Atlanta chimed in. "Last summer I had hard data—a license plate number from Bronson's snowmobile trailer. So I wouldn't forget, I kept reciting those numbers while walking that back road from the sand pit. Here at camp, Juanita heard me repeating the numbers. But no court is going to accept a remote-hearing story as hard data, so the license plate numbers at that point became soft data. No matter how accurate, psychic information is soft data, which means many people will not accept it."

"It was more complicated, though," Charlie said. "When you saw the numbers on a license plate, they were hard data. On our end, we didn't know that what Juanita heard was a license plate. And we didn't know they came from you. Once we agreed Juanita was actually hearing you at a distance, we still had to consider that they could be a zip code, a phone number, or lottery numbers. Eventually we deduced—figured out—

they made up a license plate. That's the deductive part Bando is talking about, the third process. The police took a chance and, not knowing if it was hard or soft data, ran the numbers through their computer, which matched them to Donnie Bronson."

"Exactly," Rose said. "Hard data, soft data, and the process stuff. Law enforcement is stuck using only hard data along with deductions and conclusions, though we here can consider soft-data. Smitty would call those hunches police smarts. We, not being cops, have limited access to their hard data. But we have a wealth of soft data from you—psychic data."

"Like Caroline's and your ghosts," Maggie said. "The rest of us can't see them, but we believe you two can."

"Charlie's dreams are soft data," Twait pointed out.

"I don't see how spoon bending or levitation play into this," Maggie said. "No offense intended, Atlanta, but our gifts don't provide information, hard or soft."

"True, they don't provide data," Bando said. "Which makes them not *psychic gifts* but *paranormal* gifts. Atlanta's two levitations last summer allowed her to escape Bronson and go for help. And Maggie, you combined your paranormal gift for manipulating metal with BJ's psychic gift of seeing the inside of those locks; working together you opened the padlocks. She pictured the pins and you lined them up to pop the locks."

"Why are you telling us this?" Damon asked.

"Because we're being *drawn* into this mystery and we may or may not be able to say no. We can let the police handle it—they have most of the hard data--but we're able to access soft data that they can't. The problem is, we can't disclose your gifts or it would blow your cover."

"And they wouldn't believe a bunch of teenagers anyway," Damon said.

"Probably true," Bando continued. "But whenever I can, I'll communicate it indirectly to the police."

"Meaning through that policewoman, Smitty?"

"Through any means I can, Damon," Bando answered.

After a long silence Harley said, "I don't know if this is anything, but I've concluded that Mr. Alley was hanged."

Rose said, "We haven't mentioned that yet. Why would you say that, Harley?"

"Two pieces of soft data lead me to the conclusion. First, Caroline said Alley's ghost appeared with his head tilted to the side. Second, look at Damon's drawing there. It's soft data—unless he and Atlanta are playing Hangman."

A notebook lay open halfway between Damon's right hand and Atlanta's left. On the page he had drawn a gallows shaped like a giant number 7. Under it he had placed six underlined letters as if a games-player had guessed them one at a time: H A N G E D.

"Atlanta?" Damon asked.

She shook her head.

"It was you, Damon," Harley said firmly. "I watched you do it."

"Couldn't have. That's my right side. I'm a lefty."

"Not any more," Harley answered, and said to Maggie, "Soft data. Charlie's book calls it *automatic writing.*" Then he added, "Class clown scores, spikes ball," and gave her a smug grin.

CHAPTER 17

AFTER THEY MADE their phone calls home they started a roaring fire in the pit by the ball field. Sitting around and toasting marshmallows for s'mores seemed like the right ending to Sunday.

"So, Caroline," Maggie asked, blowing on a blackened marshmallow on a stick. "What's the deal on your Mom and Dad and Bando? How'd they get together? And why'd they start up a camp for weirdos—I mean *gifted teens?*"

"In England we're called *peculiar children*," Charlie said.

"I saw that on the cover of the book on your bunk," Damon said.

"Yeah. *Miss Peregrine's Home for Peculiar Children,*" Charlie explained. "One of the girls levitates."

"Peculiar," Atlanta said. "Peculiar. Peculiar. Peculiar. Well, that describes us."

"Especially Harley," Maggie quipped.

Harley grinned. "Eat your heart out, spoon bender. It's personality."

Charlie brought them back to the question. "So we know you and your Mom see ghosts. And we know your Dad was a diving midget. Is he psychic? And what do you know about Bando?"

Harley's marshmallow melted off the stick and fell into the fire.

"Mom's got other gifts, but doesn't flaunt them. She has highly developed intuition."

"What's that mean?" Harley asked. "Like my mother having eyes in the back of her head?" Nobody laughed.

"She used to work in carnivals and circus side shows as a fortuneteller, Madame Rosario."

The others stared at Caroline.

"Seriously?" Atlanta asked.

"Yeah, seriously."

"Did she dress like a gypsy and use a crystal ball?" Harley asked, losing another marshmallow to the fire. He set the stick down. "I give up."

Maggie handed him the S'more she had just made. "This one's on me. But no more."

"She did. She dressed the part—silk dress, headscarf, and huge earrings. She worked the crystal ball, the Tarot and dolphin cards, and pendulums—all tools of the trade for psychic mediums. There are tricks, of course, but Mom says many of the fortune-tellers are truly highly intuitive. We have pictures of her in a scrapbook back home in Florida."

"Florida?" Charlie sounded surprised. "Your family lives in Florida?"

"Yeah. Free Camp is only one week long. It's something my parents and Bando developed. We get to stay the whole summer—basically a free summer vacation away from the Florida heat—for care-taking this place."

"Aren't there camps here the other weeks?" Maggie asked.

"Not since Addie and her mother drowned six years ago. Some businessman from Portland bought it and hasn't figured out how to use it yet. This is the only camp week."

"What do your Mom and Dad do the rest of the year?" Maggie asked. "Obviously they're not still performing with the circus."

"Mom's a professor at a community college outside Orlando."

"You're kidding!" Harley exclaimed, bits of Graham Cracker tumbling out of his mouth.

"You truly are peculiar, Harley," Maggie said, shaking her head.

"What does she teach?" Atlanta asked. "Cooking, I'll bet."

"Nope. You guessed figuring she's the camp cook, right?"

Damon said, "Let me guess. She has a Ph.D. and teaches Religious Studies."

Dead silence. They waited for Caroline's answer.

"Exactly right," she said.

"No way!" Harley blurted. "How'd you do that, Damon?"

Damon grinned. "For me to know and you to find out." He let Harley sit with his mouth hanging open for a few seconds. "Harley, she told me. Rose told me in the kitchen yesterday morning when I first got here. We were making the cinnamon rolls and I asked what she did when she wasn't a camp cook. It's hard data, not soft, my friend."

Caroline continued. "As you know from today's newspaper story, my Dad was a high-diving midget. He was a weightlifter, too, which helped him develop the chest and shoulder muscles that protected him in diving. He'll also be the first to tell you he had other jobs in the circus, including cleaning up elephant poop."

"So what's he do for work now?" Atlanta asked. "Midget diving and scooping elephant poop aren't very marketable job skills."

Caroline kept them in suspense nearly a full a minute.

"He's a mini-porn star," Harley wisecracked, and this time they laughed.

"Well?" Charlie pressed.

"He wrestles alligators." Once the surprise wore off, she said, "Near Disney World in this tourist trap. It's a great paying gig. There are posters of him all over the place: Mighty Twait, the Midget Alligator Wrestler. The poster shows him with his arms wrapped around this six-foot gator. The crowds love him and he loves the spotlight. It's a match made in heaven. A little applause and Dad comes alive."

Harley wanted to know if he'd ever been bit.

"A couple of nicks on occasion. You can see teeth scars on his right thigh. But he hasn't had an incident in a long time."

Harley asked if Twait hypnotized the alligators.

"No, Harley. And in answer to the earlier question, Dad seems to have absolutely no psychic or paranormal abilities."

"Hey, he somehow cast a spell over your mother," Maggie said in a syrupy voice, and the others groaned *aw* in unison.

"Does your Mom watch him wrestle them?" Atlanta wondered.

"She used to, but now she's busy with her own job. When she did, though, she'd stand behind him at the autograph table after a performance. Picture six-foot-four Mom standing behind Dad in a chair. He had a joke that always brought down the house. He'd say, 'Wrestling the alligators is easy. But consider my poor wife here. She's the one who has to catch them.'"

When the laughter subsided, Damon asked, "How do Rose and Twait tie in with Bando?"

"When Dad was a little boy—no jokes here—he was always a little boy; when he was a child, Bando was a neighbor. Back then Dad called him Uncle Bando. By some mysterious coincidence they met again later in life when Mom and Dad were in the circus. Bando joined as a mentalist using hypnotism—he calls it the power of suggestion. He was like that guy, The Amazing Kreskin. They all left the circus when Mom and Dad got married and decided to start a family—which so far includes only me."

"So Bando's a magician and a hypnotist?" Damon asked.

"Not a magician—a mentalist," Caroline corrected. "And not hypnotism—power of suggestion. He doesn't perform any more."

"Anything else?" Damon asked.

"Mom says Bando's got really strong intuitive senses, stronger even than hers. I guess he's retired. He stays in our in-law apartment a couple months in the winter. Other than that he travels—around the country and maybe around the world. He doesn't discuss it. He's got a couple of brothers, but—." She stopped mid-sentence.

"Caroline? You okay?" Damon asked.

"Nobody move," she answered. "Freeze where you are and slowly—very slowly—turn your heads and look toward the two trees out by the boys' cabin."

Everyone shifted slowly.

Harley whispered, "What are we looking for?"

"Can anybody else see them?"

Nobody could.

"I see them," a soft voice, Rose's, said behind them. "Addie Beals, Ted Alley, why are you here?"

"Mom, someone's trying to appear behind them."

"They're fading, pulling back to let him show himself. It looks like that burned man from the Horton Cemetery."

"His mouth's not moving this time," Caroline said. "He's not saying *scarecrow.*"

"He's tilting his head down. Alley did that, too."

"No, this is different, Mom. Alley's was to the side—hanged. This guy's is tilting forward on his chest. And look—he's trying to stretch his arms out to the side."

"Like a scarecrow," Damon said. "He doesn't want us to think he's just saying the word. He *is* the scarecrow."

MONDAY

CHAPTER 18

WHILE THE OTHERS were at breakfast Caroline ran computer searches using combinations of *charred, burned, scarecrow, body,* and *victim.* Google brought up thousands of articles and sites. Finally she hit upon *CrimeVoice.com,* a public information bank that listed crime stories and articles about California and surrounding states. It included media and police reports, law enforcement bulletins, and other links. Users could select a particular municipality or a broader region. While one area's police department was reporting a murder, a home invasion, and a liquor store robbery, the editor of a mountain village's online newspaper was posting a paragraph about a rabid coyote attacking a family poodle. One city had fines for violating a sprinkler ban, another a report about burglaries in a certain neighborhood. The LAPD and FBI regularly used CrimeVoice to appeal for the public's help on manhunts. The future was in plain sight: sites like CrimeVoice were fast making Post Office wanted posters obsolete.

Charred victim led her to CrimeVoice.com which had a tab marked *Cold Cases* which brought up an unsolved homicide with the latest updates.

In early August the previous summer a couple in a rented Cessna reported a brush fire in California's Armstrong Redwoods State Recreation Area near Merstin Creek. Fire personnel responded from Guerneville, a small town at the south end of Armstrong Woods' access road. While extinguishing the brush fire, they came upon the burned body of a man lying on his back, arms outstretched. His wrists and ankles had been secured to a cross of two-by-fours under him. The base had been dug in, but the fire burned through it enough that the man's leaning-back weight snapped it. Investigators were certain the body had been upright when the fire started. The victim wasn't immediately identified, so the media had nicknamed him The Crucified One.

Caroline had to stop reading and take some deep breaths. Her stomach rumbled and she tasted bile in the back of her throat. Could this California *charred victim* be the burned young man from the Horton Cemetery who had come later to the campfire?

Thanks to a Texas Missing Person report a week later the victim was identified as James Lee Terrell, Jr., a 20 year-old college student at Texas A&M. His roommates said that in late July he had taken a bus to Oregon to spend a week with friends. At the end of the visit he called to say he was going to thumb his way back through California with a backpack. After a week with no contact they called police to report him missing. Apparently he had thumbed down the wrong car or truck.

The three-year-old photo from his high school yearbook showed a clean-cut, handsome young man. A later update noted Terrell had died of strangulation by ligature six to twelve hours before the fire. He hadn't burned to death. To Caroline, it was small consolation.

She hit the print button and while the printer spat out pages, she fished two large discarded junk-mail envelopes from the trashcan. Across the front of the first she wrote JAMES LEE TERRELL JR., CALIFORNIA. On the other she wrote EDWARD "TED" ALLEY, MAINE. She took two blank sheets of paper and at the top of the first jotted in caps *TERRELL*. Below she started a column of notes and questions. *College student--Texas A&M. Hitchhiking. Was he picked up close to scene or closer to Oregon friends? How long was Terrell with killer(s). Strangled, then burned. Did killer(s) want to burn body? Brushfire--coincidence, accident, intentional? Is this about display and presentation of body? Media nickname: Crucified One. Is this Scarecrow? Crime of opportunity or targeted?* On the second blank page she wrote ALLEY and beneath it scribbled three questions. *Hitchhiking? Hanged? Crime of opportunity or targeted?* She took her notes and the newly printed articles about Terrell and slid them into his envelope. She slipped the single sheet on Alley into the other.

Then she did something completely out of character for her. She bowed her head, clasped her hands over the keyboard, and said a prayer—for James Lee Terrell Jr. and his family, for Ted Alley and his family, and for herself, her family, and everyone at Free Camp.

CHAPTER 19

After breakfast Bando called Camp Sojourner and arranged to meet with the director. Then he asked the six teens to arrive fifteen minutes early for meditation so he could make the appointment. They sat Zen for a half hour, this time without extra discussion.

"I hate to rush off," Bando said while they were rolling up their yoga mats. "But I've got to be somewhere. You've got 45 minutes before your 10 o'clock session with Rose. Bring those pendulums you bought. If you forgot yours or didn't buy one, Rose has a couple of extras."

"Bando?" Harley asked, his rolled yoga mat still in his hand. "Have you got just one minute?"

"If it's life and death, yes. Otherwise, Harley, can it wait two hours until I get back? I'm cutting it close."

Harley sighed. "I guess it can wait."

Bando grabbed Rose's car keys and was out the door.

* * *

"So we've all got our pendulums in front of us," Rose said. "Step One is to cleanse them."

"Of what—evil spirits?" Harley asked.

"Some people will tell you that," Rose answered. "But what you want to do is start fresh and fine-tune it just for you. Perhaps somebody has already adjusted theirs at home?"

"I did," Atlanta said. "Mine came with instructions. I've already used it."

"Rose," Harley said. "It sounds like you're saying it's like drinking out of somebody else's water glass."

Rose lit a small incense burner in the center of the table. "Today we'll use sandalwood incense. You can also use an herb like sage. Some people do it without smoke by leaving their pendulum out in the bright sunshine for the whole day; then they bring it in just as the sun goes down. It's important to cleanse it and charge it up the first time, but it's a good idea to cleanse and recharge it every so often, too. Now, one at a time, hold your pendulum by the chain in the sandalwood smoke."

They took turns.

"Okay, close your palm around your crystal. Let it absorb your particular rhythms, feelings, and energies. You're leaving your impression on it."

"Like downloading our DNA?" Harley asked with a grin.

"Psychic DNA," Damon said.

"So this means we can't borrow each other's pendulums," Maggie said.

"Correct. Once you program it, it's unique to you."

"Unless somebody cleanses it and reprograms it," Caroline explained. "I started with one of Mom's old ones."

"So how do we program them?" Damon asked. "We want to be able to ask them questions, right—like a Ouija board or divining rods you use to find water?"

"Since you're beginners, you want to start out basic: Yes, No, and Maybe—which is also Don't Know. When you're asking it a question, you'll be holding the top of the chain between your thumb and index finger so the crystal hangs at the bottom. Like this."

They copied Rose.

"And you'll rest your elbow on a firm surface, not your knee. A table works nicely or the arm of a chair."

They all tried it.

"Your pendulum should not be moving. Just let it hang. Now since there are three motions it can take—away from you and back, side-to-side, or in a little circle—you have to decide which motion means what. Now set them down on the table. You can decide and program yours any way you want in a minute."

They all set their pendulums down.

"The easiest way of course is to make a Yes answer like the motion of your head when you nod—away-and-back. When you shake your head No, your head goes side-to-side. That leaves the circular motion for Maybe or Don't Know."

"But you can choose to mix those up," Caroline interrupted. "Or change the code when you cleanse and recharge it next time."

"I want you to take your pendulum and go to different parts of the room, not too close to each other. Swing it away and back ten or fifteen times and tell it out loud what you want that motion to mean: Yes, No, or Maybe. Try to transmit that thought to it as you speak. Then swing it side-to-side ten or fifteen times and do it for another answer. Finally do it for the circular motion. When you finish, clasp your hand around it again and come back to your seats."

Five minutes later they were back.

"While you were doing that I put out a couple of helpful articles about pendulums, one for each of you. They'll give you an idea what types of questions you can ask and what typically doesn't work."

"Is this guaranteed?" Harley said. "Can I ask about hitting the lottery?"

Nobody laughed, but it did start a slew of similar questions.

"I refer you to the articles," Rose said. "And you can find a lot more information online or in basic books. What I'd say, though, is pendulum work takes practice."

"Seems like it'd be easy to manipulate them," Charlie said. "How do we know the answers are legit?"

"Only experience will tell you. But keep in mind that you can only ask your pendulum your own question. Damon can't ask Atlanta's question;

I can't ask Twait's question. That would make for easy manipulation, wouldn't it? The best advice is to use yours in private, so you're not influenced by those around you."

"I'm not sure I buy this whole idea," Charlie said.

"All I can say is give it a try. Each person must make up his or her own mind. That's as far as this session goes. The rest is up to you. Read the articles. Learn and practice."

Harley held out his pendulum and closed his eyes. "Are we having macaroni and cheese for lunch?" The pendulum moved slightly, started swinging side-to-side.

"What's the answer?" Maggie asked. "Did you set yours so side-to-side is No?"

"I'm not telling," he said. "For me to know and you to find out."

"Or you could ask my Mom," Caroline said.

CHAPTER 20

BANDO STROLLED THE grounds of Camp Sojourner with Pastor Rusty Hart, its director. Hart was an affable but serious fifty-something Baptist minister from Rhode Island, a perfect blend of fun and serious that everyone loved.

"They were pretty shaken up," he said, shaking his wooly head. "They're just a young couple with no real experience of death or trauma in their lives. Besides, nothing could have prepared them for this."

"For what?"

"For riding into a scene that looked like a pre-civil-rights era lynching. Except the man wasn't black."

"You think it was a lynching?"

"Well, when they phoned me from the clearing—I was the one who called the cops—that was the first thing they said. They said it was like stumbling upon a lynching."

"Who's *they*?"

"Tina and Rich Sutherland, two counselors. They had a couple hours off and went mountain-biking."

"Who called—him or her?"

"She did. But she got so upset I had her hand the phone to Rich. He described the scene. I could hear her sobbing in the background. He said it looked like a lynching. When he said there was a chair, I told him it sounded more like a suicide. As a pastor I've dealt with these things before. I've been trained to help people in crisis. Rich began to see it differently then, I think, not as a lynching but as someone taking his own life, and he calmed down. I told him to stay there until the police arrived and to not touch anything."

"What do you hear from the State Police, anything?"

"I only know what I've heard on TV, same as you. They haven't said anything about foul play, and I don't think they will. Myself, even though I wasn't there, I see it as a classic suicide, especially with the chair."

The two men stood in the moment's heaviness until Bando asked, "Will Rich and Tina leave early after this?"

"No. I offered to let them off, but they're super-dedicated."

"You wouldn't mind if I said hello to them." Bando's voice was soothing as a massage and his words more a suggestion than a question.

Rusty seemed to think the idea made perfect sense. "Let me see if they're in their cabin."

Rich and Tina Sutherland were mid-twenties and wore matching khaki shorts and green Camp Sojourner tee shirts with teakwood crosses around their necks. They were gracious and hospitable.

Tina heated three cups of water in the microwave while Rich motioned Bando to one of the four unmatched chairs around their table. It was small and round, its surface painted sky blue with a huge white peace symbol.

"This is bottled water," Tina said, setting the cups on the table. "Poland Spring is close by and donates it to the camp. Our well water has sulfur. The showers stink like rotten eggs, but it gives the kids something to complain about now and to talk about when they get back home. Oh, and the tea is herbal. I hope that's all right."

"Bottled water and herbal tea. Love it," Bando said with a warm smile. "Please sit, Tina. We camp people are always so busy, we don't have time to just be together without campers."

She sat next to her husband, which put them at the ends of the peace symbol's double spoke. Bando sat at the end of the single spoke.

They sipped and chatted. Rich was a middle-school history teacher but had applied to law school. Tina, a dental hygienist, was switching careers to acupuncture, acupressure, and massage, planning to specialize in pediatrics. Eventually the three of them grew comfortable enough to talk about the previous day.

"We took our bikes up the north trail," Rich said. "I led on the way up. We came down the east trail with Tina in the lead. She was out front by fifty yards and moving downhill fast. I heard her scream and saw her turn her wheel and dump the bike. I almost ran over her. I hit my brakes, ditched the bike, and ran over to see if she was okay. She was crying and staring at the clearing. I hadn't seen him yet. She pointed and I saw him."

Tina stifled a sob and Rich placed a hand on her back.

"What did you see?"

"A man. She saw a man hanging from a branch," Rich said, answering for her.

"Anything else?"

"The chair he used," Rich said.

"Where was the chair?"

"Close by."

"How close?"

"Not too far. Five or six feet behind him."

"Did the tree have lower branches?"

"I don't remember. Why?"

"How did he tie the rope to the branch?"

"We don't know," Tina cut in. "We didn't go any closer. I called Rusty. He told us not to disturb the scene. He called the police. A while later two State Troopers walked into the clearing from the other side. One was a woman."

"Rusty said your first impression was that this looked like a lynching, like a Ku Klux Klan hanging in the 1930s. What gave you that impression?"

"I don't know," Rich said.

"I just felt it," Tina said.

Rich pulled a tissue box off a small bookcase.

Tina took a tissue and blew her nose. "I can't talk about it anymore for awhile."

"I know this is painful," Bando said, and the couple nodded. "Would you mind if I said a prayer with you? Then I'll go."

Their faces registered relief that the meeting was over.

Bando stretched his arms over the single spoke of the peace symbol, resting his hands on its center, palms up. Tina and Rich did the same along their two spokes, placing their hands on Bando's palms.

"O Spirit, center of this wondrous universe; life-giver, sustainer, healer; we come bearing burdens, searching for grace and the restoration of emotional health. This beautiful couple has seen horror—such terrible horror. *The painful details etched in their memories seek release.*" He paused. "Help them to heal, *to let go of those images.* Empower all of us in the search for justice for this man. Thank you for the love of this caring couple, Tina and Rich, and for their ministries here and at home. Bless their future. And protect all our campers and staffs." Bando stopped.

The couple's cheeks were wet with tears. After a long moment of silence Rich declared, "Amen."

Bando hugged them goodbye as his mind developed the image he'd gotten from Tina in the prayer. He'd have to wait until he got back into Rose's car and on the road before he could examine it more closely.

CHAPTER 21

CHARLIE CARRIED A slab of coffee cake to Caroline's cabin where she was poring over the California printouts.

"You skipped breakfast and I didn't see you take anything when you came for meditation, so I brought you this."

No answer. She was totally absorbed in the files.

"Hey! Inspector Clouseau!"

Caroline's head snapped up and he handed her the coffee cake. She mumbled thanks.

He turned an overstuffed chair to face her and flopped down in it. "So what've we learned?"

"About what? Who?"

"Anything. Anybody," he said. "Mr. Alley or the ghosts."

"Well," she said, leaning back in her computer chair. "I've got nothing on Alley. But I've got something on the burned man, Scarecrow. He's a California case, a murder."

"California?"

"Yep. College kid hitchhiking from Oregon back to Texas gets picked up. He's strangled and his body is wired to a cross in a clearing in a recreation area. A grassfire starts—maybe set, maybe accidental. It burns through the base of the cross, which falls over backwards. A couple in a small plane spots the fire and they call it in. The fire crew finds the charred body while putting out the fire."

"Okay, could be Scarecrow. What's your take on it?"

"The student was from Texas A&M. He was so far from home he probably didn't know his killer. The cross tells us it's more than some driver-versus-hitchhiker argument turned deadly. If it were that, the driver would simply dispose of the body. This is planned."

Charlie sat up straight. "Yeah, why go to all the trouble of that cross?"

"And why put the body out in the open? So somebody would find it. This was very intentional, like staging a house with furniture so you improve your chances of selling it. It's posed to look a certain way. I think this killer *wanted* the body found there on that cross. It may not mean anything to us, but it means something to the killer."

"Okay. What else?"

"The crime-scene experts say it's likely the fire was intentionally started at the foot of the cross to draw attention. The body was secured to the cross by baling wire, which some farms use instead of twine on their hay and straw bales. One crime reporter speculates two bales of straw would have supplied fuel for the fire and enough wire for the bindings. The fire chief said there was no wind and the clearing was triangle-shaped, bounded by three wide dirt trails, so the fire was well contained even before they arrived. I say that wasn't luck. I say the killer didn't want a forest fire that would cover his work, which is why he chose a spot with so little burnable material. His aim wasn't to burn the body—he'd already strangled Terrell. Hay and straw burn hot and fast, and then in no time it's over. This fire was to draw attention to his tableau, his bizarre sculpture. See what I mean?"

"Which means he had to have the hay or straw in the car, and the wood for the cross, too—before he picked up the hitchhiker. He was waiting for a homeless man or a drifter or a hitchhiker when this poor college student came along."

"What he didn't plan on, though," Caroline said, "was the cross falling over, ruining his display. My guess is he wanted the body found upright."

"Like Jesus in the Bible."

"Good point, but I think it's the wrong one, Charlie. When they couldn't identify him for a week, the media nicknamed him *The Crucified One.*"

"Makes sense with the cross."

"But it's also gotten the investigation off course. It's steered them toward religious fanatics on the one hand and anti-religion nuts on the other. But what if they misinterpreted the killer's symbol? What if it isn't a religious connection? Think about it. Terrell wasn't nailed or tied. He was wired in place. Who else besides Jesus is hung up on two crossed pieces of wood? And secured with string or wire?"

"A scarecrow!"

"Bingo! The guy Addie brought through--*scarecrow*. It's James Lee Terrell Jr. Like Ted Alley, Terrell needs our help to catch his killer. The California cops are on the wrong track."

CHAPTER 22

WITH THE OTHERS scattered around the camp, Harley finally had time to relax on his bunk and reflect on the morning's meditation experience. Bando had warned them not to expect too much their first few times, that it was a practice to be built upon.

Just before the half-hour mark, though, five minutes before Bando brought them out of it, Harley had found *the zone*. He hadn't been consciously aware of anything at the time—it was the pleasant experience like the minute or two at the Horton Cemetery. But when Bando ended the meditation he realized he'd been—what was the word—*away*. The meditation experience felt like the anesthesia experience—refreshment— except that with this he had a sense of elapsed time. It was all coming back to him now; it hadn't been a dream. He had risen from the yoga mat and slipped into the camp kitchen and office. He had seen the office clock that read 9:12. He had heard Bando in the big room bringing everyone out of the meditative state, which made him go back and stand over his own cross-legged body where it sat on the mat. Other than in a mirror he'd never seen himself, his whole body, from all angles. He'd never seen the scar in his scalp at the top of his head. He was tempted to shake his sitting body and say hello, but when he tried to touch it, his fingers contacted nothing, or at least he couldn't feel any solid flesh. As the others opened their eyes, he had simply merged into himself again like a hand slipping into a glove. He appeared to come to consciousness only seconds after the rest of them. It seemed more real now in the cabin.

At the time it hadn't seemed possible, so he had decided to tell no one until he first talked to Bando. But Bando had an appointment.

Now he was itching to try it again. He moved from the bunk to the floor and sat between two beds, legs crossed Indian style, back against the wall with a pillow at the small of his back. He closed his eyes, rested his hands on his knees palms-up, and began his breathing practice. He relaxed the groups of muscles from his head and neck down through his shoulders and arms, then through his torso and legs all the way to his feet and toes. Before long he was gone. Gone.

* * *

Bando was half a mile from Free Camp near the old bridge when he found a good roadside turnout and pulled over. He shut off the engine and loosened his seat belt, closed his eyes, and took several deep breaths. Then he called up the mental snapshot Tina Sutherland had transmitted to him during their prayer. It was like being in a darkroom watching a photograph appear in developing solution; he was seeing the forest clearing from Tina's vantage point next to the crashed bike.

A giant maple tree dominated the clearing. An old tire stood leaning against its base. The first crotch of the tree was easily nine feet above the ground, all of its limbs branching out from there or above, none lower. He could see a rope tied halfway out on a main branch with its other end around Alley's neck. Alley was in gray pants and a three-quarter-sleeve Boston Red Sox shirt, his feet in jogging shoes with dark colored socks showing. His knees nearly touched the ground and his shoe tops practically dragged in the dirt, soles up. In front of him his arms hung free, his knuckles inches above the ground.

Between the body and the tree trunk sat a chair still upright. On the seat, hard to make out at a distance, lay what appeared to be a coiled snake.

Suddenly the skin on the back of Bando's neck prickled. He had the sense someone was looking over his shoulder. He turned and checked the back seat. No one. He got out and walked behind the car. No one. The cold prickly feeling subsided, so he climbed back in and drove toward Free Camp.

CHAPTER 23

CHARLIE STEPPED INTO the boys' cabin and found Harley cross-legged between the two bunks, head lolling forward.

"Harley?" He crept closer. "Harley?"

Harley's mouth slowly curled at the corners.

"Harley, are you okay?"

Harley took in a deep breath through his nose and gradually opened his eyes. He took a second, deeper breath and raised his arms over his shoulders, stretching. Dreamy-eyed, he blinked and focused.

"You fall asleep?"

"Nope. Meditating. Why?" He untangled his legs, stood, and walked to the door.

"It's almost lunchtime. I didn't see you around."

"Lunch can wait. I need to talk to Bando."

"He's not back yet."

"He will be any minute." Harley grinned. "Trust me."

By the time they crossed the ball field Bando was parking.

"Sir? Can we talk?"

The lunch bell clanged.

"Right after lunch, Harley. Come on, let's go in and eat."

Once they all sat down and started passing food Bando said, "We need to talk about Mr. Alley's death. It may seem like it's outside Free Camp's boundaries, but it looks like it's going to affect us here. How? I don't know. But certain things suggest we'll be touched by it."

"Soft data," Maggie said.

"Show-off," Harley mumbled.

Bando ignored them both. "So far the only information the public has is that Alley had Alzheimer's, wandered away, and was found dead in the woods near Sandy Creek. There's the rumor Jerry passed along that Alley was found hanged, something Damon's Hangman sketch and Caroline's cocked-head vision may support."

"Suggesting suicide or murder," Charlie said.

"I'm sure it's murder," Bando said. "We've got a very nasty person or persons out there, possibly—probably—still in our area."

Maggie raised an index finger. "So you're saying somebody hanged him?"

Bando shook his head. "Nobody hanged him. But somebody murdered him."

"How can that be?" Damon asked. "If he was hanged by somebody, he was murdered."

"I don't think so," Bando answered. "His body was found with a rope around the neck, but he wasn't hanged. An autopsy will show some other cause of death."

"What makes you say that?"

"I met with the couple who found the body. They gave me very little hard data but a fair amount of soft. If I tried to share it with the police they'd use my statements to implicate me in the murder. So it's got to stay in this room. Agreed?"

Everyone agreed.

"He was killed first and then hanged in plain sight so he could be found."

"Sounds like Terrell on the cross," Caroline said to Charlie, patting the fatter of the two folders.

"Wait your turn," Charlie whispered. "They don't know about that yet."

Bando continued. "The tree's lowest branches are out of reach, so to get up there and tie a rope around the branch, the killer would need a ladder. Nobody's going to carry a ladder from the trailhead up to the clearing and back. Also, it's unlikely Alley was alive—at least not conscious—when the killer brought him to the clearing, otherwise he'd risk Alley escaping while he climbed the tree. There was an old tire at the foot of the tree. Why a tire? I think it was part of a rope swing already on the branch. Our killer simply had to untie the tire and make the loop. I say *loop* and not noose, because an actual hangman's knot has 13 coils. What was around Alley's neck was a simple loop. That's all he needed for display purposes."

"So it's a tableau, a picture message," Rose said.

"It's staged!" Caroline blurted, unable to contain herself any longer. "The way this California killer staged his." She pulled out the files and passed them around, telling the story as the others scanned the reports.

"Both these killings were staged," Charlie said. "It's too much of a coincidence that both were found in State Forests or parks. And both victims were hitchhiking."

"I have a little more to share," Bando said.

"Sorry," Caroline said, and Charlie added, "Me, too."

"Alley's feet were dragging and his knees and knuckles were almost on the ground. If he had hanged himself or been hanged by another, his feet would have been in the air. Yet there was a chair at the scene. Why? It wasn't anywhere near the body. Why would the killer bring a chair?"

"So he could sit and admire his handiwork," Twait guessed.

"Too much extra time," Bando countered. "It adds to the risk of discovery. And why not stand and admire? No need to carry a chair in. That'd be a second trip, since he's probably already carrying a body uphill from where he parked."

"So the chair is a prop," Maggie said. "It sends a message. When somebody dies by hanging, they or somebody else kicks out a chair from under them."

"Then this is a pretty lame message," Harley said. "Trying to suggest hanging? A chair and a rope aren't going to fool a coroner."

Rose said, "We don't know how the chair fits in, but Maggie has a point about the scene. The killer is sending a message. Let's go back to the idea of a tableau. Think of icons and images. For example, look at this new California murder."

"The tableau is Jesus on the cross," Harley said.

"That's one possibility, isn't it?" Rose coaxed. "And the media took it and ran with it, calling the victim The Crucified One. That turns everybody in the direction of religion, doesn't it? But as Caroline is suggesting, is that the only picture you get from two crossed pieces of wood? Remember what she and I heard the burned man say at Horton Cemetery?"

"*Scarecrow*," Harley said. "Two crossed sticks."

"Yes," Rose continued. "Two very different icons using the same starting point: crossed boards. Now let's shift back to Alley. We've already come up with two uses for the chair—something for the killer to sit on and something for Alley to stand on. But those are the *uses* or *functions* of a chair. What if it's not useful? What if it's a symbol pointing to something else?"

Nobody had an idea.

"I just want us to remain open to new possibilities besides how it's used," Rose said. "Right now we're thinking too hard about it."

"We're all beta and not enough alpha," Charlie said, and got several thumbs up. "Maybe it'll come to us during meditation."

Bando said, "The chair may have been important for another reason. There was something coiled up on the seat, like a dead or fake rattlesnake or another piece of rope. It was hard to make out because of the observer's viewing distance. Whatever it was, only the cops and coroner's people will know. I doubt they'll reveal it to the public. I wish we knew."

When Bando didn't continue, Caroline sensed the floor was hers again. "I'm sure the burned man from the cemetery is James Terrell. But the California investigation is following the religious angle. They don't know about *Scarecrow*. Our problem is, ours is soft data, and we have no credibility with them."

"And we can't risk drawing attention to us or any of you," Twait reminded them.

"So we're stuck," Charlie said.

"No, we have another way," Bando said. "My brother Derby. He lives in California. He can't get involved directly, but he has ways of introducing new ideas into the discussion. I'll call him today. Is there anything else to be said about the California case for now?"

A hand went up—Harley's. "You have a brother?"

"Two still alive."

"And one is named Derby?"

"Nickname. He sells hats."

"What's the other one's name?"

"Shaman."

Harley's eyes widened. "Like in witch doctor, medicine man?"

"Same spelling."

Damon cleared his throat and asked, "Can we assume a connection between Terrell and Alley?"

"Good question," Bando said. "Caroline?"

"Soft data—they appeared together. I think they want us to see that even though Terrell was West Coast a year ago and Alley is East Coast this year, they're connected. Both males. Both were walking or hitchhiking. Both died in July. Both found in clearings on public land. One is strangled and the body staged to look like a scarecrow. The other is killed by some means—I'll bet strangled—and the body is staged to look like a hanging. We've got hard data from the files here; we've got similarities; and we've got soft data. What we lack is theories."

"I have another concern," Rose said. "Are these the only two?"

CHAPTER 24

BANDO MOTIONED HARLEY to one of the office's guest chairs then took the other.

"Sorry to keep you waiting all morning," Harley. "Everything okay between you and Damon?"

"Damon? What makes you think Damon and I aren't getting along?"

"I could be wrong, but I thought maybe you both had eyes for Atlanta."

"Oh, that? Well, she's hot this year, that's for sure. But I'm not blind. She and Damon have chemistry. Everybody sees it. Besides, she's out of my league for now. I'm suffering from arrested development."

"Arrested development?"

"Yeah, lack of hair on my body—and slightly lacking in emotional maturity."

"Have you had this talk with your mother or father?"

"Oh sure, with each of them separately. It was embarrassing for them and for me, but they both said the same thing: I'll grow out of it. Each person has their own timeline."

"Sounds like you have wise parents. What about you and Maggie? What's going on there?"

"Nothing. That's more like—well—it's fun to tease each other. It's verbal sparring, good-natured teasing, nothing romantic."

Bando smiled and made his hands into a small steeple, touching his forefingers to his lips. "This isn't what you wanted to talk about, is it?"

"No. It's about the meditation."

Bando raised an eyebrow. "Really? The meditation. Hmm."

"Yeah. Seriously. You wouldn't believe what I got out of it. It's amazing."

Bando said nothing.

"How can I say it? Okay, remember yesterday at the cemetery when I said I saw myself? You told everybody to withhold judgment."

Bando nodded.

"It happened again this morning. A few minutes before you ended the meditation I was walking around the kitchen and the office. The clock on your desk said it was 9:12. I got back just in time to slip into my body."

Bando's face was inscrutable. He gave a noncommittal nod.

"I wanted to talk about it then, but you had that appointment. So while you were gone I decided to try it on my own. I went to my cabin and did the breathing exercise."

Bando's face became a question mark.

"I wanted to see if I could travel farther out-of-body. So I left the cabin and slipped right through the screen door—I didn't even have to open it. And I sort of glided across the ball field and out the driveway to the road. I turned right and went a quarter mile, maybe a half-mile or a mile, I don't know exactly. *And I saw you parked alongside the road.*"

Bando sat up straight, his eyes widening.

"You were sitting there with your eyes closed. I figured you were meditating. For a second there I wondered if you were out traveling, too—you know, outside your body. So I slipped into the back seat."

"That was you! I knew someone was watching me."

"Remember when you looked in the back seat? And then you got out and checked behind the car? I started laughing but I couldn't hear myself. Must have left my vocal cords at the cabin." Harley grinned.

Bando was speechless.

"While you were standing behind the car I took off back to camp. I should have just stayed in the back seat and caught a ride with you. But it was probably better that I beat you by five minutes, because just as I got back to the cabin I saw Charlie trying to wake me up. I slipped into myself. You think I've found my gift?"

CHAPTER 25

MONDAY AFTERNOON BROUGHT the scavenger hunt everyone was waiting for. They piled into Rose's car and FreeK Camp #2, drove to town, and parked on the square by the library.

"Gather by the gazebo," Rose directed. "I'll hand out the scavenger lists after we decide who's on which team. One adult per team."

"Atlanta and I will go with Twait," Damon said before anyone else could choose.

"I'll take Rose and the class clown," Maggie joked. "That'll give us high psychic and high logic."

"I'll take that as a compliment," Harley said.

"I meant Rose and me," she smirked.

"So by default Caroline and Charlie are stuck with me," Bando said.

Rose handed out nine rope-handled shopping bags. "Let me remind you to stay with your group."

"Mom," Caroline argued. "There are times when divide-and-conquer makes more sense. Like three front doors in a row? Splitting up can work if we stay within sight of each other."

"Use common sense," Bando said. "But remember, there's a dangerous person out there."

"And there are other strange people around," Maggie whined. "Like Harley."

"Good one, Magpie," Harley said. "You'll be eating crow soon enough."

"Ooh, Magpie?" she said mockingly. "Think I haven't heard that one before?"

Rose continued giving instructions. "Remember Rule #1: *no buying.* Rule #2: *no stealing or shoplifting.* Rule #3: *no begging.* You can explain to a storeowner or homeowner who you are, where you're from, and why you're seeking your items. Everybody got it?"

Head nods.

"Okay, try to get as many items on the list as you can. Meet back here at 4 o'clock, no later. The team with the most items checked off wins."

"Let me remind you," Twait said, drawing out his words. "This is not about individual performances. It's about cooperation and teamwork."

Groans.

"And group decision-making."

More groans.

Rose handed out the lists and Twait yelled, "Ready, set, go!"

Appropriate chaos broke out.

SCAVENGER HUNT LIST

- *3 different-colored paper clips*
- *1 waffle cone (cone only, unused)*
- *2 chicken eggs, one brown and one white*
- *classified ads from any Saturday (not Sunday) newspaper*
- *1 sugar packet*
- *1 soda can (empty)*
- *1 cork*
- *5 business cards (all different)*
- *1 bird's nest (without eggs)*

- *1 banana peel*

- *1 discarded lottery ticket*

- *1 Kleenex (toilet paper doesn't count)*

- *1 Band-Aid (any size)*

- *1 apple, orange, grape, or cherry*

- *1 can of soup, beans, etc. for a church Food Pantry*

- *1 map (not hand drawn)*

- *1 bank pen, deposit slip, or other bank item*

- *1 autographed poem/rhyme (by author not associated with Free Camp)*

- *1 take-out menu*

All three teams huddled and chattered, trying to hammer out their strategies. Caroline quickly took charge of her group and led the way down the main drag toward the stores, Charlie and Bando trying to keep up with her.

Maggie overheard Caroline's strategy and thought it made sense—get the largest number of easy items from merchants first—so she convinced Rose and Harley their team should go in the same direction as Caroline's team except on the opposite side of the street.

Atlanta, Damon, and Twait were more laid-back and plopped down on a bench in front of the gazebo.

"They'll find the easy stuff right away," Atlanta said. "We can get those things later. Why don't we pick out the five hardest things and try getting those?" They checked the list and Atlanta pointed across the street. "How about starting right there at the library? Everybody else will have the Monday papers, not Saturday's. But the library has back issues. Maybe the librarian will make us a photocopy of the Saturday classifieds. Nothing in the rules says it can't be a copy."

They crossed, entered, and explained to the woman behind the desk about Free Camp's scavenger hunt then showed her the list.

"A photocopy is 10 cents, but since you can't beg or buy items, I'm happy to contribute a dime," the woman said. She found a Saturday paper in the reading room and made a copy of the classifieds. She sat down again and reached into a drawer. "And here are your three different-colored paper clips. And here's a pen that will save you a trip to a bank. But don't run off yet, because I have a First Aid kit—which gives us the Band-Aid."

The librarian became the fourth member of their team.

"Your local library and librarian," Atlanta said, "underused community resources."

The woman beamed.

"Bingo!" Twait said a little too loudly. He was standing by a literature rack inside the front door and held up a brochure. "God bless the Bridgton Area Chamber of Commerce. Check *map* off the list."

The librarian handed the Band-Aid to Atlanta and scanned the list one more time.

"Ah, the Kleenex." She pulled a Puffs box from a side drawer and plucked one. "Here you go. And how about this?" She fished a yellow Splenda packet from her pocketbook. "As it says, it's a sugar substitute."

Twait shook his head in disbelief. "You're a gold mine."

"Happy to help. I remember how awful it was for your camp last summer. Yesterday's paper brought it all up again. And now this man found hanging in the woods—at least that's what I've heard." She turned somber then recovered and smiled again. "You'd better make haste and find those other items."

"This is great," Twait said. "Can we impose on you for one last thing?" His eyes twinkled and he flashed his best playful smile.

"The men's room key?" she asked.

"No, Ma'am. Could you jot down a poem and autograph it?"

She grabbed a sheet of scrap paper and wrote: *Roses are red, violets are blue. Sugar is sweet, but Splenda is, too.* At the bottom she signed in beautiful cursive script: *Best of luck winning the scavenger hunt! Hanah*

Lonergan. "It's your autographed poem, but it also bolsters the sugar/ Splenda argument."

As they reached the front door, Hanah Lonergan didn't whisper but called out loudly, "Laundromat on the side street to the right. Business cards stuck everywhere. Bet there's a stack of Chinese takeout menus, too."

"What a community resource," Twait muttered.

The Laundromat provided them five business cards, a takeout menu, and two unexpected bonuses.

Atlanta held up a soda can she found in the trash. "This must be our lucky day. And check this out." From on top of a stack of magazines on a windowsill she held up not one but three old lottery tickets.

"What if they're winners?" Twait joked.

"Then we'll have to toss them. Can't be bringing back winners for a scavenger hunt, can we?"

"The list doesn't specify winning or losing," Damon said seriously. "It says *discarded*—which those are."

"Hey, I know we're kidding around here," Twait said. "But what if one of those tickets was a million dollar jackpot winner? Would you look for the owner? Would you split it with your friends?"

After a long silence, all three laughed.

They crossed the square to the convenience store where Charlie had bought his prepaid cell phone the previous summer. The man behind the counter listened to their story and went through the list. He gave them an apple and a can of soup.

"See that scoop shop over there?" He pointed catty-corner across the square. "That's where you get your waffle cone. Tell Lisa at the counter that Nick the Greek sent you."

They thanked Nick and got the waffle cone from Lisa who looked over the last items on the list. She reached into a glass-front cooler and withdrew a brown lunch bag. She pulled out a yogurt, a power bar, and—

"My banana," she said. "I can eat it early." She did, and dropped the peel into Atlanta's bag.

"You think the other three groups are still running their butts off?" Twait asked as they left.

"Probably," Damon said. "If we've only got three things left—the 2 eggs, the cork, and the bird's nest—I'm thinking it's a waste of time hitting businesses. No grocery store is going to split up a dozen eggs for us. But we might find a cork and the eggs in a home. Let's head away from the business district and go door to door."

The team got a white egg at the first door they knocked on. The brown egg came from the fifth house, where a shaggy-haired twenty-something insisted on opening a bottle of wine so he could present them with the cork.

"I've got a stopper for it," he said. "I'd be opening a bottle soon anyway. My parents are coming for dinner next week." He held up a bottle of Barefoot Zinfandel in one hand, a bottle of Yellow Tail Sauvignon Blanc in the other. "Red cork or white?"

When Atlanta asked about a bird's nest, he grinned sheepishly and pretended to paw through his thick hair. "Might still be one up here, but I haven't heard any chirping lately."

"I meant in the back yard," she said.

"I know. I doubt it. My back yard's pretty bare. I don't have the answer on that one."

Damon did, though. "I live here in Bridgton. If we walk another quarter mile out to the picnic park with all the pines behind it, we'll probably find one. There's always bird poop on the picnic tables. Got to be nests close by."

They thanked the shaggy-haired man and headed for Damon's picnic park.

"This is unbelievable," Atlanta commented. "One thing left on the list and we may get it. We've got to be way ahead of the others."

They reached the park. It was set back from the road and had a gravel driveway leading into a small parking lot. Four swings hung from a timber frame, two slides and a set of monkey bars not far away. A pair of portable toilets sat near the edge of the woods. There were no cars in the parking area.

"Stick together," Twait reminded.

They crossed the playground and were about to enter the pine grove when a white van slowed near the end of the driveway. It didn't turn in but slowly continued on by. Twait was used to drivers slowing down so they and their children could gawk at a midget. Sometimes they'd even stop and ask, "Are you a leprechaun?" or "Are you a midget?" But there was something different this time, something odd about this van. The passenger window was down and Twait had caught a glint of sunglasses before it moved on.

They entered the woods, eyes heavenward, searching the branches for a nest. They bore left so they'd come out of the trees on the edge of the woods nearest the road.

Nobody spotted anything. The canopy of pine boughs overhead was too thick.

"I'll double back and check along the parking lot," Twait said. "You two stay together and go that way so you come out in the meadow by the road."

They split up. A few minutes later she and Damon came out into a small field that lay between the woods and the road. They looked back up into the branches as they walked the woods line.

"Look," Damon said, pointing. "Halfway up—that dark clump. It has to be a nest."

She stood next to him and tried to see where he was pointing. "Can't see it."

He stepped behind her, bending at the knees to match her height, and extended his left arm over shoulder and past her cheek. His other hand rested on her right hip.

"See it? Sight in along my arm."

She sucked in her breath, feeling his chest against her back. His breath warmed her ear and the bare neck below it. Her heart pounded in her chest and ears.

A car horn blasted, breaking them out of their reverie. Four teenagers in an open-topped Jeep hooted and whistled. Damon and Atlanta pulled back, dreamy-eyed, and Damon waved at the passersby.

"Friends of yours?" she asked.

"No idea." They stared into each other's eyes a moment before he broke it off. "Oh, the nest. It's in this one," he said, moving to a large pine. "Eight branches up on the right. Problem is it's at the outside end of the branch where it's floppy. We need one of those cherry-picker lifts like the phone company uses—unless…."

She stared at him, knowing exactly what he wanted her to do.

"Aw, come on. Please? It's a guaranteed win. Nobody else will find a nest."

She shook her head.

"I won't tell."

"I know you won't. But I can't. It's not fair to the others."

"Atlanta, *life's* not fair. Do it. You can tell them if you feel the need to. For now just get it."

She hesitated.

"Well?"

"You'll keep an eye out for Twait?"

He nodded.

"Watch the road, in case a car comes. I need two minutes."

"I've got your back." He stepped out into the field and stood with his hands in his pockets trying to look nonchalant.

"Don't look," she said, and lay on the ground on her stomach, hands stretched out in front like Supergirl. She concentrated and a moment later floated slowly, deliberately upward, touching the lower branches with her hands on her way by. She located the nest and a minute later settled back down to earth. She dropped the bird's nest into her shopping bag. "Check."

"Amazing," Damon said and pulled her close for a quick kiss. "Got me all excited."

"You were supposed to be watching for Twait and cars coming."

"I was. Honest. But I couldn't help myself."

"Hey, you two!" Twait called from the corner of the woods. "Hope you had better luck than I did."

"We did," Damon said, squeezing Atlanta's hand then letting it go.

"We got very lucky."

Atlanta pulled out the nest. "Damon found one right under that tree. Must have blown down in the storm."

"What storm?" Twait asked.

She blushed and didn't answer.

As they started for the road the same white van passed going the opposite way back toward town. Had the driver made his delivery that quickly? He was driving faster on the return trip. Even with his driver-side window up it was clear he still had the sunglasses on. Now he held a cell phone to his left ear, blocking any clears view of him.

Twait couldn't catch the license number, but he knew it was a Maine plate on a Ford work van. He hoped he wouldn't need the information in the future. Why would he?

CHAPTER 26

I T WAS AFTER 4 o'clock when they got back to camp, so Bando gave them free time until dinner. In the office he found the answering machine blinking. Two messages.

The first was from his brother Derby. "I planted those seeds you gave me. And I scouted Armstrong Woods and the area around it. Nothing much up there except recreation areas and summer camps. Give my love to Rose and the little guy."

The second message was from Smitty. "Call my cell." She left the number.

He dialed and she answered on the first ring.

"Hi, it's me," he said. "Something new on Alley's death?"

"It's now a homicide."

"We both suspected as much, didn't we? Cause of death?"

"Strangulation, not by hanging but by garroting; coroner says the killer used a wire. Bruises on the back of the neck tell us he pulled it tight from behind."

"Anybody in custody?"

"Nope."

"Anything more from the crime scene?"

"Not yet."

"Is it public—that it's a murder?"

"If not the 6 o'clock news, it'll make the late news. Either way, it's out tonight."

"Anything else?"

"Isn't that enough? Be careful."

"Me?"

"Yes, you, all of you. He could be in your backyard."

"He?"

"Probably. Women don't strangle with a wire and hang somebody up in the woods."

"True. If he is in the backyard, whom should I call—you?"

"9-1-1. But you know you can call me anytime." From her end of the line she couldn't see Bando blush.

"Protect and serve," he said then shook his head, unable to believe he'd said something that stupid.

***

Damon and Atlanta walked to the waterfront, bringing their pendulums.

"You think they really work?" he asked, letting his crystal hang from its chain in front of him.

"One way to find out. I played with mine back home, but I'm far from an expert. Ask yours a question."

"You first," he said.

She clasped the top of the chain between her thumb and forefinger and rested her elbow on the arm of the log bench. "Are Mom and Dad trying to get back together?"

"Remember what Rose told us. It won't tell you the future."

"I didn't ask if they will, I asked if they're trying."

The pendulum hung motionless.

"Close your eyes," he said. "And no peeking. I'll watch it for you."

"I'm not going to peek." She shut her eyes.

The chain and crystal moved ever so slightly.

"Don't force it. Let it happen on its own."

"Is it moving?"

"A little. Don't open your eyes, though."

It moved away from Atlanta then back.

"Back and forth is a yes, right?" he asked.

"Right."

"Then the pendulum is saying yes, they're working on it. You can trust it or not. Move on to a different question."

She stilled the pendulum and held it out again. "Does Damon have a girlfriend in Bridgton?"

He reached out and touched her pendulum so that it moved side-to-side.

"I saw you," she said, and grinned. "I had my eyelids cracked."

"That was a trick question. And remember, technically *you* are in Bridgton." He reached toward her pendulum. "Want me to make it answer yes?"

"My pendulum knows what I meant. Try yours now, hunch guy."

"I do have hunches. But remember, I'm also the world's biggest skeptic." He got comfortable and held out his crystal. "I'm not sure I can rely on this thing."

"Back and forth is yes for yours, too, right?" she asked. "And side-to-side is no?"

He nodded. Then he closed his eyes and took several deep breaths the way he'd learned in Bando's meditation sessions. "Are the spirits of my parents here now?"

The pendulum quivered, then began a tiny circle.

Damon shivered visibly. "Ice cold behind me, on my back and neck. Now it's all around me like a cold wet coat." He stilled the pendulum.

She saw him relax. "Warmer now?"

"Actually, yes. What do you think—overactive imagination?"

"I think we should have had Caroline here to see them."

"Ghosts choose to appear to her. She doesn't just turn on her spook screen like a TV."

"Okay. Try a different question."

His face grew serious, concerned. "I'm feeling a hunch, a strong one."

"Test it."

He closed his eyes again and held up the pendulum. "Is someone else—someone other than my parents—watching us?"

The pendulum didn't hesitate. It moved away and back—yes—gathering strength.

"Are you doing that?" Atlanta asked, alarmed.

He opened his eyes and saw it swinging to and fro. He stilled it and closed his eyes again. "Is it someone we know who is watching?"

The pendulum ticked side-to-side, no. He saw it through slit eyes. "Atlanta, listen to me very closely. I want you to stay calm and don't—don't under any circumstances—look around. If there is someone watching, I don't want him to know we suspect anything. Here's what we'll do. I think whoever is out there is watching from the waterfall trail by the boys' cabin. You and I will get up and I'll put my arm around your shoulder. I'll make a sweeping gesture toward the hill and woods like I'm offering you the world. We smile and look happy—and while we're playing make-believe we scan the woods. Just follow my lead. Got it?"

"You really think somebody's watching?"

"Yes. The pendulum, if it's trustworthy, confirmed my hunch. Ready?"

Damon stood up and bowed before Atlanta with a chivalrous sweep of his arm. He proffered a hand, which she took, and she got to her feet. Then he turned her so they both faced the trail, the two of them scanning the woods the whole time.

Something moved in the bushes at the bottom of the trail. They froze. A moment later a deer stepped out and took a few steps toward the ball field. It stared at them then gracefully walked behind the boys' cabin and disappeared into the woods.

"You think that's our Peeping Tom?" Atlanta asked.

"I hope so," Damon said, and the two of them headed away from the waterfront.

Halfway up the hill, near the spot where Donnie Bronson had spied on them from his dirt bike the summer before, the watcher lowered his binoculars and smiled coldly.

CHAPTER 27

ROSE DELAYED SUPPER until 6:15 so everyone could watch the evening news in her cabin. The report confirmed what they already knew: Ted Alley had been murdered. Police were seeking the public's help and the phone number for a tip line was posted on screen. After supper everyone played kickball for an hour, then shifted over to hacky sack and Frisbee.

Bando went to the office. He was missing something, but he couldn't put his finger on it. He stretched for 20 seconds then sat in one of the guest chairs and closed his eyes and reopened Tina Sutherland's mental image of the crime scene. He saw the tire leaning against the tree trunk, the limb with the rope attached, the loop around Alley's neck. The chair sat between the body and the tire, the coil arranged on it. What was that coil?

He saw Alley's hanging body—gray pants, black socks, a Red Sox jersey, knees and knuckles nearly brushing the ground. And there—he hadn't seen it before—what was that? Tucked into the belt at the back of his pants was what—a hat? It was hard to make out from Tina's distance and angle of vision, but it had to be a cap hanging out of the belt. But color-wise it didn't match the Red Sox jersey. No, this cap was bright blue.

So now he had three questions begging answers. Was there anything like a note found on the body? What was coiled on the chair? And, if Ted Alley had been a Red Sox fan, why did he have a mismatched cap? Was that due to his mental confusion when he walked out of the house?

TUESDAY

CHAPTER 28

BREAKFAST WAS UNDERWAY when Caroline marched in. She passed around three sheets of paper. "The top page showed up on one of the California crime sites yesterday. It introduces the idea that Terrell was made to look like a scarecrow, not necessarily the Crucified One."

"Good old Derby," Twait mumbled to Bando. "A tip of the hat to him." Bando rolled his eyes.

"The second page is Alley's online obituary. It gives us his background information. That last page is this morning's news story on Alley." Caroline filled her plate and continued. "In a nutshell the article says he was murdered, which we learned from last night's news. But this goes further, saying he was strangled and the hanging was for show."

"Terrell was, too," Charlie noted. "Strangled and posed."

"How about we say *staged*," Maggie said. "Or *arranged*. *Posed* is for pictures. This is more like theater."

"Maybe," Harley said. "But he could be a photographer."

Maggie rolled her eyes. "He's not staging them for himself; it's for the public. These are like tableaus or sculptures with shock value."

"Whatever words we use—staged, arranged, or posed," Caroline said, "it looks like it could be the same killer."

"No brush fire with Alley," Atlanta pointed out.

"Maybe he learned from California," Charlie countered. "That little fire seemed like a good way to draw attention, but it burned the support beam and knocked over his display—or tableau, to use Maggie's word. That was an unintended consequence."

"So was the charring of the body," Atlanta said. "Which in an odd way may be what brought this Terrell to us."

"What do you mean?" Charlie asked.

"Think about it. Who appeared at the waterfall? Not Terrell, even though he had already been dead a year. It was Addie bringing Mr. Alley who had just died. Terrell came through to Mom and me at the Horton Cemetery—and why there—because Damon was there. Terrell appeared right where Damon had been sitting and meditating, generating alpha waves, psychic reception. I think the common factor was *burned man*— James Lee Terrell and Damon's father. I think Damon's father might have given up a chance to come through because he felt Terrell's needs were more pressing."

"But Terrell showed up again later by the campfire, with Addie and Mr. Alley," Maggie pointed out.

"Yes, and who was there? Damon. Addie helped Mr. Alley across; she didn't help Terrell across. It was Damon's father again helping Terrell to appear. Addie brought Alley at the same time Damon's Dad brought Terrell."

Bando said, "Let's go back to the similarities—not in the crimes but in the geography. Both bodies were found on public recreation lands. Why?"

"No security cameras?" Damon suggested.

"That's a good practical reason. But what if we're so focused on seeing these as crime scenes we're not seeing the bigger picture—and I really mean *picture*. Sometimes we see the painting and not the frame, or we see the painting and frame but not the wall it's hung on. But it all influences our perception of the painting. We just forget to notice what's around it."

Harley looked lost. "Missing your point, Wise One. Can you clue me in?"

"Sure. In both Maine and California we have large expanses of unpopulated land—but it's not all publicly owned, is it? What else is around there?"

"Small towns," Harley said.

"Businesses," Caroline added. "Residences, neighborhoods."

"Yes," Bando went on. "In both areas the killer needed knowledge of the woods, trails, and access roads, so he could gauge the probability of being seen. He must have lived in that part of California and this part of Maine. Which means—."

"He needed a place to live," Caroline blurted out, "and a job to pay for it."

"Correct. My brother Derby says the *surrounding* area there includes a large number of summer camps."

"Just like here," Maggie said. "Maybe the killer has a summer camp connection. Both murders happened in the summer. He could be staff."

They speculated a few minutes but concluded there was no way to check any camp connections without a name or description.

Atlanta looked over the obituary notice. "Visiting hours tomorrow afternoon and evening in Windham. The funeral is Thursday morning. Says here he was a citizen of Red Sox Nation. What's that mean?"

"Baseball fan," Maggie explained. "Boston Red Sox call themselves Red Sox Nation. You've probably seen the shirts that say *I love the Red Sox and any other team that beats the Yankees.*"

"What's BPOE?" Damon asked, looking over Atlanta's shoulder. "Says he was a lifelong member of BPOE."

"Elks," Harley said. "It's like the Rotary Club or the Moose Lodge. They have dances and you can rent the hall for a wedding reception."

"What else was he involved in?" Bando asked.

Atlanta read selected parts aloud. "Loved taking care of his yard and his flower and vegetable gardens. Enjoyed fishing and hunting. For many years owned a cabin in North Bridgton. There's a list of survivors. The family asks that memorial contributions go to Alzheimer's research."

The eating and talking continued for another ten minutes until Twait announced the day's schedule.

"The field trip will take most of the day. We'll meet by the car and van at 11 o'clock and leave for the Durham Cemetery. Rose is making box lunches for us. We'll eat, do the grave rubbing, and then head on to L.L. Bean in Freeport. On the way home we'll stop for supper at my favorite fried fish take-out place, which also has great ice cream."

Harley said, "Now das what I'm talking about," bringing hoots and applause.

"This doesn't mean a free morning," Rose reminded them. "We're combining your 9 a.m. morning meditation with the teaching session on automatic writing. Don't ask about it now; it'll make sense when we do it."

Twait said, "Hearing no objections, I'll entertain a motion to adjourn."

Being teenagers they didn't speak or raise their hands. They simply left.

CHAPTER 29

THEY ARRIVED FOR meditation and found that tables and chairs had replaced their yoga mats. Bando instructed them to each take a seat.

"Same breathing and relaxation exercises, except you'll be sitting in chairs. You won't be able to cross your legs."

Rose reached into a cardboard box on the table and withdrew a stack of drawing paper. She handed out paper, pencils, charcoal markers, and small boxes of crayons.

"Playtime?" Harley joked. "But you took away our rest rugs." When nobody laughed, he said, "So we're going to try automatic writing and drawing, right?"

"Yes, and both work off the same principle. It's about tapping into the subconscious then giving it a channel to express itself in the conscious realm."

"Will a dead person guide our hands?" Charlie wanted to know. "That was the way it was supposed to work with the Spiritualists and their séances in the 1930s."

"Probably not, Charlie. We're not talking about messages from *out there*—although I'm not dismissing that. But I don't think your parents, or Damon's parents, or Mr. Alley, or Mr. Terrell are going to have you ghost write their messages to us. That's how a lot of grieving people are taken advantage of. We're not tapping into the dead, but are trying to intentionally tap our subconscious and some of the psychic energy around us."

"Increased alpha wave production in the brain," Charlie said. "It happens in altered states. With dreams we don't control it. With hypnosis the subject doesn't control it. The only one we have any control over is meditation."

"The only one you forgot," Bando said, "is what we call daydreaming, when your mind is relaxed."

"Like when you're listening to music that you don't have to concentrate on," Maggie said.

"Could be that," Bando answered. "But I mention daydreaming because that's often when people tend to doodle. We even describe it as doodling *mindlessly*. Remember Damon's Hangman game? He didn't realize he'd done it. And it came out of his non-writing hand. Somehow he picked up an image, a symbol, a bit of soft data from the unconscious. The expression might be: *he pulled it right out of thin air*. He didn't pull it from some hidden or secret part of his brain, did he? It was more like pulling down what had been—until that moment—a very weak radio signal. You've all done that, haven't you—not been able to get a certain radio station until you either move closer or get out of a valley, or the weather conditions change. But then for a little while you can get it."

"So we're going to meditate," Damon said, "hoping to get out of that valley or to give ourselves more favorable weather—more alpha waves and better reception—allowing a weak signal to come through on this paper as words or pictures."

"Bravo," Bando said. "Maybe a combination—let's call it meditative daydreaming."

"So what are we looking for?" Harley asked.

"Nothing," Rose answered. "That's the paradox. If we give you an assignment, your conscious mind would take over the search. But we want your unconscious mind to do the work, to pull down a signal from the huge psychic energy field around you. You can't force it."

"To stay with the radio signal idea," Damon said, "would it be like trying to find an FM station on AM radio?"

"One way to put it," Bando said. "Works for me."

"So do we just sit with a pencil or crayon in hand and wait for something to take over our bodies," Harley asked. "Like Whoopi Goldberg when Patrick Swayze possessed her in *Ghost*?"

"Nobody's going to possess anybody, Harley," Bando said. "When you're all comfortably settled in a meditative state I'll suggest that you choose from the instruments in front and translate to paper any image that comes to your subconscious."

"Whatever signal we pull down out of thin air," Damon said.

"Yes," Rose agreed. "But remember, this takes practice. Some of you will be able to do it. Others will deliver images your conscious mind is holding on to. Whatever we get is okay."

"Ready to begin?" Bando asked, and while they were saying they were, he leaned to Harley and whispered, "Please stay in your body."

They did their breathing and relaxation. Around the 20-minute mark Bando gave them a suggestion that they continue to relax while writing or drawing whatever they liked. He allowed them 10 minutes and brought them back.

They discussed the experience. Several hadn't been fully aware what they were writing or drawing, but most were.

"Knowing that I was expected to produce something pulled me out of my relaxed meditative state early," one of them said.

"I drew what was on my mind," Caroline said. "I don't know if it was on my conscious mind or my unconscious. It was just right there in front of me."

Rose collected the drawings and dismissed the teens. Then she turned the papers face down and shuffled them like a deck of Tarot cards. She dealt them out, one row of three over a second row of three. The arrangement looked like a six-paned window from an old house.

"Why'd you lay them out that way, Rose?" Bando asked.

"How else could she have done it?" Twait asked. "That's really the only way that makes sense."

"Well," Bando said. "She could have gone six-across like Solitaire, or maybe a circle, or six in a line up-and-down, or a horseshoe or semi-circle."

"Those never occurred to me," Rose said.

"Me either," Twait said.

"That's interesting, isn't it?" Bando replied. "I don't know why, but it is. And I don't even know why I challenged Rose on it I just had to."

After a moment Rose asked, "Ready?" and Bando nodded.

She turned over the two center squares. They were rough sketches of Alley's obituary photo. Under one the message read: RIP Ted Alley. Under the other: Justice.

"Caroline, right? Twait said, pointing to the word Justice.

"Nope. Maggie," Bando corrected. "I watched her draw it."

The third was a tornado.

"The vortex again?" Twait asked. "Like last year with Bronson? And Damon drew one in the margin of his application. Must be him again."

"This isn't Damon," Rose said. "It's Atlanta."

The fourth drawing was of a man. He was fuller than a stick figure and his face was blacked in. But the arms, legs, and torso had no color at all.

"Burned face?" Twait asked. "Damon drawing his father?"

"Not Damon," Bando said. "Charlie. And I'm not sure why only the face is black. If this was Terrell, the body would be burned, too."

The fifth showed what looked like a multi-vehicle pileup with the boom of a crane above tangled wreckage. "This one's Damon," Rose said.

"Looks like a mass of junk," Twait commented.

Rose turned over the last sheet of paper—a ball cap with *Red Sox* across its crown. From the corner of her eye she saw Bando flinch as if it struck him in the face.

"What do you see?" Rose asked.

Bando sat back, a deep breath escaping as a heavy sigh. "My first impression is we have two drawings of Alley with no ball cap even though he had one in his waistband. Then this drawing spotlights a ball cap, but not the bright blue one in his belt." He ran his fingertips over the Red Sox cap drawing. "Is this Caroline's?"

"No," Rose answered. "Caroline drew one of those two sketches of Alley. The Red Sox cap is Harley."

"Well," Twait said. "Harley's the one who loves hats. Stands to reason he'd draw a ball cap."

"I don't think it's about Harley," Bando said. "I think it's about Alley. Something tells me that's his Red Sox hat."

"One of your strong hunches?" Rose asked.

"Yeah."

"I had the same feeling. Remember Carl Yazstremski—Yaz—the slugger the Sox had in the 1970s?"

Bando and Twait nodded.

"During the meditation I kept seeing him at the plate, swinging for the fences. I couldn't get him out of my head. Soft data to go with your hunch and Harley's drawing."

CHAPTER 30

AT 11:05 THEY set off on the field trip to Durham and Freeport.
Durham, a few miles north of Freeport, was a rural backwater best known as the place where novelist Stephen King grew up. At one of the town's ancient cemeteries the Free Campers would have lunch and try grave rubbing and—as Twait jokingly said—see what else came up.

Freeport, their ultimate destination, was headquarters to the L.L. Bean fishing-and-camping-supplies empire. The business and the town had become practically synonymous. Bean dominated the downtown but wasn't the only game in town as scores of factory outlet stores lurked in its shadow hoping to catch the customer overflow. While the ads touted Freeport as *a shopper's paradise*, one cartoonist sketched a fat birdlike couple hauling shopping bags and captioned them *the Credit-Carded Out-of-State Sale-Suckers*.

They reached the Durham cemetery and parked the vehicles across the road. Except for the cemetery there were only trees and bushes as far as the eye could see. Everyone piled out.

"Watch for cars," Rose cautioned reflexively.

There were none. The road, not even busy back in its heyday, was little more than a shortcut for locals now. For a hundred years, from mid-century to mid-century, the neglected graveyard had served the few families who made up the hardscrabble Spiritualist settlement known as The Kingdom, which Stephen King referred to in some of his horror stories and novels. Running roughly 100 feet along next to the roadside, the bone yard ran 50 feet back to the woods and was surrounded by a tumbledown rock wall.

A narrow gateway cut through the front wall, once wide enough for either a funeral cart or pallbearers squeezing through lugging a casket. Weathered fieldstone markers like small surfboards begged for attention amid an ocean of weeds and wildflowers. Others, broken off or split apart, lay gathering moss. They bore faded names and odd symbols that blurred the lines between skulls and angels.

"Watch where you walk," Rose called as she and Twait unloaded the ice chests and box lunches. "It may look a mess, but it's still sacred ground."

Charlie and Harley vaulted the rock wall while the others traipsed through the narrow gate single file. They spread out.

"These will be great for rubbings," Maggie said to Caroline. "I made one in a Revolutionary War cemetery in sixth grade. It's hanging on my bedroom wall."

"No way I'd put one up in my bedroom," Caroline joked. "Already too many spooks hanging around me."

Rose yelled from across the road, "Take a quick look around. Then come back over here and pick up your lunches and drinks. You can sit in the van or the car."

Maggie made a face. "You sure your Mom teaches college and not middle school?"

"How about if we sit on the stone wall?" Charlie shouted.

"Yeah, it's not like we're going to hurt anything," Harley yelled. "Or anyone." He gained support from a few of the others.

"Okay, okay. The van, the car, or the front wall, but that's all. The other three walls look like they might be covered with poison ivy. Be careful not to knock any of the rocks loose. This isn't our property."

"Doesn't look like it's anybody's property anymore," Harley mumbled, drawing a few laughs.

"It's still theirs," Maggie said, gesturing toward the graves.

They ate lunch, the three adults lounging comfortably in the van with the doors open, the six teens along the front wall like birds on a wire. Afterward Rose gathered everyone in the center of the cemetery and set down her box of art supplies.

"First you choose a solid stone that's not flaking—either one that's still in place or on the ground. Pick one that's not too dusty or badly cracked." She pulled out soap and water. "You wash it top to bottom, otherwise it'll streak or look uneven when somebody else comes along." She took rice paper and masking tape from her box. "Tape the paper over what you want to get the impression from. Make it firm or it'll slip and you'll get a blurry image. Then take your charcoal marker and—just like it says—rub the grave. You transfer the image to the rice paper."

She demonstrated.

"That's just the start, but you've got the idea and you can see how it should turn out. When you're finished, you remove the tape and the grave rubbing—and then last thing, you rewash the gravestone. Leave it neat. Got it?"

Heads nodded and mouths mumbled yes. Teen enthusiasm.

"The whole process should take you 20 minutes to a half hour. Now here are your supplies."

"Do we pick any tombstone?" Damon asked.

"Choose one with an interesting design. That back corner to the right will have simpler stones because it's where people buried their slaves."

"They had slaves in Maine?" Maggie asked.

"What's reported publicly is no. But some people apparently kept them. And later, if runaway slaves from other states made it here—even if they lived free—they still had to be buried somewhere when they died. This is one of the towns that buried black people in the same cemetery with whites."

"So long as they stayed in their own corner," Charlie pointed out.

"Let the graves begin," Twait quipped.

They spread out like elementary schoolchildren searching for bugs. Some sat, some squatted, some stood.

Maggie and Caroline settled on two tombstones near the slave plots. Both got excellent rubbings and began removing their tape.

"Everybody should be finishing up by now," Rose reminded, sounding like a proctor at the S.A.T. exams. "Don't forget to rewash the stones and rinse them with clear water. Please don't leave any tape on them. Clean up your mess. Leave the place better than you found it. Five minutes."

"Mom?"

"What, Caroline?"

"We've got company."

"Where?"

"In the slave section. There. At the back."

Rose looked. "I see him."

Everyone looked now, but only Rose and Caroline saw anything.

"Why's he so blurry, Mom? Is he having trouble coming through?"

"I think he's blurry because he's appearing to us naked."

"Is he—*was* he—black? He looks black from the neck up. The blurry part of him looks shiny white."

"Faded silver, I'd call it. It's like he's—what—*painted?*"

"You think he tried to paint himself white?"

"I don't know, Caroline. Can you see that square on his chest?"

"Could be a patch, some kind of bandage. You think he was a runaway slave who got shot?"

"No. He's shaking his head. I think he was answering you. Ask him another question. Hurry. He's fading."

"Are you from this cemetery?"

No response.

"Are you looking for us?"

Yes.

"Are you with Addie?"

No answer.

"Do you need our help?"

Yes. Then he collapsed into a pinhole like the screen of an old TV set suddenly unplugged.

CHAPTER 31

EXCEPT FOR MAINE'S two natural wonders, Acadia National Park and Mt. Katahdin, L.L. Bean was the state's most popular tourist destination. Given the choice of an island tour, a trip to a lighthouse, or a visit to Bean, most Maine visitors opted to shop where they could take off their shoes and stand on a piece of American retail's holy ground.

At first the teens acted like any other tourists—but then they grew bored, and quickly—because in the end Bean was still basically a big store with a kids department in a separate building next door. Several of them had been to Bean satellites in Connecticut, Massachusetts, and New Hampshire, and all of them had seen the same merchandise in Bean catalogs. The visit Rose thought would be a hit turned out to not be. An hour of exploring with little spending money made it a bust. Still, they tried to make the best of it.

Damon modeled fishing hats for the girls while Charlie and Harley hit the book department. It wasn't big enough to be called a bookstore, but it had a decent selection of paperbacks in their interest areas: Maine shipwrecks, New England ghost stories, and joke and riddle books. They had their noses in books when Twait and Rose rounded a corner on their way to the canoe and kayak section, chatting and not even noticing the boys.

A moment later a tall, muscular man hurried around the same corner, taking the turn a little too tightly so that he almost knocked Harley down. Harley kept his balance by placing a hand on the man's forearm. The man didn't look down or offer an apology. He simply gazed over Harley's head at Twait and Rose as they disappeared down the ramp.

"It's not polite to stare," Harley said.

The man looked down. "What?"

"It's not polite to stare at that man."

"The munchkin?"

"They're called *little people*," Charlie cut in. "Not munchkins, not midgets."

"Yeah, well, thanks for the lesson in political correctness, kid," the man snarled, and took off.

"He didn't even apologize," Charlie said. "He's the one who ran into you."

"I knew he wasn't going to apologize. Didn't you?"

Charlie looked puzzled. "Yeah. Now that you mention it, I did know. Jerk."

"Yeah. Jerk."

Awhile later they left Freeport and drove south on Route 1 to the fish-and-chips drive-in Twait had mentioned. They ordered at a take-out window that reeked of fried food and staked out two picnic tables on the deck. While they waited for the counter to call their order numbers they took turns tossing out questions.

"What's with the ghost at that cemetery?"

"You said he didn't seem to know who Addie was?"

"His body was painted?"

"Why was he naked?"

"How come L.L. Bean's catalogs are way better than their real store?"

"It's the models that make the catalog. It's only manikins in the store."

"You mean the men or the women models?"

"Both, I guess."

"I don't know how Rose made ham-and-cheese sandwiches taste so good."

"You were hungry. And food always tastes better on a picnic."

"And in a graveyard."

"It was the Hellman's mayonnaise and the Grey Poupon mustard."

"Too bad we didn't get to see Stephen King's childhood home."

"It's haunted."

"That's why he moved out, right?"

"Why did they call that part of town *The Kingdom*?"

"*The Kingdom* was a really bizarre religious cult that had to do with a movement called Spiritualism. King mentions them from time to time."

"You've been reading your weird books again, haven't you, Charlie?"

"I like to educate myself. Some of what I learn comes in handy."

"Then tell us why a black man would paint himself white."

"Or why someone else would do it to him."

"Caroline and Rose said grayish silver, not white."

"Didn't the villain in James Bond—that Goldfinger guy—didn't he kill a girl by painting her with gold paint. It clogged her pores so her skin couldn't breathe and she suffocated."

"Goldfinger did it because she was in his harem, but then she betrayed him by sleeping with 007. That taught her not to fool around behind *his* back."

"Whatever. She died. Her skin couldn't breathe."

"Sleeping with a guy doesn't mean you deserve to die."

"Well, what about this black man? He's dead. His skin couldn't breathe through the paint, either, I guess. What'd he do to deserve that?"

"Who says his skin suffocated? Caroline saw a huge bandage on his chest. Remember? Maybe he was shot or stabbed."

"Then he isn't connected to Terrell and Alley. They were strangled."

Someone on the loudspeaker called out the numbers for their orders. They ran to the pickup window, carried their loaded trays back, and fell upon the food like hyenas on a gazelle carcass.

It was close to 8 p.m. when they got home to Free Camp and saw a State Police cruiser pulling out of the driveway. It made a U turn and followed them to the dining hall. While everybody clambered out with gear and grave rubbings, Smitty climbed out of the police car.

"Got a minute, Bando?" she asked.

"Let's go inside," he answered. "Update?"

"Let's say it's another courtesy call."

"I'll see you all at breakfast," Bando said and he and Smitty went into the office.

The light on the answering machine blinked once then repeated.

"You need to check it?"

"Later."

They sat opposite each other in the two guest chairs.

"Top Cop is sending us out to warn the camps again. This is a strange one. Whoever this guy is—we're guessing it's a guy, since it'd take a lot of strength to lug the body to the clearing—he's a nut case."

"Any leads—footprints or fingerprints? Witnesses? Composite sketches from passersby? Maybe somebody saw his vehicle parked at the trailhead."

"Nothing yet. Alley was strangled on Saturday night. His body was carried to the clearing—likely before dawn Sunday. The Sutherlands found him that afternoon. So he needed two trips, one with the body, the other with—well, I can't tell you what else, but he'd have needed plenty of time."

Bando shook his head sadly. "It's terrible, just terrible, and scary for people around here, especially the children and teens in all these camps. And poor Mr. Alley's family—the obituary said he had a wife and son and grandchildren."

"His wife is in a nursing home. Her Alzheimer's was more advanced than his. The son—Ed junior—lives over in Standish. He's the next-of-kin we notified."

Bando shook his head again. "How can human beings do this to each other?"

"How and *why?* I just want to make sure you know we've got a bad one on the loose. And he may still be in the area."

Bando gave her a long, warm handshake. "Thank you, Alicia, for checking on us."

"You're welcome." Her mind still wasn't willingly giving up any images.

CHAPTER 32

AFTER SMITTY LEFT, the staff gathered in the dining room and Rose pulled out the sketches from the morning session.

"We were so caught up with the Red Sox cap that Harley drew we didn't give this one much attention." She held up Charlie's roughly drawn man with the blackened-in face and colorless body. "It's got to be the spirit Caroline and I saw this afternoon in Durham."

"White man, black face?" Twait asked. "Or black man, white body?"

"He showed himself in the slave section. Maybe they helped bring him through. He's trying to tell us he was black even though his body was white. I don't know what that means. Bando, while you were in talking with Smitty I asked Charlie what he was intending to show with the drawing. He said he was recalling a dream from the night before he left for camp. When I asked if he had meant to put a bandage on the man's chest, he said the body was fuzzy in his dream. But he remembered there was something like a wraparound bandage on the man's head that he didn't include in the sketch this morning."

"So he had bandages on his chest and his head," Twait guessed. "You think he was injured in the Civil War or during his escape from slavery—maybe 1860s—and was buried there at Durham?"

"Don't know. Not enough information. My gut wants me to tie him to Alley and Terrell, but I can't see a connection yet."

"Just one," Bando said. "All three have come to us asking for our help."

* * *

Caroline's Google searches using *Durham, Durham cemeteries, The Kingdom, Underground Railroad,* and *slaves in Maine* proved to be educational but not helpful. She typed *black man painted white,* expecting nothing but references to the Rolling Stones' song *Paint It Black,* which she got plenty of. But it also turned up a You Tube video, "Crazy Silver Painted Black Man Dances the Robot on Santa Monica Pier." She felt a rush of excitement and clicked on the link.

The clip reminded her of the mimes who worked the parks, boardwalks, and piers honing their performance skills for any audience they could draw in. A linebacker-sized black man with silver makeup and a silver robot costume danced for a crowd on the pier—clearly not her slender ghost. But the clip challenged her thinking. Until now her question had been: why would a person paint himself a different color? Here was one reason. Maybe there were others.

She knew it would take a while, but she decided to search out each state's crime sites. They all had pages or links for open Missing Person cases and Unsolved Homicides. She'd start with Maine, expand to other New England States, and then try the mid-Atlantic. Then she'd hit the West Coast, Alaska, and Hawaii, leaving the Midwest and South for last. Somebody had to have a posting about a white-painted black man.

While she played cyber-detective, Bando phoned Smitty on her cell phone.

"Alicia, I should have asked you outright while you were here before. Something about the Alley crime scene is bugging you."

"Very perceptive. But you know I can't release any information about the scene."

"Okay. Then let me ask something else."

"Go ahead."

"My campers want to know about Criminology 101, basic police procedure. The six of them are on edge since Alley's murder. Besides that, though, their curiosity has been stimulated. Back home they've seen CSI and the other cop shows. Now they want to know what it's really like. I'm a camp director, not a cop, so I don't have those answers. Where might I get a cop to talk to them?"

"Are you asking me to come out and talk to them," she asked coyly, "give a little lecture, do some Q&A?"

"Could you?"

"When?"

He stammered into the day's schedule but she cut him off. "How about tomorrow morning around 9:45? Any conflicts?"

"That'll follow meditation nicely."

"Okay. See you in the morning."

"Can't wait."

She held on an extra couple seconds then said, "Bye."

* * *

Caroline hit pay dirt—in New York. Once she had the basic information and a name from the Unsolved Homicides page, she pieced it together using an obituary, several tributes, a few letters to the editor, a *Suffolk Times* editorial, and other articles.

Two summers earlier the body of a black man had been discovered in a junkyard outside Riverhead, where Long Island splits into the North and South Forks. The day before, 20 miles east in Greenport, a woman had filed a Missing Person report for her 47-year-old developmentally delayed nephew, Leon Parks. He was black, and everyone around town knew him as Bike-man, because he got around either by thumb or on his antique Schwinn.

The editorials and tributes were touching. "A genuine local character," one writer said. Another wrote, "Bike-man wouldn't hurt a fly. Why would somebody want to kill him?"

When junkyard workers found him, Parks had been stripped naked and painted. The Unsolved Homicides link didn't state the paint color, but word leaked out in articles that it had been silver. Another article reported the salvage workers who found him said "he still had his bicycle helmet on, but somebody had wrapped his entire head—bike helmet included—in silver duct tape, so he looked like a cross between a mummy and a knight."

Caroline printed out everything she found on Bike-man. While the printer ran, she fished another discarded junk-mail folder from the wastebasket, marked it Bike-man/NY, and slid the printouts into it.

None of the materials stated cause of death, but she was sure it wasn't skin suffocation from the paint. Her bet was he'd been strangled, stripped and painted, then put on display.

WEDNESDAY

CHAPTER 33

AT BREAKFAST CAROLINE shared her new printouts on the Bikeman Parks murder, which stunned everyone. They were sure it was the sprit from the Durham cemetery, and they had no doubt he'd been strangled and his body staged by the same man who had killed Alley and Terrell. But there was nowhere to go with it yet.

Bando announced the change in schedule to accommodate Smitty's talk, which they welcomed. They were almost too excited to meditate.

Around 9:30 Smitty showed up in civilian clothes. She shared a cup of tea with Bando in the office then everyone gathered in the dining room. She explained about the Maine State Police in general then went into the work of the Evidence Response Team and how they would have worked the Alley scene. The teens had plenty of CSI type questions about collecting DNA, bagging and tagging, and determining the cause and time of death.

She outlined how the various Criminal Investigation Division units or CIDs around the state worked. The closest unit was CID#1 in Gray.

Caroline asked Smitty if she aspired to become a CID investigator.

"I'm pursuing that course of study. I've been on my share of construction traffic details and logged plenty of patrol miles—not that there's anything wrong with those parts of the job. But that's not why I got my degree in Criminal Justice."

"I can't think of anything I'd rather do than be a private eye," Caroline said.

"She'd make a good one," Twait said, chest swelled with pride.

"Yep. Nobody snoops like Caroline," Charlie added.

"Amen," Harley joked. "Smitty and Caroline, super trooper and super snooper." They laughed politely.

Smitty continued. "The Crime Lab is on Hospital Street in Augusta. The Forensic Biology part of it is very important to us. It's generally a three-day turnaround on DNA, which is phenomenally fast compared to other states. That's not only on capital crimes like murder, but also on property crimes—like when you take a swab swipe in a burglary case and get skin cells from a door knob or broken glass. Maine's got a lower crime rate than California or New York, so in those states DNA workups may not get into the national database for months. We're very fast."

Bando asked, "So those evidence lockers or evidence rooms we used to see on the old police dramas on TV, they don't exist anymore?"

"Oh, they still exist, but in a different way. For example, evidence warehouses still take the big stuff. Some warehouses are climate controlled, but not all. But we only use a fraction of the space we used to. That's partly because cotton swabs are used to collect DNA samples that are then bagged and tagged, so the evidence isn't as bulky. If we can get the swab sample off the window and properly document it, we don't have to take the whole window. See what I mean? A lot of it is on slides, with the information being stored on computer disks. We're more efficient."

Bando had Rose primed to ask the next question.

"Okay, take the Alley crime scene, since that's on our minds. The Evidence Response Team wouldn't leave the rope hanging from the tree, right, or other objects that were found at the scene? They'd take them in. What about the body and the clothing? Does everything go to one place?"

"The body goes in for autopsy, which generates a report. Shoes and clothing would be removed from the body, then bagged, tagged, and sent to the Crime Lab in Augusta. So would any objects found at the scene, for example a potential murder weapon or other personal effects that might or might not be the victim's—maybe gum, candy wrappers, that sort of stuff. Because it looks like the killer is still at large, anything from the Alley case has been expedited and is probably at the Crime Lab right now."

After a few last minute thoughts and questions, Bando thanked Smitty for her time and expertise, and the group applauded. Everyone had learned a lot, especially him.

* * *

As soon as Smitty was gone, Harley corralled Bando.

"Sir, I notice you haven't told the others about my gift."

"I've told Twait and Rose, not the other kids. You haven't told them, have you?"

"You told me not to, not yet."

"Thank you. I've had some concerns about it. It's not as simple as it appears."

"Then we should talk a little more about it. I borrowed Charlie's books and read up on astral projection and out-of-body travel, but I still have questions."

"I guess it's time for a crash course."

"Have you ever done it—left your body, I mean?"

"No. But one of my brothers used to."

"Used to?"

"Yes."

"Was it Derby in California?"

"No."

"Must be the other one here on the East Coast?"

"No, not Shaman."

"But I thought you said the others were dead."

Bando was stone-faced.

"Oh. Sorry."

"Harley, what you experienced is an out-of-body experience."

"Yes, I read that. Some people float above the operating table and their hearts stop, then a silver cord pulls them back in and they come back to life. It's happened with people in car accidents, too. After a crash they stand next to the car and watch the EMT do CPR on them—or sometimes they travel upward toward a bright light that they think is God, and they see dead relatives welcoming them—but then at the last second they're drawn back into their bodies."

"Those are similar to your experience but slightly different. What you're describing is called a near-death experience. It's one type of out-of-body experience. But yours isn't near-death, is it?"

"No."

"Yours is out-of-body travel, sometimes called *astral projection* or *astral travel*. It often occurs the first time—and often the only time for most people—at a moment of trauma. It's accidental in those cases—like the car crash example you gave just now."

"So basically, my soul or my spirit leaves my body and goes for a walk, right?"

"Yes. There are several ways it happens. The most common is traumatic or *unintentional*; it just happens. But some people have done it intentionally through *Bhakti yoga* and *kundalini yoga* or an exercise called the *Monroe technique*. My brother Sidat who died used meditation coupled with something called the *rollout or rotation method*. Basically, you turn over inside your body and slip out."

"Sounds like me. The first time was unintentional during meditation. I thought it was what you called *going into the zone*. After that, though, I used meditation to get to the right frequency—and I rolled out."

"You think you can do it again?"

"Don't see why not. It was easy."

"How about later this afternoon?"

"Where? On my bunk or on a mat?"

"In the back seat of Rose's car with a blanket over you."

"Why there?"

"Because we need to go to Augusta."

"Why?"

"It's where the Crime Lab is, on Hospital Street. We need to get in."

"We?"

"You."

"Isn't that breaking and entering?"

"You're not going to break anything."

CHAPTER 34

Rose and Bando's after-lunch session was on psychic awareness and developing practical intuition. They recapped the importance of using meditation to increase the brain's alpha waves. As a demonstration Rose had Maggie break out a new deck of cards, then predicted not just the colors but the suits of 39 of the 52 cards in the deck.

The cards reminded them to press her for a Tarot reading, which she at first declined, then gave in to. She pulled out the special deck and in reading Damon turned up a sequence ending with the Death card, so she stopped abruptly. She was visibly shaken, something Bando picked up on. He gave everyone the rest of the afternoon off, announcing that Twait would open the waterfront from 3 o'clock to 4:30.

Atlanta and Damon went outside while Caroline and the others set up an easel pad by the fireplace.

The adults moved into the kitchen. Bando closed the door.

"What was that about, Rose?" he asked.

"Three times I read Damon and three times the Death card came up in the same place in the sequence."

"Is the Death card about his parents? Maybe this is a way of saying they're close."

"No, it's about a death. Now."

"Alley?"

"No, in the near future. Very near."

"Damon or somebody else?"

"Don't know."

"How much credence do you give it?" Twait asked.

"Strong. Eight on a ten scale."

The three of them stood quiet for a minute, then Bando said, "Rose, I need to borrow your car again."

"When?"

"In fifteen minutes, after I change into some slacks and a sport coat. Ted Alley's visiting hours start at 3 o'clock down in Windham."

"You're going to his wake?" Twait asked.

"To offer condolences to his family from the camp."

"And to see what he can find out," Rose said to Twait.

"If there is anything to be found out."

"Back for supper?"

"No. I'll keep going to Augusta. While I'm changing, can you do me a favor? I need both ice chests, the two picnic baskets, and three tablecloths."

"Food, too?"

"No. It's for props. We'll eat at McDonald's or Burger King on the way back."

"We?"

"Yes. Harley's coming with me."

"To the funeral?" Twait asked.

"No, to Augusta, to try out his gift."

CHAPTER 35

THE FUNERAL HOME attendant held the door for Bando and directed him to the guest book. Next to it sat a framed picture of Ted Alley in a tie and jacket. Bando signed in as the director of Free Camp, Bridgton, then went into Parlor #1 and sat in the back row.

A man who looked like a middle-aged version of Ted Alley stood shaking hands and chatting with people near the open casket. A stocky woman close in age stayed close beside him. On the junior Alley's other side sat a confused-looking wisp of a woman in a wheelchair, her back to the casket, Alley's widow brought in from the nursing home. Assorted friends and relatives gathered nearby or sat in the first few rows on padded folding chairs.

Bouquets, floral sprays, and flower arrangements flanked the casket. Silk ribbons expressed relationships as well as sorrow: *Beloved Husband, Dad, Brother, Friends Forever,* and *We Love You Grandpa.* A small wreath on a wire stand read *BPOE Brother Elk.* The largest, made up of red roses, white roses, and some darker-painted ones, had been artistically shaped into a Boston Red Sox logo. The ribbon read: *Fan & Citizen, Red Sox Nation.*

Bando sat for a half hour until a temporary lull. He made his way forward to Alley's son and daughter-in-law, shaking her hand then his.

"Mr. Alley, I'm from Free Camp in Bridgton. Our staff and campers wanted me to express how sorry we are for your family's loss. It's been on their minds every day."

The son nodded and the awkward silence set in.

Bando pointed. "I love this Red Sox arrangement."

The son brightened, motioned toward the open coffin, and Bando glanced toward the body.

"Dad was a lifelong fan. He's got his Red Sox tie on. And you can see one of his many Sox caps there." Ted Alley's folded hands appeared to be clutching one close to his sternum.

"Wow," Bando said, and with no one in line waiting to speak to the family, the word wow was enough to get the son talking.

"Dad had a huge collection of Red Sox memorabilia that he either bought or got from us as gifts. He had mugs, beer steins, arm patches, posters, practice jerseys, autographed player photos, a signed Carl Yazstremski home-run ball, and a pegboard across his entire garage wall covered with ball caps." He gestured toward the casket again. "The hat he's holding is his American League Pennant hat. We wanted to put his World Series Champs hat there, but he must have lost it the day he wandered away."

The confused woman in the wheelchair sparked to life.

"He didn't lose it."

Alley leaned close to his mother. "What, Mom?"

"Ted didn't lose his cap."

"Maybe somebody took it," Bando said.

The widow tensed up—defensively or perhaps offensively, answering the challenge. Clear-eyed and lucid, she looked Bando in the eye and said, "Over his dead body." Then she relaxed and disappeared again behind a veil of forgetfulness.

Ted Junior was at a loss for words.

Bando rescued him, pointing to a floral display. "I see he was an Elk."

"Yes, he held all the offices and attended right up until two years ago. He loved his lodge and his lodge brothers. Many of them will be here tonight or tomorrow."

"Your father must have been quite a guy."

"He was. This damned Alzheimer's robbed him—and Mom—of so much."

"Robbed you, too," Bando said, and took Alley's hand in his two. The two men stood for a long moment, linked only by their hands and a shared sense of loss and sadness. "I read that your Dad loved baseball, fishing, and hunting. How about other sports--bowling, golf?"

"He bowled a little early on. I don't think he ever played golf, though. He joked that it was a stupid idea—hitting a ball so you could chase it or lose it, just so you could hit it and chase it and lose it again. He didn't even like to watch it on TV."

"Quite a testament: devoted husband, father, grandfather, lodge brother, neighbor, sportsman—and of course rabid Red Sox fan."

"All those and more. Thank you so much for coming."

Bando hugged him warmly and shook the hand of the widow. Before he turned to leave he took one last glance at the casket. It left him with a mental image he wouldn't forget—a dead man clutching a Red Sox cap.

* * *

Maggie and Atlanta had just gotten into their bathing suits when Caroline knocked on the girls' cabin door and came in. She still had her shorts and tee shirt on.

"Not swimming today?" Maggie asked.

"Can't afford to miss the computer time. There's got to be more out there on these three cases."

"So what brings you over here if you're not coming to swim?" Atlanta asked.

"I wanted to show you these," she said, and held out some computer-printed articles to Atlanta.

"More on Alley, Terrell, and Parks?" Maggie asked as Atlanta took them.

"No," Caroline said. "They're on Damon's parents and the fire."

Atlanta looked up. "I already know about this. We all do."

"What we know is what Damon told us, that his parents died in a fire. We all know you care about him, so I'm assuming he told you even more. But still, all you know is what came from his mouth. Those articles give you the story from other perspectives."

"They think he did it, don't they?" Atlanta snapped, her eyes fiery. "They think he set the fire. But they're wrong. He didn't, I know he didn't!" She threw the papers on the floor and stormed out.

* * *

Before leaving Free Camp, Bando had gleaned a wealth of information from the State Police website. Evidence Receiving Hours were 9 a.m. to 3:30 p.m. suggesting technicians would be working cases during those hours and for at least a few hours after. Alley was still a priority so all the evidence wouldn't yet be in a remote storage facility. Harley would have no access to paper files or computer information so it would be strictly about viewing what could be observed.

Bando drove past the Crime Lab once so Harley could see it and learn his way there and back. It was a low, mostly brick building with a blue-trimmed door and matching archway at its main entrance. Maine Medical Center's parking lot was three minutes away by car, 15 by foot, and somewhere in between when *astral gliding*, which Harley described as The Invisible Man on Roller-blades.

They found a parking space in the back corner of the Medical Center lot. Bando kept the car running and the air conditioning on.

"Okay, Harley. You know most of what I know about the crime scene—the rope, the tire, the position of the body, the clothing, the hat, the chair and whatever was coiled on it. Once you get inside, see what's out in the open first. You may be able to find a case number marked on something that's Alley's. If you have that case number, you can pass through one of the interior doors and locate other items tagged with the same number."

"Got it."

"You know your way there and back, right?"

"Yep."

"And you won't stay inside there more than ten minutes, right?"

"Right."

The two of them got out of the car and opened the back doors. Bando pulled out the props and set them on the ground. Harley climbed in, closed his door, and lay down across the back seat.

"Deep breathing, relaxation, and as soon as you hit the alpha state you try the rollout. These back doors will be closed, but you should be able to pass through them. I'll keep the air conditioning on, so your body will be cool enough under the tablecloths. We can't put you in the trunk; it's not air-conditioned. But we can't risk having someone walk by and notice a body in the back of the car. I'll be here when you get back." Bando covered him with the tablecloths and set the two ice chests and picnic baskets on top. Then he closed the door and climbed back in the driver's seat.

"You okay back there?"

Harley didn't answer. Bando sat waiting for the tablecloths to move again.

*　*　*

The rollout maneuver worked. Once Harley entered a light state of meditation, he recognized he was ready. It was just like turning over in bed at night, rolling from his left side onto his right side—except that his body didn't roll, only his astral body did. The car doors were hardly there. He somehow brought his astral body to the right frequency and passed through, then found himself standing—no, hovering in a standing position—a fraction of an inch above the blacktop. Time to skate.

He glided the mile to the Crime Lab, thinking how much smoother this was than the astronauts step-bouncing in slow motion across the surface of the moon. He didn't understand how it worked—he had no physical parts with which to push off from the sidewalk the way a sprinter does on a track—but he had the odd sensation that it was his touching the ground from time to time that allowed him to push forward. At first it was hard to overcome the feeling that he was exposed and someone might see him, but he knew from sneaking up on Bando's car days earlier he was invisible to the naked eye.

The Crime Lab doors, though harder to penetrate than the car doors, were a piece of cake. He assumed it wasn't about their thickness but about his energy field weakening. Did it have to do with time away from his body, or with distance from it, or both? He made a mental note to talk with Bando about it. As soon as he was inside he passed a cop at the reception window handing over a marked paper evidence bag to a blonde woman cop behind the reception desk. The cop flirted then turned and left. Suddenly Harley was there—inside one of the lab rooms. *Ten minutes inside*, Bando had said. Eight left. He had to move fast.

* * *

The time passed quickly and suddenly Bando heard a rustling behind him. He turned as Harley poked his head out from under the tablecloths and grinned.

"Un-freaking-believable!" He shook his head as if he'd just sampled the world's best chocolate. "Super sleuth! What a trip!"

Bando helped him out from under the props so he could climb through to the front passenger seat. "Take it slow. You may be a little shaky."

"I am a little. Longer runs drain the gas tank. It's the same with passing through doors and walls. It gets harder and harder after awhile. Wood's the easiest, but cement and steel—if your energy's getting low— you feel like you're going to get stuck halfway through."

"Here's that Gatorade," Bando said, and handed Harley a large bottle of blue liquid. "Replenish your electrolytes. It's warm, but my brother Sidat said it was better that way, less shock on your system."

Harley took a few gulps then switched to sipping. "Head for a McDonald's, Jeeves. Two Big Macs and some fries for the road home."

"McDonald's coming right up. So, did you find anything related to Alley?"

"I did. But I don't know what it means. The first thing I saw was a lab guy working with an evidence bag with Alley's name and case number on it. I looked for anything else with the name or case number. It looks like the Crime Lab expands into a warehouse out back, but I didn't have time to go back there. But in this room off the lab they had the tire and the chair. On a shelf above was an open crate with a couple more items that had his case number."

Bando drove out of the parking lot onto East Chestnut and started toward Routes 9 and 202. Harley swallowed another slug of Gatorade. He held out his hand, fingers extended, shaking a little.

"Okay, don't keep me in suspense, Harley. What did you see in the box? Anything we didn't already know about?"

"The ball cap—the one you said was tucked behind him. It's blue and has gold trim across the brim—sort of like a Navy admiral's but kind of soft, a yachtsman's cap, I guess. It had lettering on it: Mattituck Lions, Island's End Golf Tournament."

"Golf?"

"Yep. Golf."

"Anything else?"

"Just a little braided whip."

CHAPTER 36

It was 7:30 when Bando and Harley got back to Free Camp. They unloaded their picnic props and carried them to the kitchen.

"We're over here," Rose called from the big room where she and Twait sat facing each other. "Wednesday is foot rub night. Harley, everybody else is outside or in their cabins, probably making their calls home. Your cell phone is right there on the pass-through counter."

Harley grabbed his phone and disappeared out the door as Bando walked over and plopped down in an easy chair. He kicked his shoes off and swung his feet up onto the coffee table. "Is this where the line forms?"

"Hah! Good luck with that one," Twait said.

Bando shrugged. "Can't blame a guy for trying."

"Worthwhile trip?" Rose asked. "We figure you visited the Crime Lab. After all, Alicia practically spelled out the directions in her talk. She even mentioned the street."

"Everything but the house number," Twait said. "I don't think she'd give that workshop for just anybody. Somebody sweet-talked her."

"All right, you two, knock it off or I won't tell you what we found out."

Twait and Rose glanced at each other and rolled their eyes. "Ooh, threats," Twait mocked, and Rose teased, "Like we could stop him from telling us."

"Okay, it was a great trip. Harley was amazing. Only his third astral projection, and it was a long, difficult one. He came through with flying colors." Bando told them where he had parked and how they had used the props. "Half an hour later the tablecloths move, his head pops up, and he's grinning like a Cheshire cat. If he hadn't told me what he saw, I'd have sworn he'd been snoozing the whole time."

"Which was what?" Rose probed.

Bando told them about the chair, the tire, the charity golf cap, and the braided whip.

"Like a bullwhip?" Twait asked. "One of those things the muleskinners used on the freight wagons?"

"No. Smaller. Obviously Harley couldn't pick it up, but from the way he described it I'd say it's a riding whip or a stage prop, maybe a child's toy from a Western souvenir store. But it was a whip, not a stuffed snake or a coil of rope."

"Wasn't Alley's, I'm sure," Rose said. "Must have been the killer's."

"You think he hung Alley up and whipped him," Twait wondered, "then left it behind?"

"No. When Harley went into McDonald's I rechecked Tina Sutherland's snapshot. No bloodstains and no shred marks on the clothing. The whip was never used. It's a prop."

"Leaving it was no accident," Rose said. "This guy is deliberate about everything. He placed it exactly where he wanted it seen—not on the body but near it, not slung over the back of the chair but on it, and carefully coiled. He's like a window dresser with his manikins. Everything in the display is there for visual impact."

"So he must drive around lugging his props," Twait said, "waiting for a chance to pick up a stray manikin. Then all he has to do is kill him, dress him, and pose him."

"Fits both Alley and Terrell, doesn't it?" Rose observed. "And now maybe this black man, Parks."

"It's like he strangled them to put them out of their misery," Twait said. "So he could use their corpses like a Chicago slaughterhouse. We're not angry at the cows; we're relatively indifferent. But we need to kill them to get the meat. The slaughter is an unfortunate but necessary step in the process."

Rose shook her head sadly. "Two, maybe three men murdered—maybe more—for some crazy man's art."

"I think you're onto something, Rose," Bando said. "What is art but a message someone transmits through some medium of expression? It's their way of communicating something to a perceived audience."

"I'm no profiler, but I wonder if he's angry, maybe fixated on something or someone that hurt him, and he's trying to make a scene to show the public who he's angry at."

Bando sighed. "So perhaps—and I'm just thinking out loud here—perhaps he's shown the public three scenes, maybe more that we don't know about, and God forbid more to come. What are the three scenes showing us? I remember contemplating the Wallace Stevens poem, 'Thirteen Ways of Looking at a Blackbird,' which is about 13 perspectives over four seasons of the year. It's not 13 blackbirds but one blackbird observed at thirteen different times. One blackbird."

"Twait," Rose asked. "Remember the Georgia O'Keeffe Gallery in Santa Fe—all those magnificent paintings of the Desert Southwest? Half of them were of her favorite mountain. She painted it again and again in different years and different seasons. It was like she was obsessed with it. If she had written a poem, she might have called it 'Two Hundred Ways of Looking at My Mountain. She had to show us that mountain.'"

Bando shifted in his seat. "So our killer isn't like other murderers. He's not trying to *hide* something—except maybe his identity—he's trying to *reveal* something. But the audience, the world, we aren't seeing it."

They sat thinking awhile.

"I'd still like to know if the whip was used," Twait pressed. "A whip might also play into the Terrell case if you went back to the idea of the Crucified One."

"The only way to find out if the whip was used on Alley would be to see the autopsy report or photos," Bando said. "Closest place to find those would probably be CID in Gray. And I'm not even sure they'd have it. Besides, even if we went there and got Harley in, the report would have to be lying open on the table."

"Let's not forget about Smitty," Rose said.

Bando shook his head. "I don't see her giving us that kind of information. And we've got to be careful here. We can't even tell her we know there *is* a whip. Tina Sutherland's mental image and my gut tell me the whip wasn't used, that it was a prop."

"Got a plan?" Rose asked.

"No. But I have a question. About a hat."

"A hat?"

"Yes. Remember Harley's sketch of the Red Sox cap and how you kept seeing Carl Yazstremski at the plate? This afternoon Ted Alley's son mentioned Yazstremski while his father was lying in the casket with a Red Sox cap in his hands. He said the World Series cap went missing when Alley walked away from home the other day."

"What does that tell us?" Twait asked. "We already knew Alley was a huge Sox fan."

"That's not Bando's point," Rose said. "The point is why didn't they find the World Series hat in the clearing near the body? Why did they find some charity golf cap that wasn't even on his head?"

CHAPTER 37

ATLANTA FOUND THE articles about the house fire and Damon's parents on her bunk.

"You put these here?" she asked Maggie.

"You should look at them. There's nothing bad about Damon in there."

"How do you know? You read them, didn't you?"

"Why shouldn't I? They were on the floor. You didn't seem to want them."

"Caroline wants to break me and Damon up."

"That's bull crap and you know it. She's got no interest in Damon."

"Then why'd she dig these things up? And why'd she feel the need to give them to me?"

"It's certainly not jealousy. If she found something bad on him, why would she want to steal him away from you? Besides, nobody's made a move on him. If anything, Caroline cares enough about you to do a sort of background check on Damon, make sure he's not going to hurt you. You ought to thank her."

"Thank her?"

"Hey, don't cop an attitude here, honey. If you're pissed off at your mother or at your parents for divorcing, deal with it at home. But don't take it out on me or Caroline or anybody else here. We're your friends, not your punching bags." Maggie stood up and walked out.

Atlanta propped two pillows behind her back and began to read. The articles reported on the fire, then on the police suspecting Damon but eventually removing him from the list. She found herself reading parts of them out loud.

The first article from the *Portland Press Herald* contained an eyewitness interview with Katie Haskell, a teenager who lived across the street from Damon. "It was a warm night and we don't have an air conditioner, so Mom and I were on the porch waiting for *Two and a Half Men* to start. We heard yelling and screaming, a fight over at Damon's. He's three years younger than me and he's a really cute, really nice guy. It sounded like him and his father. His father was mean to him a lot. It's not the first time Damon got into it with his Dad. Next thing I know we hear a door slam and Damon comes down and sits on the front porch, which he's done before. His father yells down from their apartment for him to get his ass back upstairs. So Damon gets up and goes around back of the house, probably to the other porch. Mom and I figure the fireworks are over, so we go inside for *Two and a Half Men*. Well, the show gets over and I notice it's really bright like daytime out there. So I go to the window and see their house is on fire. We run outside, Mom and me, but it's too late. The whole building is in flames. I feel sorry for Damon with no place to live. I told Mom he could sleep in my bed and I'd take the couch."

Subsequent articles reported that Damon admitted to arguing with his parents and leaving the building. According to him, though, he had jogged downtown and "hung out," returning later to find the house on fire. A later article suggested he was initially a person of interest but the District Attorney quickly dropped it.

Atlanta could see that Caroline and Maggie had been telling the truth. There was nothing damning about the articles. If anything, they seemed to bear out what Damon had told the group publicly and her privately. But she wondered why Katie was taking so much time talking to reporters. Was there more going on between the two of them than she was telling the police? Why hadn't Damon mentioned Katie Haskell? She ripped up the papers and was about to throw them in the wastebasket, but at the last minute stuffed them in her backpack and stormed out of the cabin.

* * *

A light rain started around 8:30, forcing the campfire inside to the big fireplace. They roasted marshmallows and drank hot chocolate, but the mood wasn't as upbeat as it had been at the last campfire.

Bando filled everyone in on the trip to Windham and Augusta, revealing Harley's gift. They had a lot of questions about out-of-body travel and wanted to do a meditation session right then so they could try it themselves. Bando said it could wait until morning.

"Does this mean Harley can stick his head through the girls' cabin walls and see us showering?" Maggie asked.

"You wish, Magpie!" Harley jabbed, laughing. "It'd be like looking Medusa in the eye. I'd turn to stone."

The conversation about invisibility went on for a while and ended with them making Harley promise not to peep.

Once the silliness was out of the way, a seriousness set in the way it can at a New Year's Eve party after a few drinks.

Atlanta said, "Caroline, Maggie, I'm sorry I got mad at you two today." She glared at Damon then turned back to Caroline. "You were right to give me those articles."

The girls nodded and Caroline said, "It's in the past."

Atlanta continued. "We can't let things divide us, not now anyway. Remember the final dinner last year at that motel? We were together. We had a bond. It took all of us, all of our gifts, to survive Donnie Bronson. No single gift alone was enough. We made a pact we wouldn't *disclose* our gifts but would use them to *help* others. Remember? And do you remember how my cousin Mo proposed that toast? He mentally lifted that glass no-hands and got our attention. And while it was floating up there he proposed a toast. He said 'to FreeK Camp.' Remember? And we all clinked together, 'to FreeK Camp.'"

Every throat was in a knot except Damon's.

"Well," he said. "I wasn't part of the group last year, and I can't mentally raise anything, but I can propose a hot chocolate toast. To those of us here: may we use our gifts together to catch this murderer." They all lifted their cups and proclaimed, "to FreeK Camp"—except Atlanta who bit her lip and looked away. Suddenly she turned, filled with resolve.

"Well, Ted Alley is dead," she said. "James Terrell is dead, and now another man, Leon Parks, is dead, all murdered. The three of them are begging us—the FreeKs—to help. The time for marshmallows and hot chocolate toasts is over. Some force has called us and our gifts together in this place and time—and I don't mean just our psychic and paranormal gifts but also our brains, our bodies, and our teamwork. We have to help now before somebody else dies."

No one breathed, including Twait and Rose. Atlanta's eyes were like lightning, and everyone waited for her to tell them what came next.

"Caroline has more information—in case anybody's interested."

Caroline held up a sheaf of papers.

In two minutes everyone committed. They dragged in the easel pad and prepared for a long night.

"There's a red Magic Marker around here somewhere," Harley joked. "But I hear it only writes the letter K."

Everyone laughed and then got to work.

Caroline laid out everything on the Parks junkyard murder and any updates on Terrell and Alley.

"Let's assume it's the same killer or killers," Atlanta said. "A single serial killer would be my guess, but we can't rule out a pair or a willing accomplice. Parks, the black man found in a New York junkyard two summers ago, is victim #1." She wrote it on the easel pad. "Terrell, who died last summer, is victim #2. Ted Alley this summer is victim #3."

She ripped the sheet off the pad and taped it to the wall. On a fresh new sheet she wrote *Similarities* and listed everyone's observations as they called them out.

- Staged (weird tableaus)
- Strangled. (Need to verify whether Parks was.)
- All men

- All hitchhiking or on foot, probably accepted rides voluntarily
- All in summer
- Alley and Terrell in public recreation area clearings; Parks also in isolated place
- None of the 3 areas had cameras except maybe junkyard (How to check?)
- Appearances: all made to look like they died of odd causes—Alley by hanging, Terrell by crucifixion or burning, Parks by paint pore-suffocation. Reality: probably all strangled (reminder: confirm Parks)
- Terrell and Alley found in areas with high concentrations of recreation-related businesses and summer camps. Parks near suburbia, dumped in junkyard (Q: Are there recreation areas or summer camps nearby?)
- All 3 bodies probably transported and staged at night
- Atlanta tore off the sheet and taped it on the wall. "We can add to it as needed."

She started a fresh page: *Differences.*

- Alley and Terrell white, Parks black (Q: Did killer paint Parks white because he needed all whites?)
- Ages (Terrell 20s, Parks 40s, Alley 70s)
- States: NY, California, Maine
- Parks single, Terrell single, Alley married but apart from wife in nursing home
- Alley with Addie Beals at waterfall; Terrell at Horton Cemetery; Alley and Terrell with Addie at campfire; Parks at Durham cemetery in black section.

Atlanta stuck the third sheet to the wall by the others. On the next blank page she wrote: *Observations and Questions.*

- Killer must be strong enough to carry bodies uphill or long distance
- Strangles grown men. Is he military or government trained (like Seals, Special Ops, CIA, police)? Or does he stun

or chloroform them first? (Wouldn't have to be especially strong or specially trained in this case.)

- Does not appear to know victims. Staging planned, props ready, but partly these are crimes of opportunity that he's ready to carry out
- Does not appear interested in torture
- If props ready, good chance vehicle is truck or van (space & concealment needs)
- Props suggest pre-planned tableaus. Parks—silver paint, paintbrush, duct tape. Terrell—2 wooden 2x4 crosspieces, matches or lighter, one or more bales of hay to burn, baling wire to be used to connect crosspieces and to bind hands and ankles. Alley—chair, whip.

"And let's not forget Alley's ball cap switch," Bando said. "His World Series Red Sox cap disappeared and a golf charity event cap took its place on the body. Alley's son told me his father didn't play golf, wouldn't even watch it on TV. We need to check it out. Mattituck Lions, Island's End Golf Course."

"It's another prop," Charlie said. "But why?"

"Caroline, can you Google it?" Bando asked.

"I will," she answered. "But I can save us some time right now. When I checked out the Bike-man story, I got a map of eastern Long Island." She shuffled through her Parks file. "Here it is. Mattituck. It's one of the little towns between Greenport where Parks lived and Riverhead where he was found. So Mattituck ties together Alley here in Maine with Parks in New York. That's hard data the cops can use."

"So the golf hat came from where Parks lived and died," Atlanta said, and wrote notes on the easel sheets. "How it got here to Maine is another question."

CHAPTER 38

THE HOUR GREW late and once Caroline begged off to hit the computer, the others faded. Harley hung back to chat with Bando.

"I just wanted to say thanks—for letting me do something really big, the Crime Lab."

"Nobody else could have done it. And you did it well."

"Thanks. You were right."

"About what?"

"About losing strength, about melting through doors."

Bando said nothing.

"After I got back to the parking lot, I could barely get through the car doors. It was like the Boston Marathon and hitting Heartbreak Hill at Mile 19. I was tired and I almost got stuck passing through. The back door took everything I had. I think maybe the Gatorade helped. I know the Big Macs sure did."

They laughed.

"But you did get back."

"Yeah. And I feel great about it. On the trip home I didn't say anything, but I started thinking—what if my astral body did get stuck halfway through a door or a concrete wall? What if I—it—my astral body—can't make it all the way back to my physical body? What if it's like you swim away from shore until you're almost out of sight of land, and then you find yourself too exhausted to swim back? You can see the land way off, but you're worn out and nobody's around to help."

"I guess the answer is experience, just like knowing how far out to swim. You learn by training, by observing yourself—and by not taking foolish chances. That way you keep a little reserve in your tank to draw on."

"So you're saying practice—practice traveling out of body? Build myself up like—like Twait did with weights?"

"It would seem to make sense, Harley, but I honestly don't know. As much as I meditate, I've never been able to travel out-of-body."

"But you said your brother Sidat did?"

"Yes."

"Was he good at it?"

"Exceptional."

"Was he like a crime fighter? Did he use his powers for good?"

"He worked for the government. He'd never say exactly what department it was for, though."

"He was a spy?"

"Maybe."

"What happened to him?"

"We don't know. We suspect he stayed out-of-body too long. By the time they notified us that he was at Walter Reed Hospital, he'd already been comatose for three months. They asked our permission to remove him from life support."

"So they declared him brain dead?"

"No. They didn't. He wasn't brain dead. He had brain activity, but he was comatose. We insisted they keep him on life support, but in the end they insisted it was their decision, not ours, because technically he was government property. They took him off everything except water. He still survived another 95 days without food."

"I didn't know that was possible."

"The government never said anything about him traveling by astral projection. But Shaman, Derby, and I were pretty sure that's what he'd been doing for them. We figure he left his body in a low-pulse, meditative state to conserve energy—life force."

"Like a computer going into sleep mode when you go to bed?"

"I suppose. Most people think of a bear hibernating in winter."

"So they let him die? People have come out of comas after 15 or 20 years, haven't they? I mean, if they're not brain dead they can."

"True. But in his case, for whatever reason, they let him go."

Harley's face looked pained. He mulled the idea.

"Did you see him after he was dead? Did you see him buried? Or did they just tell you they disconnected him then buried or cremated him?"

Bando looked puzzled, then disturbed, as if he were searching his memory for something elusive.

"You're sure he's not in a secret facility somewhere, like a warehouse? I mean, maybe they told you that to get you off their backs. Even if they gave you his ashes, how could you be sure they were his?"

Bando nodded. "I'll have to recall the circumstances again in detail when I see Shaman and Derby. You'd better get going now if you're going to get any sleep tonight."

"Wait, one last question. Let's say your brother's physical body—or *my* body—died and was then buried or burned, but the astral body was out traveling. How long can astral bodies, um, *tread water*?"

As soon as Harley left, Bando called Smitty who was less than a half hour away.

CHAPTER 39

A FEW MINUTES LATER Caroline marched into the big room with her parents behind her. Harley had done a U-turn in the yard, sensing something was in the air.

"Bando," Rose called into the office. "Caroline's got something on the golf cap."

They sat down and Caroline reported.

"The Mattituck Lions are like the Rotary Club or Kiwanis. They do local projects and fund charitable causes. Their summer fundraiser is a golf tournament held at the Island's End Golf Course. Guess where it is? It's in Greenport, Bike-man's hometown. If you pay to play, you get a golf cap."

"But Bike-man couldn't afford golf," Harley said.

"No, but he could have gotten the cap from a Goodwill Store or somebody could have given it to him. He was a local character. Let's say it was his and he had it on when he was killed."

"So the killer takes it off him the way he took the Red Sox cap off Alley?" Harley asked, perplexed.

"Let's not conclude that yet. We don't know that he took Alley's hat. Alley could have legitimately lost it before he was picked up hitchhiking."

"But," Twait cut in, "it gives us one theory—musical hats. The killer moves one victim's hat to the next victim, and so on."

"Only problem with that," Rose said, "is the timeline." She pointed to Atlanta's easel sheet on the wall: Parks/NY/#1, Terrell/California/#2, Alley/Maine/#3. "If it was musical hats, the golf cap would have gone from Bike-man Parks to Terrell, then maybe a Texas A&M hat of Terrell's to Alley. Why would he skip one?"

Caroline grabbed the Magic Marker and made a note on the easel sheet: *Musical hats? Did Terrell have a hat—maybe Texas A&M? (Check this out).*

Bando said, "Let's go back to the premise that Bike-man's killer wanted a prop for a later killing, but he didn't know which tableau would come next. He doesn't think of them one at a time, but has a cast of characters in mind and a variety of props in his vehicle. After all, the connection isn't between victims; it's between tableaus. This is about his art."

"How about this?" Rose suggested. "Maybe the cap wasn't Bike-man's at all. It was the killer's. He's a charity golfer who lived on that part of Long Island or at least played golf while passing through."

Caroline wrote a new note on the big pad: *Was killer a golfer? Did he live near Parks two years ago?*

"How can we know where the killer lived without knowing his name?" Harley asked. "And we still have the question: *Why leave a golf cap in place of a baseball cap?*"

Twait said, "*We may know* a hat connects Parks and Alley, *but the police don't know.* They should. If they're trying to match DNA from Alley's crime scene to a national databank, it might save them some time if they try matching it to DNA from Bike-man's scene. And if the fire didn't destroy all the DNA at Terrell's scene in California, they might link all three."

"How do we tip them off?" Harley asked, looking to Bando. "Your brother Derby again?"

"I've already asked Smitty to stop by. She ought to be here in about ten minutes. She can get the ball rolling tonight."

"I have another thought," Harley said. "Does this Lions Club have a website that lists the players in their tournament each year?"

Caroline stood up fast. "Hold that thought. Back in a flash." She ran out.

Rose wrote on the easel pad: *Lions Club golf rosters.*

"Good thinking, Harley," Bando said. "Maybe Caroline can see if there are rosters from other golf tournaments near Terrell's scene, too. And we can check for golf fundraisers here in Maine. If our killer really is an itinerant charity golfer his name might show up in several places."

"What we need is access to more computers," Harley said.

Twait suggested, "Last year the kids used a couple at the library. We already know the librarian. We can check in the morning. The library opens at 9 a.m. I can drive a couple of you in. I've got errands I can do while you're there—we need a couple of bags of anti-algae stuff for the lake. I'll swing back for you and we'll be back in time for lunch."

Caroline popped back in with printouts. "Got the Lions Club golf information for the last seven years."

Harley said, "Hello, Nancy Drew."

THURSDAY

CHAPTER **40**

THE NEXT MORNING Smitty called Bando before breakfast.

"Those names you shared with me last night? And Caroline's printouts? Wow! We're onto something. After I got off shift I spent the whole night running that down. Can we talk somewhere this morning?"

"Sure. Where? What time?"

"I've still got more to check out, and I'm looking a bit worse for wear with no sleep, so I want to grab a shower. How about 9 o'clock at McDonald's in Windham?"

"Sounds great. We're skipping meditation so the kids can go to town this morning. I'll see you in Windham."

* * *

Twait stopped in front of the library and dropped off four teens. Caroline and Charlie stayed behind with the computer.

"Look for me between 11:15 and 11:45," Twait reminded. "These errands won't take all morning. If I'm done early I'll sit out here and read my newspaper and drink my coffee. But 11:45 at the latest. Rose won't appreciate us being late for lunch." He pulled FreeK Camp #2 away from the curb and drove south on Portland Road toward Tru-Value Hardware.

* * *

Back at Free Camp Caroline ran computer searches while Charlie compared seven years of rosters from the Mattituck Lions golf tournaments. He drew a line through those golfers who took part every year, narrowing the lists to those who were one-timers, particularly in the year Bike-man Parks was murdered. He got down to 47 one-time names.

"I've got a phone number for the Lions Club event chairman," Caroline said, and got up. "I'm going to call him. You keep checking Maine golf events and see if any of the New York names turn up in Maine."

Charlie took over the seat and the screen.

Caroline went to the office and dialed the chairman's number.

"Mr. Mellas? Hi. My name is Caroline and I'm calling from Maine. I need your help on a golf story. You chair the Mattituck Lions tournament, don't you?"

Jake Mellas sounded like a man in his seventies. He was pleasant and eager to help.

Caroline first had him recount the background of his club's fundraiser—this was his fourteenth year chairing it—then listened to his litany of difficulties involved in the running of such an event.

"I'm particularly interested in not last year but two years ago," she said. "I have several of your rosters that I found online. When I compare them year-to-year, I see that the usual suspects appear in the top twenty-five finishers. Looks like you've got plenty of talent out your way. I noticed many of your golfers have Long Island courses as their home clubs, which tells me your returnees are fairly local, right?"

"If by local you mean Long Islanders, then yes. Mostly Suffolk County with a few from Nassau. This is not a big PGA Tour event, so we seldom get an out-of-state golfer. It's a charity event. I know most of them by face and name."

"Do you have the roster from 2 years ago close at hand?"

"Almost at my fingertips, but not quite." Mellas excused himself from the phone for a minute then came back on. "Got it."

"I'm wondering about a couple of those one-time names."

"You suspect irregularities in your Maine tournaments? Are you seeing the same people?"

"Not quite sure what we're seeing. Can I ask you about a few we've got flagged?" Caroline went through the list.

Mellas had partial recollection about some of the names. Caroline took notes next to each one. It seemed to be going nowhere.

"What about your 145th place finisher, David Osbourne? Hometown is Shelter Island, home course is Quinipet."

"Osbourne? Oh, yes. I remember that situation. He wanted to play so badly—said he was working at the Methodist summer camp on Shelter Island, which is a 10-minute ferry ride from Greenport. Quinipet isn't really the name of his home course; it's not a golf course at all. It's the name of the Methodist camp. Anyway he said he loved supporting charities, but he didn't have an established handicap. And as a summer worker he had no home course. If you saw him play you'd believe it. The guy was no golfer. We bent the rules to let him in, and he had to guarantee us he wouldn't claim a prize even if he placed. That's why his home course is listed as Quinipet. David Osbourne—he said call him Ozzy Osbourne. Wasn't Ozzy Osbourne the rocker who bit the head off that bat in a concert?"

"Can you describe him?"

"Tall, maybe six-foot, kind of muscular but no bodybuilder—dark hair with probably a dash of salt, I'm guessing mid-forties. Why?"

"I'd like to be able to recognize him if I see him here. Last question. Did he get one of your free hats?"

"Everybody does. It's in the registration packet with our complimentary Lions Club tees."

Caroline thanked Mellas and said goodbye. Then she ran back to the cabin, bumped Charlie off the computer, and searched *David Osbourne golf*, *David Osbourne camp*, and *David Osbourne*, hoping it was his real name and that he was still using it.

*   *   *

After following Twait's van from the camp to the library, the man in the white Econoline could hardly believe his luck. Fate never failed him. He adjusted his sunglasses and pulled out, following FreeK Camp #2 at a distance.

CHAPTER 41

BANDO TURNED INTO the Windham McDonald's and saw Smitty sitting outside at a cement picnic table, a red and white umbrella cranked open above it. She was in her street clothes. He parked, walked over, and sat opposite her. There were two paper cups on the table. She pushed the one with the lid his way.

"Tea. No sugar, no milk. I just brought it out, it's still hot."

"Thanks." Bando opened his tea, dunked the bag a few times like he was fishing with a hand-line, and set the wet bag on the discarded lid. They sipped awhile without speaking.

"So where do we start?" he asked, pulling out a small notepad and a pen.

Smitty answered with a notepad that held a stubby pencil in a plastic loop. "Just want to make clear that this is my personal pad, not my Trooper pad."

"Does that mean we're off the record?"

"Not necessarily," she said. "Let's start with Alley."

"Okay. I know more than you think I know, but I can't reveal how I got the information."

"I'm guessing the teens."

"The teens?"

"They're smart. They like playing detective, especially Caroline. I could see it about them when I did the workshop."

Bando kneaded his forehead. He hesitated, weighing the need to share.

"Am I right?" she pressed.

"Right about what?"

"That some of your so-called unexplainable information and ideas comes from them."

"It does, yes. But these are special teens, not just smart. They possess unique gifts, which is why Twait, Rose, and I have the camp. Our job is to teach them, to help them discover and develop those gifts. There are those who wouldn't hesitate to exploit them. And by the way, I can't divulge their gifts."

"I wasn't expecting you to, just as I can't pass you information on open cases. I know a little about the camp. I did my homework after the Bronson mess. Twait is a former circus diver who now wrestles alligators near Disney. His wife Rose is intelligent and well educated, but she must have once had a wild side that drew her to circus and carnival work as Madame Rosario the fortuneteller. Then she got her degrees and settled down to raise a family. She not only teaches World Religions but a few nontraditional courses like Water-witching and Dowsing, ESP and Practical Intuition, and Reiki and Energy Healing. It makes sense she'd work with kids with psychic or unusual gifts. You, on the other hand, I couldn't find out much about you except that you had a run as a circus hypnotist. I can't even find out your last name. Even your Florida driver's license—which I see uses Twait and Rose's address—has only the one name Bando on it."

"It works for Madonna, Adele, and Cher. Good detective work, Alicia." Bando finished the last of his tea in a large gulp. "Shall I share my own detective work?"

She nodded.

"I know that when you found Ted Alley, you found a little whip coiled on the chair. Tucked into the back of his belt was a blue golf cap that came from a charity golf tournament run by the Mattituck Lions Club on Long Island."

"So you did figure a way to get into the Crime Lab."

"I never went in. Cross my heart."

"But you accessed the information."

"Yes. And thank you for the workshop you did for the kids."

"I had a hunch if you knew where it was you'd find a way to get to it."

Bando pushed his empty paper cup around the table with his finger. "Thank you," he said quietly.

"You're welcome."

"Now I need facts on a different murder, but I have no way to get it. Last night I gave you Caroline's printouts on James Lee Terrell Jr., the college student murdered in California. Do you agree that his body was staged in a way similar to Alley's?"

"I do. Bike-man Parks was staged, too. I've checked them out. The hard part is linking the three."

"I need to know if Parks was strangled, too."

"Can't say," she answered, nodding her head slightly.

"Was a hat found at that scene?"

Her head moved side-to-side.

"Okay," he said. "We know Parks was found sitting propped up against a junk car in a salvage yard. His body was painted silver from the shoulders down and his head was wrapped in silver duct tape from the eyebrows up. Were there any other props besides what was found on the body?"

"You mean like an empty oil can about six feet away, which is something you might expect to find in a junkyard anyway?"

"Is that a for-instance or an answer?"

She shrugged. "Can't say."

"Okay, Parks had a bandage on his chest. What was under it? Was he stabbed or shot in addition to being strangled? Was it functional or just another prop?"

"Long Island law enforcement may be withholding that piece of information. Interesting question to check out, though."

Both notepads were still blank.

"Give me a couple of phone numbers where I can reach you," Bando said.

She simply stared.

"Oh, come on," he said, almost grinning. "I've got to get something in writing from this exchange."

Smitty smiled, wrote four phone numbers on his pad, marking the last one HOME, and left.

CHAPTER **42**

TWAIT TURNED INTO True Value Hardware, parked in front, and went inside.

The man in the white Econoline continued on by and made a U-turn then came back by the blind side of the store. He backed the van in almost to the back boundary near the bushes so it faced the road. He got out, opened the hood, and propped it up. Then he went behind the van, opened the twin doors, and removed a set of jumper cables. He carried them to the open hood and attached a red and a black cable to his battery, leaving the other red and black ends hanging loose. He went to the driver's side, reached in, and rummaged between the two front seats for a box. Finally he walked to the corner of the building to wait.

Twait came out carrying two plastic pails of algae fighter. He put them in the camp van, climbed up onto his booster seat and was about to strap on his extenders when he heard a voice.

"Excuse me, sir?"

A big man in sunglasses stood by Twait's window.

"I left my headlights on while I was inside ordering paint and my battery ran down."

He pointed past the corner of the building. The front of a white van was visible, hood raised, a pair of cables hanging down over the grillwork.

"I've got the jumpers hooked up already, but I need another vehicle to jump it. You won't even have to get out of your van, sir. I'd sure appreciate it."

"No problem. Be right over. My battery is on the left. Easy enough to match up."

"Thanks a million," the man said, and walked to his vehicle.

Twait backed FreeK Camp #2 away from the front of the store and maneuvered it so it was nose to nose with the disabled van. He pulled his hood release latch from inside then waited for the stranger to raise FreeK Camp's hood and attach the jumpers.

But the man was nowhere to be seen.

"Hello?" Twait called out the window.

No answer.

"Mister?"

Still no answer.

Twait looked toward the Econoline's the open driver-side door. A pair of feet hung down. They were twitching.

"You okay over there?" Twait called loudly, at the same time opening his own door and setting aside his leg extenders. He slid off the booster seat and climbed down to the ground. "Mister?" He walked between the two vans. "Hey, mister, you okay?"

A raspy voice gasped, "It's my heart. Angina attack."

Twait stepped around the door and saw the man lying chest-down on the seat, arms and head between the seats.

"I'll call 9-1-1."

"No. No. My nitro pills are right here. Can't … quite … reach them. Can you help me? Squeeze around me on the floor—between my seat and the gas pedal. The bottle's … right … here."

Twait wriggled in under the steering wheel as the man had directed. When he was wedged partway in, the man lifted himself up and raised something in his right hand. Before Twait could utter a word, he felt the surge that preceded the blackout.

CHAPTER 43

CAROLINE AND CHARLIE spent an hour Googling golf rosters for *David Osbourne/Osborne/Osborn* without success. With that angle exhausted they went to WhitePages.com and turned up 22 David Osbournes nationwide. Many also had phone numbers, some had addresses, and a few listed the age of the householder and gave names of other household members.

Jake Mellas had said Osbourne looked middle forties, so Caroline narrowed the range to 35-55, cutting the list to eight they followed up on. Several David Osbournes were mentioned in business articles; another was a coach in a Little League story; yet another was a triathlon participant. But none of them looked like they might leave their everyday lives to spend three summers in three different states. There was no hint of an itinerant serial killer.

"Let's give up on phone numbers," Charlie said. "Try name only."

When Caroline ran *David Osbourne,* Google automatically considered spelling variations. The search engine returned 58,700 possibilities including the late black actor Ossie Davis, rocker Ozzie Osborne, and TV's fictional comedic stuntman Super Dave Osborne.

"How about *David Osbourne criminal record?*" she wondered aloud, and typed it in. That took them to jailbase.com and similar sites, but when they tried a name, it gave them only come-ons for paid search services. Investigating serial killers could be expensive.

"Caroline, what if we're off track? What we've got is the name of a bad golfer from one charity tournament, not necessarily a killer."

"No. This is too coincidental, Charlie. This Osbourne worked a summer camp less than 40 miles from where Parks was found. Maybe we can't find a phone number listed because he doesn't have a permanent address. He wouldn't have needed one if he had access to the camp's phone."

"Then why don't we call the camp? The man might still be there."

Caroline's face lit up. "That never occurred to me. We need a phone number for Camp Quinipet, Shelter Island, New York. While you do the search, I'll go find my Mom. This time we need her help."

Five minutes later Caroline and Charlie sat in the office watching Rose dial the number.

*　*　*

The two library teams took their searches in different directions from Charlie and Caroline's.

Harley and Atlanta worked the Terrell/California case, revisiting Caroline's old sites for updates and following up any fresh links.

"Looks like Derby's message hit home," Atlanta said. "Everybody's running with the scarecrow angle."

Before they shut down their computer, Harley scrawled a few notes. *Scarecrow. Hay/straw. Fire.* Atlanta took the pencil from his fingers and added: *What was he wearing?*

Maggie and Damon put their time into Bike-man Parks. They read all the eulogies, tributes, and editorials they could find.

One man wrote that "if you took Bike-man's bike and foot mileage and laid it all in a straight line, it'd go ten times around the equator." Another said, "Nobody knew or loved the East End better than Bike-man."

A pilot for the Shelter Island Ferry said in an interview, "Bike-man loved riding around Greenport. But Greenport is flat, no hills. So two or three times a week he'd take the ferry to Shelter Island, coast down those big hills for a couple hours, and come back home. He was such a simple soul we never had the heart to charge the poor guy. I'm pretty sure none of the other pilots or pursers did, either. He sure did love those hills."

Maggie jotted a note. *Lived in Greenport. Traveled to Shelter Island a lot with bike. Found dead in Riverhead. Did they find his bike? Where?*

* * *

Rose put down the phone and looked over the desk at Caroline and Charlie.

"Quinipet's director says Osbourne was an excellent maintenance man, but he was only there the one summer. They'd love to have him back. When I said we were considering hiring him here, he said he'd highly recommend him. When I told him Osbourne had forgotten his resume but suggested we call Quinipet for an outdated one, he volunteered to fax us a copy. So now we wait."

CHAPTER 44

BANDO GOT BACK TO camp a little before noon expecting to see everyone on the porch waiting for lunch. He saw only Charlie.

"Charlie, where's the van?"

Charlie shrugged.

Rose appeared at the screen door.

"Where's the van?" Bando repeated. "The library detectives running late?"

"Got a problem. Maggie called. They're still at the library waiting for Twait. He probably found an audience somewhere. Charlie, would you tell Caroline we're moving lunch to 12:30?'

Rose updated Bando on Caroline and Charlie's Osbourne searches and the forthcoming Quinipet fax.

The office phone rang. "That could be the fax now," she said, and ran for it. A moment later she came out. "Maggie again. Still waiting on Twait."

"I'll go for them, Rose. Four can fit in your car. Twait must have broken down somewhere."

"He'd have called, Bando," she said, her face showing more than a hint of worry. "You know he always calls."

* * *

The four teens were waiting on the library steps when Bando arrived. When Damon held the back door for her, Atlanta ignored him and got in front. He climbed in back with Maggie and Harley.

"Still no sign?" Bando asked. "He didn't call the library?"

"Nope," Atlanta said. "I guess he didn't call the camp, either."

"Not before I left. But he never carries a cell phone, so if he did have trouble, he'd have to wait for help or find a landline. Did he tell any of you where he was going?"

"He just said errands," Harley said. "Something about a hardware store and algae killer."

"Did he say which hardware store?"

Nobody knew.

"We'll give him the benefit of the doubt," Bando said. "If it's a transmission or something major, he'll find a way to get the van to a repair shop. He'll call and let us know what's going on sooner or later."

Not just Bando but everyone checked for traffic—hoping to see a battered blue van. As they pulled onto the street Bando asked, "So, what did you dig up?"

Atlanta reported, "We found some new websites and blogs on Terrell. They're rethinking the staging idea—shifting from crucifixion to scarecrow. We came up with a new question: *What was Terrell wearing?*"

"You think he may have been naked?" Bando asked. "Like Parks? Painted?"

"Can't tell from the reports," Harley answered. "But it's doubtful. Ted Alley wasn't naked. As Atlanta said, though, we do wonder what he was wearing. Alley had on jogging shoes that were his and a cap that wasn't. The killer not only stages but partially dresses his victims. Did he add something to Terrell's dress?"

"I'll see if I can find out."

Damon spoke up. "Maggie and I found out Bike-man loved hills, but his hometown didn't have any. So twice a week he took his bike across to Shelter Island on the ferry."

"And here's news you're not up-to-speed on yet. Caroline and Charlie found out Shelter Island is home to Camp Quinipet, which is where a fellow named David Osbourne worked summer maintenance—the same

David Osbourne who played in the Mattituck Lions golf tournament. The camp director is faxing us Osbourne's old resume so we can get some information."

"We've got to notify the police," Atlanta said.

"I called Smitty before I left camp. So they'll be tracking him down."

Damon continued his report. "We came up with a couple of questions ourselves. *Did they find Bike-man's clothing, and if so, at the junkyard or somewhere else? And did they find his bike, and where?* From what you just told us, I'll bet the bike's underwater near Quinipet."

"I'll see if I can get answers to those, too. I'll call Smitty again when we get back."

* * *

When they got back to camp, there was still no word from Twait. Rose had sandwich makings out, so the teens sat down to lunch. She herself only nibbled and sipped.

Bando phoned Smitty. He missed her at the barracks, where the dispatcher told him to try CID in Gray. But he was five minutes too late there, too, and finally reached her on her cell. He relayed the teens' questions.

"I shouldn't tell you this," she said. "But I will. Parks' bandage hid a huge hole. Somebody made a mess—probably trying to remove the heart like they used to do with suspected vampires in the Colonial days. He stopped when he couldn't get past the bone. The Medical Examiner's report said Parks was already dead when the extraction was attempted."

"There's a consolation," Bando murmured. "Why bother?" They were silent for a moment before Bando continued. "Rose called the camp director at Quinipet, where David Osbourne worked the summer Parks was killed. He's sending us a fax of the guy's old resume. Not here yet, so I guess he's still trying to dig it out of his files."

"We'll get the New York State Police to knock on the director's door, too, and get one. But you may get your copy first. If you do, here's my fax number. Anything else?"

"Yes, one big thing, Alicia. Twait dropped four kids at the library around 9 o'clock and went to do some errands. He was supposed to be back for them no later than 11:45. We haven't heard from him. This isn't like him."

"The kids okay?"

"They're fine. I picked them up in Rose's car. They're eating lunch. But something's wrong. I mean come on—three hours to do a few errands? Even if he broke down miles from civilization, he'd find a way to flag down a ride or get to a phone."

"No cell?"

"No."

"Okay, it's 12:45, so he's barely an hour overdue."

"Too soon for a Missing Person Report?"

"Do we have reason to think anyone is out to get him?"

"No."

"Okay then, even if this Osbourne is the one we're looking for, he'd have no idea anybody's checking him out, right?"

"Right. But Alicia …"

"What?"

"I've got one of those feelings. Twait is in trouble. I know it. Can you help?"

"I'll get our people on it right now. I'll keep you advised."

Bando hung up. He was barely out of the kitchen when the phone rang again. He picked it up, listened, talked, asked questions, and hung up. When he walked out to the dining room this time, everyone stared up at him.

"Bando?" Rose asked. "You okay? You're white as a ghost."

"Who was that?" Caroline asked.

Bando sat down slowly. "The hardware store on 302. They tracked us down by the name on the van. A clerk went out for lunch and saw it idling next to the building. No driver in or near it."

Rose and Caroline began to sob.

CHAPTER 45

BANDO, ROSE, AND Caroline took off for True Value knowing the State Police would already be there, checking the van out. The three of them could answer questions, give a report, and see if anything was missing or different about the van.

In the dining hall the teens were numb, their worry about Twait draining their energy. No one seemed able to even raise a new question about the three murders. Their attention spans were shot.

Then in the middle of their funk, Atlanta said, "If Twait's been taken by the same guy, he's getting bolder."

"I don't know if he's bolder," Charlie said, "but he took a bigger risk this time. Think about it. He drives around carrying the props, but he still has to get some unlucky hitchhiker alone. He's prepared, but he requires opportunity and a low-risk place. *A hardware store isn't low-risk.* It's a business, with staff and customers coming and going, maybe a door camera, traffic on the road. Why would he suddenly go high risk?"

"Maybe he's in a hurry," Maggie suggested. "Is he on a time schedule?"

Atlanta stepped to the easel pad and wrote: *Why increase the risk?* Below it she put: *Time pressure to complete pattern?*

Damon said, "Maybe he couldn't miss this particular window of opportunity."

"What window?" Harley asked, anger in his voice. "Like he had to kidnap somebody today, this morning, before noon?"

Atlanta snapped her fingers. "That's it! What you said, Harley. He didn't have to kidnap *somebody*—he had to kidnap Twait. And he had to do it while Twait was alone, away from all of us. He saw this as his only chance to isolate him—and that made him take a bigger risk. This time it wasn't random. He specifically chose Twait."

They sat stunned.

"But why?" Harley asked. "Why not somebody else?"

"Exactly," Atlanta answered. "Why not somebody else? Why not another hitchhiker? He did it because Twait is different, looks different."

"He needed a midget!" Harley blurted out.

* * *

Smitty turned into the True Value parking lot from the south as Bando, Rose, and Caroline pulled in at the north end. Two marked cruisers and an unmarked car were already on the scene. Two uniforms and a plainclothes policeman and a plainclothes policewoman stood talking together within a tape-cordoned perimeter. A photographer snapped pictures near the driver's door of the van.

Smitty was in street clothes but had her badge on her belt. She motioned Bando, Rose, and Caroline to the edge of the crime scene tape and introduced them to the lead investigator, whose name was Perkins.

"We're not treating it as a Missing Person case," Perkins said, "because of the scene and because of the Alley murder. We're considering it a kidnapping. I've got somebody in the store now checking the video surveillance cameras. Front door camera first, then the ones over the cash registers."

"What about a parking lot camera?" Bando asked.

"Don't have one here. Most of the businesses on 302 don't have outside cameras because it's a busy enough road that they don't get kids drinking, parking, and smoking weed. If we're going to see anything outside here, it'll be the little glimpse we get from the front door camera."

"How about the front door cameras from other businesses?" Caroline asked.

"Nothing close enough," Perkins said. "I understand he's your father, miss, but try to be patient. The clerks have confirmed that your father was inside and made a purchase, so he'll show up on camera. Whoever was watching him may have also been in the store, and if so he'll turn up on video. We'll identify and interview other customers from the tape, too, and see if they can tell us anything."

"What about the van?" Smitty asked.

"The store clerks left it idling right there until we arrived. We turned it off after we checked for explosives. The hood latch had been pulled, but the hood wasn't raised. Even though your camp van is facing that row of bushes across the back of the lot, the front bumper is more than a full car length away from them. The bad guy's vehicle was probably in that space, something the cameras wouldn't catch."

"So Twait pulls the camp van up face-to-face with another vehicle," Smitty said, "trying to help—probably thinking he's going to jump a dead battery."

"As likely a scenario as any at the moment, Trooper Smith."

"Then the bad guy grabs Twait but leaves Twait's van running, because he doesn't dare step out into the open where he can be spotted. Plus he doesn't want to leave fingerprints."

"That remains to be seen. We'll dust anyway. If you're right, it suggests Mr. Twait got out of his van and was somehow lured or forced—perhaps at gunpoint or knifepoint—into the other vehicle."

Bando and Rose gave statements to Perkins and inspected the van while Caroline and Smitty walked the perimeter.

"Smitty," Caroline said, her voice quivering. "I'm really, really scared."

"I know you are. But your Dad is tough, and he's going to be okay."

Caroline bit down on her lip, fighting back tears. She sniffed.

"I'm so afraid this man will do something—tonight. Then tomorrow—tomorrow somebody will find Dad's—." She couldn't bring herself to say it. Then she forced herself to verbalize the worst. "He could be dead already." She began to weep.

Smitty pulled her close. "That's not the case and you know it, Caroline. This guy needs your Dad for something. I told you, he's going to be okay." She held Caroline for a while. "How could he not be okay? Look who's on the case: you and me, ace detectives."

Caroline tried to force a smile and rasped, "You, me, and a bunch of FreeKs."

They turned back to the van as Bando and Rose were walking away from it. Perkins was thanking them for their help.

Caroline froze, stiffening.

"Caroline, what is it?" Smitty asked.

"By the van."

"What?"

"Alley, Terrell, and Parks. It's the first time I've seen all three together."

Smitty didn't question the vision. Instead she asked, "Why are they here?"

"I don't know."

"Are they trying to tell you something?"

"Their lips aren't moving. But they're right by the driver's door."

"Are they trying to tell us something?" Smitty repeated.

"I think it's what they're showing us. First, this connects them to Dad. Second—and I hope this is right—they're showing me Dad isn't with them. Yet."

CHAPTER 46

TWAIT TRIED TO move, but his muscles didn't want to work. He sensed he was on his right side, his arm twisted under him. He forced his eyelids to open and close, but it made no difference. Wherever he was, it was pitch black. His brain struggled to piece things together.

There was the man asking for assistance. And there was the white van—was it the one that drove past when Damon found the bird's nest on the ground? He remembered seeing the jumper cables hanging down and a man draped across the driver's seat begging for help—something about the nitro pills he'd dropped. There was the squeeze under the steering wheel that trapped him between the seat and the pedals. Why hadn't he gone around to the other door? Why had he done exactly what the man told him to do? He'd glanced up just in time to see something that looked like a gun in the man's hand—and then pain, blindness, and unconsciousness. And here he was. But where was here?

Another memory surfaced, too, but it felt like a later one—blinding brightness, a flood of sunlight. Was there a memory of the opening of a van's rear doors? He had no recollection of being thrown there, but he must have been, and so the sunlight had to be when the man checked on him. There it was—a quick image of a man in silhouette then the gun shape again coming at his chest, and then the pain, blindness, and unconsciousness like before. It was beginning to make sense. The man who had disabled him—probably with a stun gun—had transported him from the hardware store to this location. The transfer from the van to whatever pitch-black prison he was in now had required a second stunning.

His shoulders ached from having his wrists handcuffed behind him. There was no wiggle room, because his chest and shoulders were so muscled and his arms shorter than most people's. The arm that was between his body and the floor had gone numb, so he rolled onto his stomach to regain circulation. Exhausted, right cheek against the floor, he wanted to drift off to sleep or unconsciousness again. He wasn't sure if his eyes were open or closed, so he fluttered his right eyelash against the floor to see if he could feel it.

"I'm alive," he muttered, and gave a little laugh. "Now what?" He closed his eyes again. Just a few minutes rest.

He had no idea if he actually slept and if so for how long. Nothing had changed. Ah, not true. Two things were different: salt and moisture. He licked his lips and tasted the sweat and salt on the surrounding skin. He was perspiring more than when he had first come to. Whatever his prison, it was heating up.

He struggled to get to his knees, but the cuffs binding his arms against his body made it almost impossible. He worked his forehead up against a metal wall and managed to get to his knees then to his feet. His head didn't hit anything above, so he couldn't tell how high the roof was. He rose up on the balls of his feet but still touched nothing, so he tried jumping, also without making contact. But he did feel a slight spring to the floor and a side-to-side swaying that told him he was either in a vehicle or a trailer, probably the latter. He backed up until his foot touched another wall. It had to be a small cargo trailer.

He felt behind him, following the walls until he discovered the door. His hands were too low to feel for a handle, so he used his face. No handle on the inside. He felt his way around further to see if there was a side door for loading. No luck. With his hands pinned behind him and no door or loading door to kick at, he lacked any real possibility of muscling his way to freedom.

The handcuffs wouldn't pull apart. They were metal, good old police handcuffs, not the ones his magician friends escaped from so easily. Besides, he didn't have a hidden key or a hairpin.

He checked the floor again—smooth wood like his hardwood floor at home. He wasn't going to pry up a board and go out the bottom.

He licked his lips, tasted the salt. His throat was dry. He was dehydrating. He didn't know if the box was airtight and without cracks, but it appeared to be. Maybe there was no light coming in a crack or vent because it was nighttime; he had no way of knowing. In cuffs he couldn't even press the button to light his watch dial.

He backed up against the side and knocked softly then harder. Maybe he could draw the attention of a passerby or even his abductor. If the man opened the door, he might be able to barrel past him like a human cannonball then set out at a dead run. He'd have a chance in a footrace. If it failed, at least cooler fresh air would rush in.

He tried yelling, but the walls contained the sound.

He ran at the door with his shoulder lowered. It didn't budge and he only hurt himself. Jumping up and down and rocking the trailer brought no one. He listened intently for the sounds of civilization—wouldn't it be ironic if the trailer was parked in a U-Haul lot—but it only made him more certain the man had removed him from the world of living beings.

He lay back down on his side near the door, raising a leg now and then to give it a couple of kicks. Eventually he gave up, moved to a corner, and in the close moist heat sat in the yoga position. He slowed his breathing and meditated, lowering his heart rate and reducing his oxygen consumption.

He had to trust his captor would be back. The man had a twisted logic and a set of rules to go with it, but it was logic nonetheless. That logic had to say: *the little man can't die of heat stroke or suffocation; he has to be strangled.*

CHAPTER 47

THEY ALL HEARD the phone ring, but it was Atlanta who ran for it. When it didn't ring a third time she realized it was an incoming fax. The machine pressed out a transmittal page and a two-page resume. She scooped up the sheets and carried them back to the eager group.

The name at the top was H. David Osbourne. The address was c/o Julia O. Wilson in Overland Park, Kansas.

"He goes by David but it's not his first name," Charlie pointed out. "Which is why he didn't turn up when Caroline and I ran searches. We need to find out what the H stands for."

"And Julia O. Wilson," Atlanta said. "Friend or sister?"

"I'm guessing mother," said Harley. "The guy's a loser."

"Like you and the rest of us?" Maggie quipped.

Damon shrugged. "Oh, come on. It's got to be his mother. He lives at home with Mom. First husband died and she remarried. The middle initial O is for Osbourne. If it isn't the remarried mother, I'll bet the sister married a Wilson." He looked up at Atlanta, who looked away.

"Damon's logic makes sense," Charlie said. "This guy jumps from job to job, especially summer jobs, so he's all over the country. His Mom's house is where he keeps his winter clothes and his comic books. I mean, why pay rent on an apartment you're only using eight or nine months a year?"

"He lists a phone number," Atlanta noted. "Could be his cell." That stopped the conversation.

"That'd be too good to be true, wouldn't it?" Charlie asked, verbalizing the question on all their minds: "Think that's still his number? The resume is three years old."

"It could still be his mother or sister's," Maggie said. "You can't tell from where it is on the resume whether it's there to call him or them."

Atlanta went back to the easel pad. "Let's slow down. We'll go through it and take notes. Once we have a list of things to check out, we can divide it up and attack it."

She wrote four items on the pad. *What does H stand for? Julia Wilson—check phone and Google. Phone number on resume—use reverse lookup for name. Call number?*

"It says here he graduated Emporia High School, Emporia, Kansas in 1986," Charlie said. "He majored in theater at Kansas City Community College, Kansas City, Kansas."

Maggie asked, "What do you think—major in theater and minor in costume and set design? I mean, look at what he's doing. He's a scene dresser. He'd know about theatrical supplies, costumes, and props. This has to be our guy."

Charlie held up the resume. "His work history shows a half dozen different teacher aide jobs. Those are school-year jobs that give him summers off. He's listed a slew of summer jobs that are at either church camps or summer-stock theaters." He scanned it further. "Five years ago he had a summer job for a theater company in Santa Rosa, California. And four years ago he worked for Camp Cazadero, a United Church of Christ camp that I'll bet is to close to where they found Terrell."

Atlanta made a note on the easel pad to check out both locations. "So we know he was at the Methodist Camp Quinipet in New York two summers ago when Bike-man was killed. What we can't tell from the outdated resume is where he was working last summer when Terrell died. But we can probably assume from his California jobs he was familiar with the area. Did he skip a year in California to work on Long Island

and kill Parks, then go back to California last year and kill Terrell?"

"What the resume doesn't tell us," Damon said, "is where he's working this summer. My guess is Maine, either at a camp or a summer theater."

Atlanta wrote: *Check camps and theater companies for Osbourne.* Then she added: *Have Bando get police up to speed*—and underlined it. "If he doesn't get back soon, we'll call them ourselves."

The group divided up the tasks and fanned out.

* * *

An hour later they reconvened. It hadn't taken long to get some of the answers.

Santa Rosa, where Osbourne had worked in theater, was south of Guerneville, home to the fire department that found Terrell. Camp Cazadero, where he had held a summer maintenance job, was a camp and conference center west of the Armstrong Woods crime scene.

"I found an online obituary," Charlie reported, and held up a printout. "Five years ago Julia *Osbourne* Wilson—you were right, Harley and Damon, she's the mother—died in Overland Park, Kansas at the age of 70. She was predeceased by her second husband of 20 years, Truitt Wilson, and her first husband of 23 years, Herbert 'Herb' Osbourne, both of whom, it says here, she loved dearly. She and Herb were blessed with twins in 1966, Herbert *David* Osbourne who survives, and Clarissa 'Issy' Osbourne who, and I quote—*was in the house when it was taken up in the deadly Emporia dinnertime tornado of June 8, 1974 that killed 6 and injured 220.* They actually put that in Mrs. Wilson's obituary."

"Wow," Harley said. "What a way to go."

Damon unfolded a Maine road map with marks on it. "Harley, Maggie, and I got this off the office wall and drew a 100-mile radius around Bridgton. We broke the cell phones out of the desk and the three of us divided up the list of camps and theaters. You can see about sixty on the map. Here's the checklist for the ones we phoned. Nobody's got an Osbourne—not a Herbert, not a David. If he's working in Maine, it's not with them."

"I tried the phone number on the resume," Atlanta said. "No luck. It was the area code covering Overland Park, Kansas, where the mother was living when she passed away. The lady who answered—she sounded pretty young and had a baby crying in the background—said she's had the number for about three years. I asked if she ever got calls for Herbert Osbourne, David Osbourne, Julia Osbourne or Julia Wilson. She said no."

CHAPTER **48**

IT WAS 3:30 p.m. when Bando, Rose, and Caroline returned from the hardware store. They trudged up the dining hall steps as if mounting a gallows. The teens offered hugs and asked questions.

"Give them a chance to catch their breath," Atlanta ordered. "Harley, you're closest—three cups of hot tea. Give them the big couch."

They settled in fast and Rose reported what they had seen and talked with the police about.

Caroline told of the three ghosts by the van. "They were shoulder to shoulder—Terrell, Alley, and Parks—right by the driver's door. So the three murders are connected. The good news is Dad wasn't with them."

"That's a good sign," Harley said, stating the obvious for everyone.

"The fax arrived," Atlanta said, and passed photocopies to Bando, Rose, and Caroline. "We found an obituary for Julia O. Wilson, his mother. She died a few years ago. After you take a minute to look over the resume and the obituary, we'll tell you what we've learned since we checked it over."

It took Bando less than thirty seconds. "Is this number his or Julia Wilson's? Is it still working?"

"Not working," Atlanta said. "I called. It was reassigned. The woman who has it now said nobody's ever called for an Osbourne or a Wilson."

Bando took a copy of the resume and the obituary and started for the office. "Be right back. Got to get this to the police."

Smitty was back at the barracks when Bando called her. She gave him the dispatcher's fax number. He transmitted the resume and the obituary.

"Tell those kids I said they do good work," Smitty said. "I can see something coming through now. I'll look it over, make copies, and get everyone going on it. How are you all holding up?"

"Rose is worried, scared, and worn out. Caroline is trying to stay upbeat by throwing herself into the information, figuring she'll find the devil in the details. The others are worried, too."

"And you?"

"Worried, angry, and frustrated, because I can't see a connection between Alley and Twait. If the same guy picked up Parks, Terrell, and Alley, why lay a trap for Twait? And if he is the same guy, did he take Twait so he can--?" Bando didn't finish. "My brain draws a blank, but my gut tells me it *feels* wrong. But why would he want to kill Twait?"

"As somebody once said *feelings are facts*. Your gut is telling you something, and I think you're right. We've got to get to Twait fast. You want me to see if the boss can assign you a patrolman to watch the camp tonight?"

"Thanks, but I don't think so. He's already got Twait, and there's no reason to think any of us are in danger. This guy isolated Twait from the rest of us. We've stressed to these campers the need to stick together. They will."

"Okay, but if you change your mind, call me."

"I will. Right now they're waiting for me. Rose needs some rest, so I think I'll give her a break and have somebody else make supper—something simple like grilled cheese with tomato soup. Show up around 6 o'clock and you can join us."

* * *

A knock on the trailer wall brought Twait out of his low-pulse state.

"You still in there, little buddy?" a muffled voice asked with a laugh.

Twait struggled to his feet in time to hear the door latch. He braced his foot against the front wall. Once it opened, he'd try barreling past the man. He waited, wanting to time it right.

But the door opened only a crack, letting in a shaft of light.

"Got to keep the padlock on, little buddy. Wanted to give you some of this fresh air, though. Sorry it's so hot and stuffy in there. Must be starting to smell like a locker room."

"Let me out," Twait croaked. "What have I ever done to you?"

"Nothing. And you can just forget the human battering-ram thing. As I said, there's still a heavy-duty lock on this door. I've got to go out for a couple of hours and wanted to make sure you still had breathable air. Time to close you up again. As I said, sorry about the heat."

Twait pushed off from the wall, his short, muscular legs driving him forward. He hit the door with his right shoulder and ricocheted back, falling on his handcuffed wrists. The door slammed and latched again.

"Told you so, little buddy. Got to go now. Got a date with you-know-who."

CHAPTER **49**

H E WATCHED THE dining hall from his same hiding place off the waterfall trail, alternating between the naked eye and binoculars. No one came out except the midget's wife and the redheaded girl who had to be their daughter. They had gone to their cabin. This was his fourth recon of the camp since he spotted the diving midget in the newspaper. Seeing the girl pluck the bird's nest off the branch had been a lucky accident; he'd been observing Twait. Dame Fortune had always favored him.

A Maine State Police cruiser came up the driveway and a woman in uniform got out. He'd seen her there before. She climbed the steps and knocked on the screen door, said something, and went inside.

* * *

Bando and Smitty met in the office to fill each other in.

"Let's start with Terrell, the college student," she said. "He wasn't naked or painted. Some of his clothing wasn't burned, like the back of his shirt that was between him and the cross. He had on a checked flannel Woolrich shirt—long-sleeve XL, way too big for him—and extra roomy coveralls. His hiking boots were size 9, a perfect fit."

"Coveralls? Like farmers wear?"

"Yes."

"How about a hat?"

"They think there was a straw hat, like a sombrero or a panama, something floppy. It was pretty well burned."

Bando scrunched up his face. "Something doesn't add up. The hiking boots fit, but nothing else did. And he wouldn't be hitchhiking with a floppy hat. How big was Terrell?"

"Five-eight, 145 to 150."

"So the boots were his, but the shirt, coveralls, and hat weren't."

"I agree. Want to hear about Parks?"

Bando nodded.

"Clothing never found, bike never found—even though an antique Schwinn would stick out in a yard sale or a Goodwill Store. The entire area East End of Long Island was searched. If the bike was there somebody would have spotted it."

"So the clothes were burned, buried, or went into a dumpster. And the bike is at the bottom of a pond or a bay because it's too easy to ID. It's near Shelter Island, close to Camp Quinipet."

"Anything yet on Herbert David Osbourne?"

"Not yet. But it'll come. We just got it. Give our people a little more time."

"I will. Can your guys give Twait a little more?"

* * *

The watcher heard the dinner bell. The midget's wife didn't leave her cabin, but the daughter went to the dining hall. So all six teenagers had to be in the main building with the director and the lady cop. This was the perfect time to set up the diversion. He crept down the hill behind the boys' cabin.

CHAPTER 50

WITH SMITTY THERE for supper the teens were unsure what they could talk openly about, so they tried to go with small talk. Smitty's phone rang and after she answered it she got in her car and left. Bando took a second grilled cheese sandwich and moved to his office. Maggie and Harley began clearing the dishes while Caroline and Charlie scooped ice cream for sundaes.

Damon moved close to Atlanta. "Can we talk?"

"About what?"

"You're stonewalling me."

"Am I?"

"Can we just please go outside for a minute?"

She gave him a stony look then announced to the others, "Be back in a few minutes," as she and Damon walked out together.

The watcher was back in place, hiding and observing. He thought he'd seen this connection developing by the pine forest when the girl had levitated, but he hadn't known it was this serious. He had thought he was going to have to wait until midnight for the blonde and the frizzy brunette to fall asleep in the girls' cabin. But this new development could work to his advantage. He pulled his duffel bag closer and unzipped it.

Damon steered Atlanta across the ball field and toward the waterfront.

"What's going on?" he asked.

"What do you mean?"

"I thought we had something going between us, chemistry, a psychic connection—*something*. Since last night you haven't given me the time of day. You're all business on these murders. In fact, that's when it started, when you stepped up and suddenly became the rah-rah leader of the team."

"In case you haven't noticed, my friend Caroline's father has been kidnapped—he may die. That kind of demands our attention, don't you think?"

"It does, yes. And we're all working on it, and on the other cases. But I'm talking about you and me. There's something going on here. What's wrong?"

"Nothing." She turned away from him but didn't head back to the dining hall. She stood still. "I had a feeling I shouldn't have come out here with you."

He placed a hand on her shoulder. "What's different from yesterday? I've told you everything, a lot more than I told the others. I told you I didn't set the fire, I swear. So what is it?"

She smoldered another few seconds. "You didn't tell me about Katie Haskell, your little girlfriend across the street."

"Katie?" He grabbed her arm and forced her to turn his way. "Katie? What the heck are you talking about?"

Her eyes were like fire. "Stop it! You're hurting me." She pushed him away.

"Atlanta?" a voice called from the porch of the dining hall. "Everything okay?" It was Harley with Charlie right behind him. When she didn't answer right away, the two of them started across the ball field. "Atlanta?"

"Everything's fine, guys. I'll be right in."

The boys kept coming.

"You sound upset," Charlie said.

"She's fine," Damon snapped. "Back off."

Charlie and Harley stopped.

"Why don't you both come inside before the bugs come out?" Charlie said. "Dessert's ready."

"Give us ten minutes," Damon said in a now calmer voice. He looked at Atlanta. "Please? Just talk to me."

She glared then softened. "Just a few minutes, guys. Save us some dessert. We're just going for a little walk."

"You know Bando's not going to be happy about this if he finds out," Charlie said, turning back toward the dining hall.

"You go ahead, Charlie," Harley said. "I've got to hit the little boys' room. And I need to dig out a book from my backpack. I'll be in soon."

Atlanta and Damon went one way for the beach and Harley trotted toward the boys' cabin. Charlie headed for the dining hall.

The watcher waited, hardly able to believe his luck. He picked up his duffel bag and crept toward the beach.

In the boys' cabin Harley lay down on his bunk and started his breathing exercises.

*   *   *

"Okay, look Atlanta. Katie wasn't my girlfriend. She was a neighbor, an older girl who always had a crush on me—more like an obsession, really. It was flattering at first, but it got old really, really fast. There was nothing there, not like what's between us."

Those were the only words Damon got out as the watcher caught them from behind, stunning Damon first. He crumpled onto the sand face down. Before Atlanta could get off a scream he jolted her in the lower back by her kidney. She fell across Damon's limp body. The man quickly tucked the stun gun back into the duffel bag, slung Atlanta over his shoulder, and disappeared down an overgrown path beyond the boathouse.

Harley witnessed it all—the man he'd seen at L.L. Bean sneaking up, the double stun-gun attack, the two bodies on the beach then Atlanta being carried off. He had tried to yell a warning, had tried to torpedo the man—but without vocal cords and a body he was useless. He had reflexively reached for his friends as they fell, but he was like a ghost and had no substance. Now he stood over Damon, watching the man carry

Atlanta away. He had to get help, had to run back to his body and sound the alarm. He was about to take off for the cabin when he heard Charlie call "Atlanta, Damon, Harley! Dessert!"

He looked again at the overgrown trail where the man had disappeared with Atlanta. He was the only one who knew where they had gone. And now the man might get away.

Suddenly a pop like a gunshot came from the boys' cabin. Charlie looked in that direction and yelled, "Harley? You still in there?" Then he yelled toward the dining hall, "Everybody, come quickly! Something's wrong! Help!"

Bando emerged onto the porch followed by Caroline and Maggie. "What's wrong, Charlie?" he called.

"Harley went to the bathroom and I heard a shot." As the words left his mouth he saw flames licking around the back corners of the cabin.

Bando saw them, too. "Fire!" he shouted. "Fire! Maggie, call 911. Caroline, get the big fire extinguisher from the kitchen. Charlie, go wake Rose up and grab the small fire extinguisher from her cabin. Everybody move! Now!" Bando approached the fire.

"What about Atlanta?" Harley shouted. "And Damon's over here!" Nobody could hear him. He had a choice. He could run to his body, roll in, and escape the fire under his own power so he could tell the story. But if he did, the man would get away with Atlanta. If he pursued the man, he'd have to trust the others to get his body out of the fire.

The fire spread quickly from the back of the dry wood-shingled cabin to the sides and the roof. Bando was poised to run in, but the intense heat held him at bay.

Harley took off past the boathouse and down the overgrown trail as fast as he could glide. Minutes later he found himself practically on top of the man as he was throwing open the back doors of the white van. He threw Atlanta's body inside. Harley saw Atlanta's face, saw the man's face, and watched him duct tape her wrists and ankles. He watched the man pull out a bottle and pour some of its contents onto a cloth that he held over Atlanta's mouth and nose. Then he duct taped her mouth and covered her with some sort of blanket. He closed the doors, attached a padlock, and hurried to the driver's seat.

Harley stuck his head through the steel rear door, took a quick inventory of the contents, and backed out. He stared at the license plate and began repeating the numbers as the van drove off.

CHAPTER 51

THE REGULAR FIRE drills and Bando's clear instructions paid off. Caroline and Charlie attacked the fire on the cabin's two sides, reducing the intensity of the heat wall so that Bando could race in and drag Harley off his bunk and out the door. Rose arrived in time to help him move the boy's limp body to the ball field.

"He's not dead, is he?" Rose asked.

"No. He's breathing."

"Smoke inhalation? Why isn't he moving?"

"It's not smoke. I'm guessing he's out traveling."

The cabin roof was aflame now. Charlie and Maggie emptied their fire extinguishers and retreated. From a distance came the sound of sirens.

Charlie, Maggie, and Caroline came and stood over Harley.

"Is he dead?" Maggie asked.

"We think he's out traveling," Rose answered.

"What about Atlanta and Damon?" Bando asked. "Where are they?"

"They were outside having an argument," Charlie said. "Harley and I heard them and tried to get them to come back inside. They seemed calmer and said they'd be in soon. Harley said he was going to the bathroom and wanted to grab a book from his backpack, so I went back to work on dessert. Last I saw Atlanta and Damon, they were together going toward the beach."

Bando said, "Rose, you and Maggie see if you can find them. Check in the boathouse, too. Then there's that old trail that goes behind the boathouse and out to the road. Maybe they walked out there. Hopefully the sirens will get them to turn around and come back. Caroline, you meet the fire trucks. Charlie, let's get Harley into Rose's cabin before the EMTs get here and try to revive him."

Bando and Charlie were laying Harley on Rose's couch when two fire engines and a rescue vehicle arrived. They drove up the driveway and Caroline motioned them onto the ball field.

"Stay with him, Charlie," Bando said. "I've got to go deal with the fire, rescue, and the police."

As Bando left, Charlie said, "I hate to say it, but this is one time I hope Atlanta and Damon are together."

The first thing Bando saw outside was Maggie leading a paramedic toward the beach. "He's over here," she was saying. "I think he's having a seizure." Bando followed.

There on the sand lay Damon, spastically trying to get his muscles and his mouth to work. A second rescue squad person came down the hill to the beach and the two paraprofessionals took over.

"Where's Atlanta?" Rose was asking. "Damon, where's Atlanta?" When he said nothing, she said loudly to anyone within earshot, "Anybody seen Atlanta—blonde with streaks in her hair and pierced jewelry?"

No one answered.

Harley wanted to. He stood looking over the shoulders of the paramedics. But nobody could see him, and nobody could hear him reciting the license plate number.

Smitty was the first Trooper on the scene. She gathered Bando, Rose, and the three teens together.

"Charlie and Harley are in Rose's cabin," Bando said. "I think Osbourne grabbed Atlanta when she was out for a walk with Damon."

"I'll get your stories in a minute," Smitty said. "Let me call this in first." She pulled out her cell and started talking into it as she walked toward her cruiser.

"I don't think this is a seizure," one of the paramedics said. "Looks like the kid was hit with a stun gun. He took a real wallop. We don't have to transport him, but it'll take some time to shake this off. Sir, ma'am," he continued, looking up at Bando and Rose. "Are you the parents?"

"We're the camp staff," Rose answered. "So we're *in loco parentis.*"

"I understand," the man said. "But you may want to notify the boy's parents."

"We will once things calm down," Bando said.

With no reason to hang around, Harley glided toward the boys' cabin. The fire department hadn't saved much. It was wet and stank of soot. He looked through what was left of the door. His body wasn't there. He checked the edges of the ball field. No body. He approached the rescue truck. Had he died from smoke inhalation? He stuck his head through the side of the rescue truck to see if he might be lying on a stretcher or in a body bag.

Suddenly from behind him he heard—no, sensed in his head, or was it in his ears—a man's voice saying, "The little cabin with the lights on. You're with Charlie." He turned and found no one there. He glided toward Rose's cabin, looked in and saw Charlie sitting over him. His astral body breathed a sigh of relief and a few minutes later so did his physical body—together again at last.

CHAPTER 52

"HE TOOK ATLANTA," was the first thing Harley spit out. "He stun-gunned Damon and then Atlanta and took her in his van." He started reciting the numbers and made the sign for writing. When Charlie handed him a pen and paper he wrote down six numbers plus *Maine plate, white Ford van.* "Get that to Bando or Smitty fast."

Charlie took the note and walked to the door, then turned back. "Next time you go traveling, you might want to let one of us in on it."

"Sorry. Next time I will."

"And just in case you're wondering, Bando pulled you out of the fire. We carried you in here so the rescue squad wouldn't try to resuscitate you. You're welcome!" He disappeared, slamming the door behind him.

* * *

The Fire Department declared the damaged cabin uninhabitable and cordoned it off with tape. Two State Police CIDs arrived and after learning Atlanta was gone extended the perimeter with crime scene tape to include the waterfront.

Rose, Bando, and Smitty huddled near the dining hall porch.

"My cabin, Rose's, and the dining hall are outside the tape," Bando said. "So we have places to sleep tonight—if any of us can. We were already sick with worry about Twait. Now he's got Atlanta."

Smitty said, "One of the CID guys says it appears the fire was touched off by two incendiary devices under the back corners of the cabin. They probably worked off either a timer or a remote signal. The fire was a diversion. My guess is the devices will be what you'd find on a movie set."

"Installed by somebody with a background in theater?" Bando asked.

Smitty nodded. Her cell phone rang and she answered it. "Wait, let me write this down. Okay, go ahead. Registered to whom? Give me the address and phone. Somebody already ran it down? Okay, anything else I can use? Thanks, Margie." She clicked off and said, "FBI's in on this now. They've got enough to tie the three murders together."

"Anything on Twait?" Rose asked.

"No. Sorry."

"Sounds like that plate number paid off," Bando said.

"It's a painter down in Casco, Red Saunders. Somebody just interviewed him."

"And?"

"He's old, pretty much retired, has had the van for years. Does the occasional cash job for friends and locals. He's got a new assistant—Ozzie—who paints for cash, uses the garage apartment, and has the van most of the time. Our interviewer got a description of Ozzie, who will no doubt turn out to be Herbert David Osbourne. Red said he doesn't feel he can let them into the garage apartment without Ozzie's permission, so they're waiting on a search warrant."

"Which takes how long?" Rose asked.

"Within the hour."

"Osbourne and the van weren't there?" Bando asked.

"No." Seeing Rose's face fall, she said, "Top Cop has everybody on this, Rose. If Osbourne's on the road in that van--."

"How long do you think he'll stay on the road, Smitty?" Rose said bitterly. "This is his big night. Otherwise he wouldn't have taken the two huge risks he took today. If he's not already off the road, he will be soon. He's out there setting a stage. He'll do it tonight. You know he will. And then tomorrow somebody will find Twait and Atlanta."

* * *

Smitty hit the road, leaving a Crime Lab van and a police car. Bando, Rose, Charlie, and Maggie gathered in the dining hall on the soft furniture, where Damon was recovering on the couch. Bando plopped a pile of cell phones on the coffee table.

"Caroline and Harley on the computer?" he asked.

Charlie nodded.

"What are the phones for?" Maggie asked.

"So you can call home and tell your families what's going on."

"Any camp can have a cabin fire," she answered. "Why worry our parents if we're all safe? They'll be here to pick us up at noon tomorrow anyway."

"This isn't some accidental fire at a summer camp," he said. "That fire was deliberately set. And we have two people kidnapped, Twait and Atlanta. The man who took them murders people. We can't hold back this information. I've got to call Atlanta's mother right now before she hears it from the police or on the news." He walked toward the office. None of the teens reached toward their phones.

Ten minutes later Bando walked out looking drained.

"Her mother's on her way, isn't she?" Rose asked.

Bando nodded. "She's very upset. She didn't want her to come back in the first place—but Atlanta convinced her. And I promised she'd be safe here."

Caroline and Charlie hurried in. "We have something."

"Bando just called Atlanta's mother," Rose said. "She's on her way."

"Well, I'm sorry, Mom, but this isn't just about Atlanta. It's also about Dad. We can't just sit here. Harley and I have something."

"What is it?" Bando asked.

Harley started. "When Osbourne was duct-taping Atlanta, I checked out the back of his van. There was this huge silky nylon bag with a drawstring on top and grips all around it."

Caroline cut in. "The bag was marked *Aerostar*. And next to it was a *T3-017*, which turns out to be a burner made by *Balloon Works*. Osbourne is going to launch a hot air balloon!"

"I saw something else, too," Harley said. "A Dunkin Donuts box. But it wasn't up in the front seat; it was in the cargo hold by Atlanta. I stuck my face right through the box. It was full of lollipops all connected by plastic wrappers, like a string of paper dolls. When I pulled back, I realized the box said Munchkins."

Something clicked for Charlie.

"That's it," he blurted, and the words started coming so fast he nearly tripped over them. "*The Wizard of Oz*. Munchkins, Lollipop Kids— Twait." He pointed to Atlanta's easel sheets on the wall. "I see it now. Terrell was the Scarecrow."

Bando interrupted. "Smitty said he had bib overalls, a flannel shirt, and straw hat. They were too big because they weren't his. Osbourne needed one-size-fits-all props to carry around, because he didn't know how big his victim would be."

"And Bike-man Parks was his Tin Man," Maggie burst out. "With a bandage over his heart and an oil can by his body. Osbourne spray-painted him silver and duct-taped his bike helmet to his head."

"So who is Alley, the Cowardly Lion?" Harley asked.

"Yes," Bando exclaimed. "Yes he is. Get it? Lions Club! The hat was in case we missed the other clues: the chair and the whip. Rose, how could we old circus people not see that, the tools of the trade for a lion tamer?"

"Remember his mother's obituary?" Caroline pointed out. "His sister died in the house taken up in the Emporia tornado. It all fits."

"Maybe he's angry at the characters who are keeping her from coming home," Rose said. "So he's eliminating them."

"But why take Atlanta?" Harley asked.

"She flies," Maggie answered. "She's the witch."

"How would he know that?" Harley asked.

"He must have seen her levitate during the scavenger hunt," Damon said, now able to form his words again. "I didn't find the bird's nest on the ground. I saw it in a tree and got her to go up for it. A white van drove by right after. He must have been stalking Twait when he saw Atlanta levitate."

"Okay," Harley said. "So that explains why he had one of those funny little corn-husk brooms in his van. I thought it had to do with chimney sweeping work."

"If I had to guess," Charlie said, "I'd say he's planning a launch after first light, so he can get pictures."

"Pictures?" Maggie asked.

"Has to be. He doesn't pose his victims just so people can find them. He wants something more permanent, a legacy to himself. He's been taking pictures of the entire cast. It's either painting or photography. Didn't we see on his resume that he worked as a school photographer?"

"Let's say you're right about a balloon launch," Harley said. "We have no idea where."

Caroline jumped up. "Google. Word combinations. *Maine yellow brick road, Maine Oz, Maine rainbow, Maine Dorothy, Maine wizard.* The rest of you stay here and brainstorm—see if you can come up with other search words. Play word association using *The Wizard of Oz.*" She disappeared out the door and Bando headed for the office to update Smitty.

CHAPTER 53

ATLANTA REGAINED CONSCIOUSNESS and feeling. She realized that when she tried for a deep breath the air came in only through her nose. She could work her jaw but not her mouth. She had no recollection of it being taped though she knew it must be. She was on her stomach with her head turned to the left, right cheek against the floor. Her shoulders ached and when she tried to move her arms she discovered they were pinned behind her at the wrists—more tape. She tried to move her legs, finding she could flex them at the knees. Her ankles had been taped.

Wherever she was, it was dark. She felt some sort of rough fabric stretched tightly over her. It had to have weights sitting on it close at her sides. Cement blocks maybe? The air under the covering was warm and thick from her breath and her skin was damp. She tried to relax and take even breaths through her nose as if sitting Zen with Bando.

If she could turn on one side, she thought, she might be able to loosen the cover and see where she was, but the weights still kept her pinned. She managed to turn her head, resting it on the point of her chin. When that began to hurt, she rested her head on the other cheek.

It occurred to her that rocking side-to-side might draw the fabric in from under the weights, so she tried it, but with so little wiggle room it was difficult and the weights didn't budge. She noticed that the floor moved slightly, and beneath her the metal felt ribbed—front to back channels like she'd seen in the beds of pickups or cargo vans. That had to be where she was. She rocked harder, sensing that her efforts were gradually increasing the space under the cover.

A rattling sound—could it be a padlock—stopped her. It was followed by the sound of a door opening near her feet then the creak of a second. She'd been right. It was a van.

"I figured you were waking up," a man's voice said. "Saw the van swaying. You can stretch out a little once I get that balloon and that burner off the drop cloth. Time to set them up."

She felt the van drop slightly as he stepped up on the bumper.

"Excuse my reach."

She heard him struggling to drag something soft but very heavy across her calves and Achilles tendons.

"Sorry. That was the bag with the balloon. I said balloon, but it's actually called the envelope." He grabbed her taped ankles and moved her legs to the side the balloon had been on. "*Pardonnez moi, mademoiselle,* but now I need the burner." Something scraped the ribbed floor. "Afraid you still can't go anywhere, but this will make it easier to stretch your muscles. Back soon."

She heard the latch of one door, the slam of the second, and the click of the lock.

The cover was looser now but was still over her. She tried to grip it behind her and after several unsuccessful tries found herself pinching a piece of the cloth between her right thumb and forefinger. She held tight to it and slowly rolled her body, drawing one side of the drop cloth closer to the middle. Once she'd made nearly a full rotation, she released her grip and repeated it. She didn't want to jellyroll herself inside it. After four rotations she suddenly could see. She was on her back staring up at the ceiling of the van.

The light was dim and barely came in through the front windshield and two front side windows. It was a panel van. Even the rear doors were windowless and solid. A metal meshwork separated the cargo area from the front, creating a large cage. No way out except the double back doors.

She worked herself up to a sitting position and slid forward to look out the mesh. Moonlight revealed trees and bushes closing in on both sides, but straight ahead the moon glinted off water. The van was at the end of an overgrown woods road or fishing access on a lake.

A shadowy figure interrupted her line of sight with the lake. It crossed several more times. The man was unpacking his silk balloon and burner near the shore.

She couldn't find anything to help her get free of her bonds. If the man had had tools, he had taken them out. She pressed her face against the cage and began sliding her cheek and tongue over the metal grid work inch-by-inch, hoping to locate a jagged edge on which to rip the duct tape. She wondered if Twait was in a different cage.

CHAPTER 54

IT WAS THE middle of the night and Caroline was still running searches. Rose had taken a blanket and pillow into the office so she could stay by the phone.

Charlie and Harley walked in.

"Here's the Odd Couple now," she said. Next to her lay a notebook with keywords she'd tried, notes next to them.

"What's NG?" Harley asked, pointing to the letters next to *Oz, Maine.*

"No Good." She continued searching. "How's Damon doing?"

"Better."

Charlie scanned the notes. "I've learned to read her shorthand. *Maine yellow brick road* brought up a daycare in South Berwick. Same search turned up the *Tribute to Elton John* concert in Augusta. *Judy Garland, Maine* was NG, but *Garland, Maine* is a town northwest of Bangor that has a Garland Pond. Judy Garland was the actress in the movie."

"Did she try *Wizard* and *Wizard of Oz?*"

Charlie ran his finger down the list. "She did. *Wizard of Oz,* the musical, was performed at the Old Port Playhouse In Portland, the New Surrey Theatre, and the Collins Art Center at the University of Maine. The Broadway version, *The Wiz,* played at the Maine State Music Theatre in Brunswick. Camden did a Community Sing-along featuring the songs from the original movie. *Over the Rainbow* childcare center is in Bangor. *Emerald City* Gift Shop is in Portland."

"He could have a connection with those theaters, right?" Harley asked, trying to sound hopeful. "That's why she wrote them down."

Caroline pushed back from the keyboard. "Forget the theaters. He's going to an isolated area. That's his pattern. And now we know his theme—Wizard of Oz—which is why he took my Dad and Atlanta. I was searching those words because I was sure—or I was hoping—he'd follow through on the theme."

"For the final act," Harley said, and regretted it immediately.

"You try *wizard, Maine*?" Charlie asked without much enthusiasm. He wasn't even sure where the words came from.

Caroline sighed and keyed in: *Wizard, Maine.* Google brought up a link about a yacht designer on the coast and a Wizard Pond in Hancock County. She clicked on the second link.

"Wizard Pond," she reported. "Down East Maine, up coast from Mount Desert Island and Bar Harbor, hours from here." She clicked the map link. "Backwoods fishing area, no roads. Between Schoodic Bay and Tunk Lake."

Charlie told her to hit the map zoom.

She did. "Damn, look at this."

Charlie and Harley leaned in.

"*Wizard* Pond," Charlie said. "And right next to it—a mile away—is *Rainbow* Pond."

"That's got to be it," Caroline said. "Wizard, rainbow, out in the wilderness. It's too coincidental. Bando's got to get the cops on this."

They were out of the cabin and racing up the dining hall steps before the cabin door slammed shut.

CHAPTER 55

THE SOUND OF the door latch roused Twait. He blinked a few times but saw nothing.

"Don't bother getting up, little buddy," the voice outside said, and laughed. "And don't rush the door again. The padlock is still on. Just changing your air. Got to love this night air, eh?"

Twait looked to where he thought the door might be cracked. He blinked again. Blackness. If it was open, there was no difference as far as light.

"Must be late," he croaked.

"Actually, it's early—about 3 in the a.m., sunrise in 2 hours. I've pretty much got everything laid out."

"For what?"

"Sunrise. Dawn. Should be perfect light."

"For what?"

"Pictures."

"People are looking for me."

"I'm sure they are. But guess what? They've been looking since yesterday morning—what's that, roughly 18 hours—and they haven't found you yet. Now they're looking for the flying girl, too. But they haven't found her, either. Guess they're—" His voice changed to off-key and sing-song. "*Lookin' for love in all the wrong places.*" He stopped himself. "Country song. Recognize it? Hey, I never claimed to be a singer. I'm more of an emerging artist. I studied theater, but my real gift is photography."

"Photography? Have I heard of you, seen your work?"

"Not yet. I'm on the way up, though. As I said, I'm an emerging talent. I've got a tour de force about to be unveiled."

"You said you've got the flying girl."

"The blonde who grabbed the bird's nest. I don't know how she did it, but I know you didn't have time to rig stage wires. That made my day."

"You're the guy in the white van."

"Yep. I followed you to L.L. Bean and the next day to that park. Kept an eye on you with my binoculars. I was waiting for a chance to cut you out of the herd, but then abracadabra, there was my witch. Problem is, I couldn't handle two of you at once. So I waited and trusted Lady Luck to give me a shot. Sure enough, she sent you to the hardware store this morning. After I had you, it was just a case of going after the girl. I was meant to have you both."

"Where is she?"

"Close."

"You haven't hurt her?"

"Just clipped her wings. She's in my birdcage."

"Birdcage?"

"Yeah, in the back of my van, same one you were in."

"And I'm in a trailer, aren't I?"

"My boss's work trailer. I cleaned it out for you. I thought about drilling a hole in the side to give you an air vent, but I didn't want to ruin the resale value if my boss ever sells it. It's his property, not mine, and I was raised to respect another person's property."

Twait knew he was talking to a man with an odd set of values and boundaries. He murdered people but considered property rights.

"So why have you taken us? She and I haven't done anything to you. Are you waiting for a ransom? Is this about money?"

"Money? There's no ransom. You're the Mayor of Munchkin Land, little buddy, one of the Lollipop Kids. I saw your picture in the paper and knew I had to have you in for my collage. The flying girl is my good witch, Glenda."

"Are we talking *The Wizard of Oz* here?"

"You are the bright boy, aren't you? A midget in body you may be, but in brainpower you stand with the giants. Of course it's the Wizard of Oz. You're the first one to get it. Well done, little buddy."

"I catch the reference, but I really don't get it. What's the Big Picture?"

"Of course you don't get it. You can't yet. Nobody can—until I show all the panels together. After you two, I'll be ready to unveil it."

"Unveil it to who?"

"To anyone who appreciates photographic art."

"Will Glenda and I appreciate it?"

"Aw, come on, little buddy. Do I have to sing *if I only had a brain*? You know the answer. You and Glenda are the last two panels."

* * *

Atlanta's cheek was bleeding where she'd gouged it on the mesh's sharp edge. The duct tape still dangled from her cheek, but at least she could breathe through her mouth. Her first instinct had been to cry out for help, but she had stopped herself. He was the only one nearby. With ankles and wrists still bound she didn't want him to answer with fresh tape—or something worse.

She heard the latch again and lay back down on her side so the taped cheek faced up. He'd quickly see she had worked herself free of the drop cloth, but that didn't seem to matter. Hopefully he wouldn't check the mouth tape. She just wanted him to look in on her and go away.

He cracked the door.

"You are a good witch, aren't you?" he asked then cackled. "Just joking. Doesn't matter, really. For my masterpiece, you'll be Glenda, the Good Witch of the North. That's not your real name, of course, but your real name doesn't matter. Nobody knows who Mona Lisa was. It adds to the mystery. I bought a crown and a wand for you—like in the movie—and I have a witch's broom even though Glenda didn't have a broom. That was the Wicked Witch of the West. But you can pose with it anyway—artistic license—to show everybody's got a good side and an evil side. Maybe somebody will appreciate the nuance. I love costumes and props. As I told your munchkin friend, I studied theater but my first love is art—photography. The Ansel Adams black-and-whites were just the best, don't you think? You know who Ansel Adams was?"

Atlanta didn't move or answer.

"You and Munchkin are going to take a hot air balloon ride a little after dawn. That's about two hours from now. I told you about the envelope, didn't I? It's all stretched out along the shore. I'll let you see how pretty it is after I get the air heated up. The hot air forces it into the upright position. When you see the flame inside it at night, it's called a glow. It's beautiful, shines through the balloon. Wait until you see it with the sunrise behind it. This'll make for fabulous pictures. I can't wait."

It was all Atlanta could do not to open her mouth and scream.

"You and Munchkin are about to become famous—just like those hicks Norman Rockwell put on the *Look* magazine covers."

The door closed and latched. Atlanta could hear him singing off-key as he walked away: *somewhere over the rainbow.*

CHAPTER 56

BANDO WAS NODDING off in the office when the phone rang. The clock read 3:10 a.m.

"Free Camp. Bando."

"It's Smitty. We got the warrant. We're in. The guys are lugging his computer to the van now. Listen to this. There's an artist easel in the corner, but it's not a canvas that's on it. It's an old window—like those artsy wall hangings you find at craft fairs—three panes over three. It still has the glass in it and looks mostly blank."

"What do you mean—mostly blank?"

"Two panes are clear glass and four are white. Oh, wait. It's not white paint; it's white paper. Oh, I see, it's turned away from me. Let me flip it around."

Bando heard her gasp.

"Alicia? Are you okay? What is it?"

Her voice was shaky. "My God, Bando. This is unbelievable—four photographs, close-ups of Alley, Terrell, Parks, and some woman—all death poses, eyes open. This guy is sick. He thinks death is art."

Without him asking for it Bando's mind brought up Tina Sutherland's mental photograph of Alley. That was bad enough without seeing the close-up Alicia was seeing. He didn't need to see Terrell and Parks. Whatever she was viewing had to be grotesque, the demented Osbourne attempting to capture the faces of death in a bizarre series of tableaus. *Thirteen Ways of Looking at a Blackbird. Six Faces of Death* up close and personal, in your face.

"You said some woman. Isn't it an 8-year-old girl in a tornado?"

"No. It's an old lady submerged in a bathtub. He shot the picture looking over the two faucets. They're blurry and out of focus, but you can make them out. The woman's face is underwater at the other end of the tub, where the image is sharpest. He wanted to get her face. Right under the faucet knobs you can see she's wearing a pair of black pointed-toe boots—creepy. She looks like a—."

"Witch," Bando finished.

"Yeah. Any idea who she is?"

"No, but it fits the theme. She's the Wicked Witch. If those four photographs are arranged sequentially in time, she was killed first, then Parks tin man, Terrell the scarecrow, and Alley the cowardly lion. Maybe the FBI and your other connections can find out who she was."

"The bastard," Smitty hissed. "Osbourne probably didn't even know her. He killed her to pose her. And now he's ready to pose Twait and Atlanta. I get the Munchkin angle, but why Atlanta?"

Bando was silent then said, "She's blonde. I guess she looks like Glenda, the Good Witch. Any word from Wizard Pond or Rainbow Pond?"

"Nothing. Frankly I'm not sure it's the right location. It's a long haul from Bridgton and we had the word out within a half hour after he took Atlanta. If he'd gone in that direction, they'd have caught up with him by now. Either he switched vehicles or he's holding them somewhere else."

"I think you're right. Anything else?"

"Yeah. I just noticed—the pictures are signed. He's put initials in the bottom right corner."

"DO or HDO?"

"*OZ*, both in caps. I've got to hang up. The guys are coming back up. I'll call with anything new."

* * *

Maggie sat up fast, disoriented. She'd nodded off. She was on one of the beanbag chairs in the dining hall.

Opposite her Charlie was sleeping sitting up on the couch. Suddenly his eyes flew open. "We were all in a HumVee driving up a dirt road. There were mines everywhere. I dreamed it."

Harley was sitting in the easy chair. "The phone rang once a few minutes ago. I think Bando is talking to somebody, probably Smitty."

The three of them walked toward the office. Bando was just hanging up.

"Smitty?" Maggie asked, and he nodded. "Any word?"

"Wizard-Rainbow isn't paying off. On the positive side, they searched Osbourne's apartment and have evidence linking him to all three murders plus one we didn't know about."

"Tell him your dream, Charlie," Maggie urged.

Charlie did.

"It doesn't sound precognitive," Bando said. "But it's certainly symbolic."

"Not just frustration or anxiety?"

"I don't think so. Sit down a minute, right here facing me. Meditation position." Bando sat on the floor.

Charlie and Maggie watched them face off.

"Close your eyes and do your breathing, Charlie. Relax. I want you to listen to my voice—like we're doing a guided meditation."

Charlie relaxed as Bando took him back into his dream.

"I don't want you to focus on the roadblocks or the obstacles. Forget the mines. Forget the bumps. Are you in the front or the back of the HumVee?"

"Front. You're driving."

"What do you see now?"

"Wide dirt road, trees on both sides. We can barely see ten feet ahead of us."

"Why? Is it foggy?"

"No. But you have those low fog lights on. Do HumVees have fog lights?"

"Doesn't matter. What's above us?"

"Brightening sky high up, brighter to the right."

"So it's close to dawn and we're heading generally east, maybe northeast. Now look at the dashboard, just above where a radio might be. See a Global Positioning System?"

"No."

"A GPS. It's there on the dash halfway between you and me. See it now?"

"Yes."

"Is the screen showing a left turn or a right turn ahead?"

"Curving left, then it straightens out, then it splits."

"Is the name of the road displayed?"

"No."

"Positive?"

"Yes. Not there."

"At the top of the GPS is our destination. What is it?"

"Doesn't say. No print."

"Then what's there?"

"Colors. A rainbow."

Maggie caught Bando's attention and pointed to her ear.

He understood. "Charlie, are you hearing anything? What are the sounds around us? Can you hear Atlanta or Twait?"

"Not them. I hear beeps and a woman's voice. It's the beeps and that lady you hear at the supermarket when they scan your groceries. Now it's stopped."

"The supermarket?" Bando asked. He waited.

"Yes, it's that fake woman's voice inside the grocery scanner. She sounds like the other fake woman in the GPS."

"What's she saying?"

"Please continue scanning. Help is on the way. Please continue scanning. Help is on the way. Please continue scanning."

Maggie sprinted out the door and a moment later found Caroline bleary-eyed at her computer keyboard.

"*Rainbow* was right!" Maggie blurted. "Charlie dreamed a rainbow on a GPS screen. But we jumped at the wrong Rainbow. We were searching *Wizard* when Wizard Pond and Rainbow Pond popped up together—so we figured it was too good to be a coincidence. That was our mistake—we stopped the search. But we were searching *Wizard*, not *Rainbow*. *Continue scanning*, Charlie's dream says. *Help is on the way*. We never tried *Rainbow*. Search it."

Caroline entered *Rainbow, Maine* and a list of links came up.

"Camp Rainbow in Ellsworth is for kids with cancer. Rainbow Federal Credit Union has 4 branch offices near here, including South Paris. But that means security cameras and people. Rainbow Lake is in Rainbow Township, Maine, near Mount Katahdin. That could be it— middle of nowhere, lots of forestland. We can get Bando to call the cops on both Camp Rainbow and Rainbow Lake. But both are hours away."

"There's got to be something else," Maggie insisted. "Search *Rainbow Pond* in case the one by Wizard Pond isn't the only one."

Google turned up several, including one in Cumberland County.

"Isn't this Cumberland County?" Maggie asked.

"Got to be the one."

Rainbow Pond was an isolated 14-acre pond in the Steep Falls Recreation Area west of Sebago Lake. The road ending near Adams Pond was the closest access point. It looked on the map like a half-mile hike in from the trailhead.

Caroline printed the directions. "It's almost 4 o'clock. Thirty-eight minutes driving time plus hike time. Bando needs to tell the cops about all three Rainbows—the camp in Ellsworth, the town by Mount Katahdin, and this one at Steep Falls. But my money's on this one. Let's go."

CHAPTER 57

WITH THE CAMP van impounded for evidence, Rose and the five teens had to squeeze into Rose's car while Bando called Smitty with the new Rainbows.

"I'll get it into the system. Everybody who's available is out on this. I'm advising you not to drive up there, Bando, but if you disregard and go—and if Osbourne is there—don't take chances. Do not engage this man under any circumstances. I'm officially off duty but still in uniform here at the barracks. I'll take my own car and hope not to see you at Rainbow Pond."

Bando hung up and ran to the van. In no time they were on blacktop exceeding the speed limit.

Caroline asked, "Flashlights?"

Everybody had one.

"We've got our cell phone screens, too," Maggie pointed out.

"Weapons?" Charlie asked. "Osbourne's got a stun gun and maybe a real gun. I grabbed this." He held up a fireplace poker from the dining hall.

Maggie held up Rose's meat cleaver from the kitchen.

"Fire extinguisher," Caroline said. "It's empty since the fire, but I can still swing it and dent this guy's head."

"Swiss Army knife," Harley said, and held it out in front of him like he was advertising a tube of toothpaste for the camera. "Big blade, little blade, scissors, flat-tip screwdriver, Phillips screwdriver, can opener—oh, and corkscrew."

"In case Osbourne offers us wine?" Maggie said, shaking her head.

They all chuckled nervously.

"Good one, Magpie," Harley responded. "When I'm scared, I tend to blab on."

"Perfectly understandable, Harley," she answered. "We're all nervous and afraid. Damon, what did you bring?"

"I wasn't thinking. But I just found this under the seat." He held up a long, silky black cylinder about a foot long.

"That's Mom's car umbrella."

No one knew what to say, so they rode in silence for five minutes, stomachs doing flip-flops. Finally Bando spoke.

"There's an important question below the surface here—about using a weapon and hurting another human being. The answer may be different for each of us, which we'll find out when the time comes. But remember, we have another powerful weapon."

"The element of surprise," Charlie said. "He doesn't know we're on to him and we're coming."

"I think Bando meant our psychic gifts," Caroline said. "Although I've got to say, tonight it might be better to be able to swing a poker accurately than see a ghost."

"Individual gifts are important," Bando said. "But they have limits."

"Okay," Charlie said. "So we have our gifts, we have surprise, and we have numbers. All we need now is a plan."

A moment later Bando said, "It's not exactly a plan, but I do have an idea."

* * *

Osbourne had carefully arranged the nylon envelope on the tarp he'd laid down. Balloon class had taught him the tarp was a necessity in areas where rocks, exposed roots, and stumps could tear the balloon's fabric. Once the burner was lit and began heating the air in the envelope's throat, it would gradually inflate and pull itself across the tarp until it bobbed upright over the gondola. The two-person basket held the two propane bottles that fueled the burner. He had used three mooring lines to secure the balloon—one around a beach boulder, one tied to a washed-ashore tree trunk by the water's edge, and the last to a stump on the upper fringe of the beach.

He'd never gone aloft in this model, but he'd been up in a similar one at balloon school. It would take 20 minutes to fully inflate it. After that he simply had to turn down the burner and let the balloon wait for him to finish setting up and taking his shots. The balloon at sunrise would be the perfect backdrop for these final two tableaus.

But this time it would be different afterwards. He wouldn't have to depend on some hiker, fisherman, or camp counselor to stumble upon his art and alert the world. After the staging and shooting he would max the burner, release the moorings, and send his work heavenward over the rainbow. Then he'd hook the van to the trailer and go home to wait for the news stories. And in a few months he'd anonymously ship his six-tableau masterpiece to the Metropolitan. He could visit it often there and watch people's responses.

His only regret was that he wouldn't be at the Portland Jetport control tower to see the look on the air traffic controller's face when somebody in a private plane reported two bodies—a dead Munchkin and a dead witch—hanging from the gondola of a hot air balloon with Judy Garland's pig-tailed face silk-screened on its side.

The time had come to light the burner.

CHAPTER 58

BANDO LEFT BRIDGTON Road and picked up the Pequawket Trail.

"Should be the fourth left," Caroline said, and began counting them down. "There's Rock and Hard Place. There's Quarry Hill Road. Nellie Lane. Slow down."

Bando turned on Acres of Wildlife Road, which ran the west boundary of the Steep Falls Preserve.

"Long, winding, dirt road," Caroline said. "But no landmines."

After the first mile the road narrowed and grew steeper. Potholes and washboards appeared.

"There they are," Bando said, and shifted Rose's car into low gear. It jittered and stuttered its way up the sharp incline. Steep Falls hadn't gotten its name for nothing.

"Which reminds me about the lights in my dream," Charlie said. "No brights at this angle or he may see us coming."

Bando switched to fog lights. They passed the Adams Pond access and drove another 500 yards. The sky was brightening above and to the right just as in Charlie's dream. The fog lights illuminated two trailhead markers, so they parked and got out. One sign read Rainbow West, the other Rainbow East. Both looked as if they had once been logging trails.

"I don't see the white van," Bando said. "He's either hidden it or driven it in by one of these trails."

"But which trail?" Maggie asked.

"East," Damon answered.

"How do you know?"

"A strong hunch," he answered.

"I can second that," Caroline said.

"You have a hunch, too?" Damon asked.

"No. Addie Beals is standing right there."

"How's Harley doing?" Bando asked.

Charlie stuck his head in the open back door to check. "He's long gone, out on recon."

"Okay, let's get his body out here," Bando directed. "You and Damon help me get him on my shoulder."

"I'll carry him," Damon insisted. "I'm stronger than both of you."

"You sure you're up to it?" Bando asked.

"I'm fine now. Feeling much better."

Bando and Charlie slung Harley's body over Damon's shoulder in a fireman's carry.

"No sign of Smitty's car," Caroline observed. "I wish we had her, but we can't wait. Let's go." "Flashlight beams down and no noise." She started down the path under the dark canopy of branches. They fell in behind her.

CHAPTER 59

TWO WHACKS ON the trailer jarred Twait back to reality. Before he could get to his feet the door swung open.

"Rise and shine, little buddy! School picture day."

A flood of bright light blinded him. He shut his eyes and ducked his head to the side. It was too bright to be sunlight. He realized Osbourne was shining a high wattage flashlight at him, keeping him blinded.

Twait was dehydrated and weak. His mouth and throat were sandpaper dry. His shirt stank of sweat and his pants of urine and excrement. With someone at the door wielding far more power than he had, it was tempting to beg. He was sure the man had either a stun gun or a pistol in the other hand. But Twait was in no mood to be submissive.

"Did you bring breakfast? I'd like my orange juice first, please, and my coffee with my meal."

The bright light looked red-orange on the inside of his eyelids as the man brought it closer to his face. Would the man strangle him now? Would it be with a rope, a belt, a wire, or his bare hands? He was prepared to kick the man in the groin as soon as he felt his breath close. He drew his legs back, poised. A jolt of high-voltage electricity hit him square in the chest.

* * *

Harley's body twitched on Damon's shoulder.

"He's back," Damon whispered, and Charlie helped him lay the body down on the trail.

Harley blinked and sat up slowly. He cleared his throat softly several times, as if he needed to internally reconnect the wires in his voice box. The group gathered around him.

"What did you see?" Bando asked softly. "Hurry."

"He was going for Twait when I left—inside a trailer. Twait's got handcuffs on and his arms are behind him." Harley sketched a map in the dirt. "Here's the lake. Our trail comes out at the beach here. There's Twait's trailer. Atlanta is way over here in the back of the white van. It's like a cage in back and has a padlock. She's not hurt. There were pieces of duct tape on the floor, so she must have chewed it off."

"What about the balloon?" Bando asked.

"Right here by the water's edge. It's inflated and ready to go. It has a huge picture on it—that girl who played Dorothy."

"Judy Garland," Maggie said.

"Yeah, her. Anyway, the passenger basket has the heater above it. Three ropes hold the whole thing to the ground. Tree stump at the edge of the woods here, boulder on the beach here, and old log by the water's edge here."

"Is that it?"

"His stage props, the Munchkin and witch stuff, are on the beach by the balloon. He's got two digital cameras on a flat rock; one's fancy, the other's a cheapie."

"Anything else?"

Harley shook his head.

"Let me remind you," Bando said, "that our goal is not to confront Osbourne but to keep Twait and Atlanta—and ourselves—safe. We have two ways to go about this. The first is to slow him down until the cops arrive."

"What's the second?" Maggie asked.

"Every artist needs his canvas, every director needs his stage," Charlie said.

"So we take away his balloon," Caroline finished. "Let's go."

CHAPTER 60

OSBOURNE SAT TWAIT up against the gondola basket. He placed the string of plastic-wrapped lollipops around his neck like a Hawaiian lei and set the Dunkin Donuts box on his lap making sure *Munchkins* showed for the camera. Finally he placed the rope from the gondola basket around Twait's throat and pulled it snug under his chin. It thrilled him to think of the balloon lifting off with Twait and the girl swinging 10 to 20 feet below the basket. He stepped back to admire his work and shook his head.

"Want to catch the light." He tenderly placed his hands under Twait's jaw and turned it slightly. "You don't want them seeing your 5 o'clock shadow."

He lined up the Glenda props: the cornstalk broom, the crown, and the wand. Then he picked up the stun gun and started for the van.

"Pay no attention to that man behind the curtain," boomed a theatrical male voice.

Osbourne froze. He glanced around the beach and up into the trees but saw nobody. He thought the voice had come from somewhere near the cargo trailer. It couldn't be Twait.

"Who's there?" he called.

From farther down the beach came the sound of music, faint, as if it were coming from a tiny speaker. He listened closely and heard nasally Munchkins singing: *Follow the yellow brick road; follow the yellow brick road; follow, follow, follow, follow, Follow the yellow brick road.*

He returned to his duffel bag and drew out a small pistol that he tucked in the small of his back. He started down the beach like a gunfighter, the stun gun hanging down in his right hand and the pistol in hiding.

"Somebody mocking my balloon?" he yelled, closing on the source of the music.

Nobody answered. The song kept on. Now it was Judy Garland singing: *Because, because, because, because, because. Because of the wonderful things he does. We're off to see the wizard, the wonderful Wizard of Oz.*

He made his way uphill to the edge of the woods, following his ears. When the sand turned to firmer dirt near the darker trees, he shined his flashlight at waist level expecting to confront someone in the shadows.

But the music came from the ground. Five feet away in the bushes he saw a dim light. The song repeated. He reached down carefully and picked up an iPhone—someone had downloaded the song and placed the phone there—a diversion. He grabbed the phone and sprinted back down the beach, tossing the phone into the water as he ran, arriving out of breath. Twait hadn't moved. The chloroform after the stun gun had done its work. The balloon appeared undisturbed. Had his witch gotten free? Was it her cell phone?

He walked fast toward the van and saw the lock was still in place. He had the only key, so she must still be inside. He reached for the lock, but before he could grab it, the lock started rapidly clattering as if it were angry. Then as suddenly as it had started, it stopped. He spun around to make sure no one was behind him. He was alone. He reached for the lock a second time. Again it shook and clanked violently on the hasp. He pulled his hand back. The lock stopped. He shined the light in a semi-circle.

Nobody.

This time when he reached for the lock, he did so with lighting speed as if he were a child catching frogs on a pond bank again. He gripped it in his fist and could feel it struggle against him. But he held on. The movement stopped. He tucked the stun gun into the front of his waistband, slid the key into the lock, and snapped it open. As soon as he flipped the hasp free of the metal keeper he refastened the lock so it couldn't attack him. He placed a hand on the door handle and was about to open it when he felt somebody tugging at the pistol he had tucked in the small of his back. He reached back and grabbed it as he turned.

Nobody was there. Nobody was tugging at the pistol.

He tucked it tightly in his front waistband next to the stun gun and opened the van door.

His flashlight lit the birdcage. Strips of ripped and chewed duct tape littered the floor. Otherwise the cargo hold was empty, the flying girl gone. Impossible. How had she done it? And where had she gone? He needed her to complete his masterpiece. She was the sixth pane.

He aimed the beam at the front seats in case she had bent the mesh back and squeezed through. Could she be hiding on the driver's floor where he had suckered Twait? He caught a reflection in the rear-view mirror but didn't react. Now it made sense.

"I guess she flew the coop," he said, dragging out his words. "A bird in the hand is worth two in the bush." He backed away from the open door and pretended he was about to slam it. The lock rattled again, impotent. Suddenly he drew the stun gun from his waistband, held it in front of him, and aimed it at the ceiling just inside the door. He pulled the trigger and the bird fell out of her nest, landing hard.

He chloroformed Atlanta, scooped her up, and carried her to the gondola, where he leaned her shoulder-to-shoulder against Twait. He placed the crown on her head, arranged the magic wand on her lap, and set the broomstick against her shoulder. He took a second rope loop and fastened it snugly around Atlanta's neck, tilting her head just so as he had with so many schoolchildren. He stepped back and reached for the better of the two digital cameras.

"I'll get separate shots for my collage once you're dead. If I took them now with you still alive, it would be artistic deceit and I'd feel terrible. But I can't waste this chance. You're so cute together—like Raggedy Ann and Raggedy Andy. What a Hallmark card it would be—touching and yet humorous. I could also submit it to my old high school yearbook.

Most Popular? Best Dancers? I know—Most Photogenic."

He shot the pictures from several angles as the dawn broke and the sun peeked over the treetops.

"Okay, you two. The light will be perfect soon. Time to get serious."

He set the good camera down and tucked the smaller one into his shirt pocket.

"Who wants to go first?" he asked, pulling a piano wire out of the duffel bag. "I'll take your silence as no preference." He wrapped the wire around his hands. "You first, little buddy."

"Hey!" yelled someone behind him. "Aren't you Oz, the famous death artist?"

He turned and saw a longhaired boy in wire-rimmed glasses standing not 50 feet away. He was brandishing a fireplace poker, trying to look menacing.

"About time somebody recognized me, kid," Oz said. "Your phone music was clever and your lock-rattling trick was unique, but if all you've got is technology, a magic trick, and that steel rod, you're seriously outgunned."

"Who said he's alone?" a girl's voice called from the boulder securing the mooring line. It was the red-haired girl from the camp, the midget's daughter, making samurai moves with something.

"Looks to me like you've found a piece of driftwood," he scoffed.

"The police will be here any minute," said a man's voice so close it startled him. A dripping longhaired, Asian-looking man rose from the lake like the Creature from the Black Lagoon. "Let them go."

"Three of you—an old man and two kids? While I admire your pluck, I'd point out that I have a stun gun and a pistol."

"You underestimate us," Caroline said, and set her samurai stick aside. She loosened the mooring line, then planted her feet against the big rock and held the line tight. The gondola shifted slightly, scraping the beach. In her best damsel-in-distress voice she mewed, "I just don't know how long I can hold this."

"You don't want to do that, girlie! Even if you let go, I have two other lines holding it. Tie it back up and walk away home before you get hurt."

"Afraid we'll ruin your shot?" Charlie mocked.

"There are still only three of you."

"You can't count, Ozzie Bear," said a new boyish voice. Someone rose up from hiding behind the driftwood tree trunk that held the second mooring line. "See this? Swiss Army knife. Sharp." He began sawing at the line.

"Don't!"

The line severed, leaving Harley with the line wrapped around his hand while he scissor-gripped the driftwood trunk between his legs. The gondola basket shifted more, changing Atlanta and Twait's poses.

"You people must be stupid!" Oz roared. "You must all be stupid. See those nooses around your friends' necks? The other ends are tied inside the basket. Release those lines and the balloon goes up and you hang them. Doesn't bother me. I can still snap some realistic shots as they leave the ground. You want to be their executioners, go ahead. It's your choice and their funeral."

"Walk away, Great and Powerful Oz," said a woman's voice near the trailer. "Your shots are ruined and doing this won't bring back your sister."

"What sister?" he asked.

"Issy," Rose answered.

He laughed until it became an insane cackle.

"Listen to her," a girl called from the tree line where the third line was tied. She shined a flashlight on something silver in her other hand. "My friend Beaver Cleaver says you should release his friends. Just jump in your van and we'll let you go." She poised the meat cleaver over the rope.

Oz scanned the scene. He had crazies everywhere—in the water, on the beach, by the trees. They were like the army of plastic soldiers he'd once set up in his sandbox.

"You're making a big mistake. You're going to be responsible for killing these two. You're *hopelessly* outgunned. Look." He showed the stun gun in one hand and the pistol in the other.

"Let them go," Harley yelled in a cracking adolescent voice. "Now!"

"You people have no idea of the importance of art or how much power it holds over me. I have to be creative. I'm losing this perfect light—perfect, don't you see? Secure those lines in the next thirty seconds so I can get my shot lined up again or I'll shoot the munchkin and the witch. Or you can let the lines go and hang them. Thirty seconds—starting now!"

Behind Osbourne in the gondola a head noiselessly appeared. Two arms, one with a death's head tattoo held apart a lasso and dropped it over Oz's shoulders and arms, the intent to keep them at his sides. But Oz pulled his hands in to protect the stun gun and the pistol. He brought them up through the loop, leaving the rope around his chest, then turned with the pistol up, looking for a target. Something blunt poked him below his left eye. He winced and pulled away from the pain. Seconds later he tried again, turning in the same direction. Something black exploded in his face like a thousand startled bats fleeing a cave.

"Damon, jump!" Bando shouted. "Now!"

At the cry of Now, Harley and Caroline let go their lines and Maggie brought the cleaver down hard, severing the third mooring rope. The balloon hesitated as if unsure what to do next. It was free of its tethers except for the ropes around Twait's and Atlanta's necks and the third around Osbourne's chest. It groaned and scraped the beach, deciding to lift off from the shore.

Oz realized a thousand bats weren't flying in his face; it was a suddenly opened umbrella. He turned and saw Damon balanced on the back of the basket, one hand on the burner control for balance. The jet of flame increased as he pulled it and locked it in position. Oz raised the pistol and watched as Damon fell backward in slow motion, disappearing behind the basket with a splash.

Bang! A single shot split the air. Oz recoiled. His pistol fell into the gondola and the stun gun dropped onto the beach. With great effort and disbelief he forced himself to turn and face the beach, straining to see who had shot him. None of the teens had shown a gun, nor had the adults. The weapons they had shown were primitive. Oz sank to his knees, scanning the beach, and finally saw through blurring vision someone in a police uniform near his van. He collapsed beside Twait and Atlanta as the basket crunched across the gravelly beach into the lake, eventually breaking free of the water's suction to rise into the early morning sky.

The balloon's ascent took up the slack in all three ropes—Twait's, Atlanta's, and his. But Twait and Atlanta's quickly tumbled free of the basket and fell into the water, leaving the ropes connected only to their necks. Osbourne's line, its other end tied around the propane bottles, tightened under his arms and around his chest. It dragged him backward over the water past Damon and Bando then briefly across the lake's surface. Finally, with blood turning his shirt crimson, he lifted off into the air under the balloon like a tail on a runaway kite—up, up, and away into the sunrise with Judy Garland.

* * *

An hour later near the trailhead markers an EMT treated Twait as Rose sat holding his hand. A second EMT worked on Atlanta while a wet Damon hovered over her with a blanket around his shoulders, watching.

Bando and the other four teens stood giving police their statements as Smitty explained to a CID man how she came to be on the beach when she was off-duty and why she had fired the shot that struck the balloonist Osbourne.

* * *

About the same time police received a call from the Portland Jetport saying a private pilot over Freeport had reported a bloodied man suspended from a runaway Judy Garland balloon. The pilot didn't know if the man was dead or alive, but he looked badly wounded. The pilot also estimated from the wind direction that the balloon would eventually touch down in the Atlantic.

FRIDAY

CHAPTER 61

I T WAS ALMOST 10 a.m. before everyone was released and allowed
to return to camp. With no sleep they were all running on the
fumes of their sunrise adrenaline. They grabbed muffins and juice to
hold them and used Twait's and Bando's cabins to clean up. Parents
arrived through the morning. At noon everyone gathered in the dining hall for lunch: 10 large pizzas ordered by Smitty and delivered by
Slices and Ices.

The teens talked as they ate, but with so many parents around, no
one dared mention psychic or paranormal gifts. Giving their stories to
the police had been sort of a dress rehearsal.

Charlie led off. "On the way there Bando came up with a plan.
Maggie downloaded that Wizard of Oz song onto her iPhone, which by
the way is still at the bottom of Rainbow Pond. We arrived and Harley
ran ahead to scout the lakeshore so we'd know the lay of the land, which
helped us fine-tune the plan."

Caroline picked up the narrative. "We got to the end of the trail and
saw my Dad sitting against the basket. Atlanta was locked in Oz's van.
Dad, it was scary. We didn't know if he had stunned you or killed you. All
Mom and I knew is you weren't moving. It was horrible."

Rose sniffed and wiped away tears.

Maggie said, "I thought maybe I could get Atlanta out of the van
when Oz went to check out the iPhone, but it had a padlock on it. So

I hid in the bushes and watched. I was only twenty feet away from you, Atlanta."

"I heard you rattle the lock a few times," Atlanta said, winking. "There was no way you could get in."

Charlie continued, "So Bando's job was to sneak through the woods and leave Maggie's iPhone up the beach to create the diversion. That's when I yelled *Pay no attention to that man behind the curtain.* I have no idea why I said that. I was adlibbing."

Bando said, "I turned the phone to max volume, hit Play, and set it in the bushes. I went further up the beach past a point of land where I slipped into the water—which by the way was very cold. I dog-paddled out a hundred yards then worked my way back toward the balloon until I could swim in close to it. Then I waited."

"I could see the top of your head," Harley said. "You looked like a crocodile waiting for a baby water buffalo to show up at the riverbank."

"When Osbourne checked out the music," Damon said, "we all ran to our positions. I jumped into the basket and scrunched down by the gas bottles. First thing I did was to loosen the inside ends of the two nooses. They were tied around the propane bottles. I looped them around loosely so they fall off with any kind of tension. There was an unused rope on the floor, so I made a lasso with one end and tied the other end to the gas bottles."

"We didn't have time to grab you, Dad," Caroline said. "Atlanta was locked in the van and Osbourne was coming back up the beach. You'd have been dead weight and we'd never have been able to outrun him."

"I understand, Caroline," Twait said. "It was a good plan."

"It was," Maggie said. "And we stuck to it. We hid and waited, hoping to stall him until the police arrived. Our backup plan was to take away his stage—the balloon."

"Wish I had seen it," Atlanta said.

"Me, too," Twait said.

"When Oz came back," Maggie said, "he went straight to the van. He had some trouble with the padlock, and that bought us some time." She winked at Atlanta.

"He eventually got it open and stunned me," Atlanta said. "We know now that he used chloroform, too. Next thing I know I'm being revived by the paramedics in the parking lot."

"I have to admit," Maggie said, "there was a brief moment when he was messing with the lock and I was so close by in the bushes—"

"What?" Harley interrupted. "You're not going to say you thought about using the cleaver, are you, Magpie?"

Maggie nodded. "Just a passing thought. But when it came down to it, I just couldn't. I saved it for you, Harley."

Everyone laughed.

"How'd you get the duct tape off, Atlanta?" her mother asked.

"When I first came to, my wrists were taped behind me. My mouth and ankles were taped, too. But I found this jagged edge on the mesh at eye level, which is how I cut my cheek. I hooked the tape on my mouth onto the sharp edge and ripped it partway off so I could breathe. Then I realized I could use my teeth to chew the rest of the tape off. Problem was, I couldn't get to my ankles or my wrists. So I got back down on the floor and I balanced on three points—my knees and my forehead—and I did the muscle relaxation and breathing Bando taught us. It took me a long time, but I finally slipped my arms under my lower body and feet. *Voila*, wrists in front! Chew tape. Free wrists. Rip tape off ankles. But then he zapped me before I could scratch his eyes out."

Atlanta's mother looked at her with amazement.

Charlie picked up the thread again. "Once he carried you out and set you up next to Twait, we knew the timer was ticking. We had no choice but to show ourselves."

They each told their part in the finale.

"Lucky he wasn't much of a target shooter," Harley said. "We kept popping up like those cardboard bad guys on a police shooting range."

"Ozzie Bear?" Maggie asked. "Where'd that come from, Harley?"

"From Fozzie Bear on *The Muppets*. The voice was Frank Oz— Fozzie. Get it? Hey, some of us say strange things under stress. What can I say? Was that any dumber than your Beaver Cleaver?"

Everyone roared.

"You know what I don't get?" Maggie's father asked. "You said there were two trails to choose from. You got lucky and guessed the right one. But when Officer Smith arrived later, how did she know which trail to take? Did she flip a coin?"

"I didn't know at first," Smitty answered. "But then I saw the empty fire extinguisher bottle Caroline had left to tip me off."

"Well, you all took a huge risk," Harley's mother said, choking up. "But you acted bravely. Foolishly but bravely."

"We acted as a team, Mom," Harley said. "And in the end, it was Damon here who hid in the basket and dropped the lasso over Osbourne. And when Oz pointed the pistol at him——." Harley turned and looked at Damon, "I can't believe you poked him in the eye with an umbrella. And then—whap—you opened it right in the guy's face. It was so awesome, dude." Harley gave him a high five that Damon returned.

"He was going to try again," Damon said. "But Bando yelled, 'Damon, jump. Now!'" And I fell backwards into the water. A second later I heard a shot and thought he'd hit me. But then I realized it couldn't be me, because I had already bailed out."

"When I heard 'Now!'" Maggie explained, "I thought it meant chop my rope."

"Harley and I thought that was our cue, too," Caroline said. "We let go our lines."

With all eyes on Bando, Atlanta asked, "So what did you mean when you yelled 'Now'?"

Bando shrugged and gave a sheepish I-don't-know grin. "I thought I was just yelling to Damon—jump now!"

The conversation hit a lull until Bando said, "We know what happened next. Even with Damon out of the line of fire, Osbourne would have turned the gun on Twait and Atlanta. This was a guy who had already murdered at least four people. Smitty had no choice but to shoot." He looked in her direction, but she glanced away and down, her mouth tight. "I want us to be sensitive to Smitty's situation. She had to shoot a human being today."

"Just in the nick of time," Harley said. "If she hadn't, Damon, Atlanta, and Twait might have been goners—and maybe some of us."

"The shooting may have been justified, Harley, but it's still a shooting.

She wounded—probably killed—Osbourne. She took another life. And she's got to deal with that, make peace with it. By all means thank her, but be sensitive. Alicia, do you want to say anything?"

She cleared her throat and when she spoke she managed to sound somewhat dispassionate. "They had to take my gun and put me on mandatory administrative leave. That's standard procedure. Then there's counseling while the internal investigation is in progress. My boss and I are confident they'll find the shooting justified. I don't regret it." Then she looked around at the parents and Charlie's grandmother. "I want you folks to know that these kids of yours have been amazing. They not only cracked the mystery; they also pulled off the rescue. They fed us ideas and information all week. You should be so proud of them. Talk about your Wizard of Oz. They showed brains, heart, and courage."

Twait said, "They are indeed quite a group."

Smitty's phone rang, so she stepped away to take the call. She wandered toward the office and was gone ten minutes.

"They just found the balloon," she said when she returned. "It landed at sea twenty miles past Matinicus Rock."

"That's way out there," Damon said. "Osbourne?"

"Still tied to the balloon. Dead, probably the gunshot but maybe drowned."

"Anything more on him?" Twait asked.

"Yes. The woman in the bathtub was his mother. It was ruled a suicide at the time, because she had mental health issues. But the coroner back then didn't have the photograph from Osbourne's window-frame tableau. Myself, I'm guessing even if he didn't kill her, he was the one who dressed her for the picture."

"What about the sister—Issy?" Caroline asked. "The one sucked up with the house in the Emporia tornado. Mom wondered if that was what got him off-track on the Wizard of Oz obsession."

"There is no Issy. Herbert David Osbourne was an only child. The sister never existed. Maybe she was a fantasy. And the Osbournes never lived in Emporia, Kansas. They were always in Overland Park. That resume said he graduated from Emporia High, but it was Overland Park.

He was probably the one who wrote the mother's obituary. And who fact-checks an obit?"

"This is one for the books," Harley said.

Bando changed the subject. "We're trying to get this group together again over the Columbus Day weekend, but not here. Harley's mom here has invited us all to their place. We can't wait a full year again to decompress. The camp property is being sold, so we have no plans for Free Camp next year. I don't think having these couple of hours now is enough."

Atlanta's mother said, "That's a great idea. But I think it should be just the staff and kids. That way you can talk more freely."

Atlanta looked stunned. Her mother smiled. Everyone agreed.

"I'd like to invite you, too, Smitty," Rose said. "You'll still be on administrative leave then, and you need to talk with somebody besides other cops and a shrink. You need to talk with us."

Silence. Then, "I'll think about it."

"Seriously?" Bando asked.

"Seriously."

* * *

In September a woman from Brunswick turned in a small digital camera to State Police. She and her children found it while grave rubbing at the old Durham Cemetery. She had no idea how it got there, but found it stuck in the ground in the slave section of the graveyard, as if it had been dropped from far above. When she clicked through the photos in hopes of finding an owner, she found the shots too gruesome to view—faces of death. She guessed the camera must belong to a Crime Scene photographer. It made its way to the Crime Lab, which linked it to Osbourne.

The newest image, the teacher said when she turned it in, was of a man who "looks like Death himself." It was a self-portrait taken at arm's length. Above his drooping head a length of rope reached to a rattan basket, and beyond that was a hot air balloon. The man's eyes were half-closed, but he had managed a frightening, almost self-satisfied grin for the camera.

CHAPTER 62

IN OCTOBER THEY spent the long weekend at Harley's talking, reading, snacking, and sitting Zen each day—doing the emotional work they needed to.

Atlanta and Damon spent a lot of their time together, and she announced he'd be joining her family for Thanksgiving. She hadn't gotten her tattoo after all and had dropped most of her pierced jewelry.

Smitty stayed all three days. Once the group swore her to secrecy, they let her in on what had really happened during both the Osbourne and the Bronson debacles.

Damon said, "After all this, though, I'm still looking for a gift that will help catch my parents' killer."

"Open your eyes," Atlanta said.

Damon looked puzzled.

"This group is a gift, Damon. We just caught a killer, didn't we? If we did it once, we can do it again."

"Yeah, why stop at one?" Smitty said. "And now you have a cop on your side."

* * *

Monday was unseasonably warm, so the last meal was a barbecue on the patio. When they finished eating, Rose retrieved a cardboard box from the house and set it on the table.

"Before I open your surprise I have a good news/bad news announcement. The bad news is the camp has been sold and the new owners have other plans for the property—not a camp."

"So no Free Camp next summer?" Harley whined, his voice deep with disappointment.

"Sorry," Rose answered.

Everyone moaned and groaned, including Smitty who asked, "But you'll be coming back to Maine, right?" Her eyes flicked quickly toward Bando then back to Rose. "The four of you, I mean."

Rose and Twait shrugged.

Bando cleared his throat. "I'm trying to work something out for January—a couple of teaching sessions at a New Age bookstore in Portland."

"Where will you stay?" Smitty asked. "I mean, maybe we could meet for dinner."

Bando nodded. "We could do that—if we want to go out. Can you cook?"

She grinned. "Can you?"

The teens rolled their eyes and Maggie changed the subject. "So what's the good news, Rose?"

"The good news is you're all invited to our house in Florida. You can come alone or all together, like over a school break in April. We're not far from Disney."

That got a buzz.

"I could visit my father," Atlanta said. "You could meet him, Damon." She squeezed his hand.

"Can we watch Twait wrestle an alligator?" Harley asked.

"If I'm not inside one by then," Twait joked, and they laughed, feeling relaxed again.

Rose turned their attention back to the box. "I saved the best for last," she said, and shook the box dramatically several times then turned it over and shook it some more.

"Apparently it's not wine and wine glasses," Maggie joked. "So we won't need Harley's Swiss Army corkscrew."

They laughed. Rose took a knife and slit the top of the box open.

"What is it?" Harley asked.

Rose withdrew a folded gray tee shirt and shook it loose. She held it up for everyone to see. Printed across its back in bold blue letters—except for the capital K that was blood red—were the words *FreeK Camp*. In smaller letters below: *Bridgton, Maine*. "Since the camp has been sold, I had *Bridgton* put on for this year's and last year's participants. I already mailed shirts to last year's campers."

"What's it say on the front?" Twait asked, eyes twinkling.

"Oh, almost forgot," Rose said with dramatic flair and turned the shirt around.

Across the left breast in the same dazzling colors it read: *Proud to be a FreeK.* Under that in white letters: *Caroline.*

Everyone clapped as Caroline accepted her shirt. Then, to more applause, Rose handed them out one by one including her own and Twait's and Bando's.

Damon was next-to-the-last. When he took it he gave Rose a warm hug, during which she heard herself whisper in his ear, "*Damon, if you ever need a place to stay—*" He whispered thanks and sat back down next to Atlanta.

"One left," Rose said, and everyone glanced around. She unfolded it and held it up for all of them to see. "*Alicia.*"

Smitty was in tears.

The End.

We trust you have enjoyed *FreeK Show: Where Nothing Is as It Appears.* In case you haven't read the FreeKs series opener, *FreeK Camp: Psychic Teens in a Paranormal Thriller*, it's available in hardcover, library hardback, paperback, and e-book. Steve Burt's award-winning weird tales collections, the Stories to Chill the Heart Series, include *Odd Lot, Even Odder, Oddest Yet* and *Wicked Odd.* His inspirational fiction collections include *A Christmas Dozen* and *Unk's Fiddle.*